5A

DEAD MAN'S BOOT

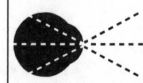

This Large Print Book carries the
Seal of Approval of N.A.V.H.

DEAD MAN'S BOOT

PATRICK DEAREN

THORNDIKE PRESS
A part of Gale, a Cengage Company

Farmington Hills, Mich • San Francisco • New York • Waterville, Maine
Meriden, Conn • Mason, Ohio • Chicago

GALE
CENGAGE Learning®

LIBRARY OF CONGRESS CIP DATA ON FILE.
CATALOGUING IN PUBLICATION FOR THIS BOOK
IS AVAILABLE FROM THE LIBRARY OF CONGRESS

ISBN-13: 978-1-4328-4591-9 (hardcover)
ISBN-10: 1-4328-4591-8 (hardcover)

Published in 2017 by arrangement with Patrick Dearen

Printed in the United States of America
1 2 3 4 5 6 7 21 20 19 18 17

For my friend, Jim Bradshaw

CHAPTER 1

Along a river as barren as a grieving man's soul, the square toe of a boot sticking out of the ground was a striking sight.

Actually, on the Pecos in Texas on this September day in 1869, any reminder of civilization was unusual. There was the beaten cattle trail bearing upstream, all right, along with fresh wagon tracks that the gusting wind had yet to sweep clean. But not since Fort Concho, one hundred sixty miles east, had twenty-four-year-old Clay Andrews seen anyone.

It was a hell of a lonesome country to watch a sun sink across, but hell had been a part of his life ever since that dark moment outside San Saba. Clay still couldn't believe Molly was gone, still couldn't come to grips with it, not even with all the images so powerful in his mind: wrists and blood and straight razor against dark-stained quilt.

A sister shouldn't die that way. No

7

eighteen-year-old girl should, but he had found her lying there, pale and cold, a draft drawing strands of her golden hair toward an open window at her shoulder.

A part of Clay wanted to keep on riding, letting the stocking-footed bay carry him ever farther from the blowing flies that had found her through the window. He wanted to gig the jaded animal until both of them were as dead as Molly. But, he supposed, there would be time for that later if he ever found the answers.

Right now, he needed to make camp and rest — he and the bay and the dapple gray packhorse that trailed at the end of a rope — and the boot was as good a place as any.

Clay figured the Pecos for the crookedest river in the world, a treeless, sheer-walled canal slithering through an arid country scorched by the sun. As he turned the bay off-trail and pulled rein only yards from the sudden bank, he could see the low-hanging sun glimmering a dozen feet below in a brief straightaway between sculpted earthen walls. This was no place to lose footwear, but there it was, a marker smack-dab in the middle of hell's back acre.

Clay had the towrope in hand as he stepped down, his underslung boot heel digging into the alkali soil. There was little danger of the exhausted horses straying, but he went ahead and half secured the reins and rope around a small pedestal of dirt supporting a clump of saltgrass.

But that wasn't the only precaution he took. Against the front housing of the saddle, a Colt 1860 Army revolver caught sunlight as it dangled from the horn by a leather loop. The cap-and-ball .44 was loaded with only four rounds, and Clay wished now that he had cast more balls before setting out. Not doing so had been his way of hoping he would never have to use the revolver, but he felt better as his hand closed on the walnut grip. Indian country would make a man think.

He slipped the eight-inch barrel inside the waistband of his duck trousers and knelt to the boot. The calfskin upper was cracked and caked with dirt, suggesting that it had been there a long time. At first the boot resisted his tug, even though most of it was exposed. But when he took it heel and toe and applied more force than he should have needed, it broke free — with a detached foot inside.

Good God.

Clay dropped the boot and shrank from it as if it had been a rattler. He stumbled back all the way to bank's edge and sank to the ground, twisting around to break his fall with his hand. Under his hat brim, he could see a cauldron of muddy, red water down and away, racing by in ominous silence, but Clay could hear his heart hammering like churning hoofs.

With a look over his shoulder, he wondered why it hadn't occurred to him that this might be a grave. After all, a boot didn't just appear from nowhere in such a forsaken place.

Turning back into the briny wind that rose from the stream, Clay drew his knees up, supporting his elbows, and found his lowered brow with his hand. There was a measure of physical relief in shielding his eyes from the torturous glare, but hiding from everything around him served only to make it easier to see inside himself.

Desecrating a grave.

He never would have done it. It was wrong, heinous, and it shook him to the core to think that someone might do the same to Molly's grave. She had rested in the shade of a live oak for three months now, the wooden box granting no protection against grave-digging worms that must have long-since distorted her innocent face into a loathsome grimace.

It was an awful picture, probing the

depths of his grief, and his trembling shoulders bent even more as his fingers grew wet against his stinging eyes. Just how many people had he lost that terrible day? Had it been only Molly, his last blood kin? Or had he also lost someone who had been like a brother to him for as long as he could remember?

He was afraid to find out, but the prospect of going through life, suspecting and not knowing, was even more terrifying.

That was what had driven Clay here, across so many miles of frontier to a wasteland that would as soon see him scalped as let him pass. He had tempted fate ever since leaving Fort Concho and bearing west up the Middle Concho. The threat had heightened as he had trailed up Centralia Draw and crossed a neck of the Staked Plains, ridden under the bluffs of Castle Gap, reached the Pecos and the crossing point of the Comanche War Trail. Even though he had turned upstream on the river's east side a day ago, he felt no safer.

If only his bullet bag was as full as his powder flask . . .

Wondering, Clay looked back at the boot. Whoever had buried the man in such a shallow grave had done so hastily, as if anxious to move on from all the dangers that this river posed. Might they have been in too great a hurry to check his pockets for pistol balls?

It took all of Clay's willpower, but he dragged himself up and started for the grave. He kept his head down, not wanting to look as his jingling spurs tolled off his steps, but finally a worn boot sole with rotting stitching lay before him. Troubled by what he contemplated, he skirted it and stopped at the almost imperceptible depression laid out along an east-west axis. A dusty haze moved across it, ever changing with the gusts.

With the side of his reluctant foot, Clay scraped a twelve-inch line across a dead man's home.

Home.

Was a three-by-six and a shroud of dirt all that anybody had to look forward to? Could all a person's work and dreams, the struggles and hopes, end in dilated eyes staring and never seeing again?

Clay could still picture the blue of Molly's eyes, looking off into eternity, into nothingness.

He started to drag his foot across again, but then shuddered and could do no more. Four rounds or forty, if a grave like this was a person's only reward, he had no right to disturb it.

But Clay did have an obligation. Turning, he reached for the boot to rebury it, only to see from this angle that more than a human appendage was inside. He could make out the drawstring of a leather pouch, an unusual thing for a man to carry in his boot. He cocked his head so he could inspect without touching. Something gave bulk to the pouch, but without doing more, nothing would tell him if it contained pistol balls.

Clay stretched out his forefinger and thumb, seeking the drawstring, avoiding the remains. He came within an inch only to hesitate, pondering his reaction if someone were to rob Molly's body of her treasured locket.

He glanced around as if expecting someone to deny permission. He saw a scurrying lizard, the exhausted horses, a twisting dust devil — and a puff of dust that blighted the downriver horizon, a crosswind spreading it by the moment.

Clay went cold and straightened. This wasn't a low-hanging cloud or rising sandstorm, but a sign that he better heed. He suddenly felt so vulnerable, and for good reason. He was caught in an open plain with a ridden-down horse, there was a boiling river with unscalable banks at his back, and he didn't have enough rounds in his Colt to rustle up a decent jackrabbit stew.

Seizing the pouch, he stuffed it inside his hickory shirt as he rushed for the horses, all thoughts of burying the boot forgotten. His frantic bolt spooked the animals, but he calmed them with a word and took reins and rope. Hooking the revolver over the horn, he stepped up into the saddle and gigged the bay upriver, fleeing the troubling sign in the sky.

At the next bend, he intersected the beaten wagon road and took the struggling bay up it, the dapple gray at rope's end resisting. Clay didn't know how much of a lead he had, and a glance back over the packhorse's ears couldn't tell him. But with both animals faltering, he knew it wouldn't take much to ride him down.

As he pressed the bay for more than it had, Clay searched for an arroyo, an outcrop, a hint of brush up out of the floodplain, any place to make a stand. But the Pecos flowed through pure alkali too sterile to support more than scrub mesquite and prickly pear, and too flat and thirsty to nurture drainages.

This was a good place for a shallow grave, all right.

The alkali rose from the trail in a fine

powder that enveloped him and crawled down his collar. To whoever was behind, it would be as sure a sign as their dust was to him. But his only other option would have been to pull rein and wait, and that was no option at all.

Molly again grew powerful in Clay's mind, and he wondered if she would be able to answer his questions herself before this was over. Maybe there was no other way for this to end. Maybe some passerby would find his own boot sticking out of the ground. Maybe if he never made it to that cattle outfit at the Narrows on the Pecos, he could at least die still hoping that he had lost no one but Molly.

Through the rope, Clay could feel the dapple gray weaken more with every stride. He knew that a packhorse tired quicker than any other, for its load couldn't work in tandem with its gait the way a rider could. But Clay grimly held on, even as the force taxed his grip and wrenched his arm. Then the gray stumbled, jerking the rope from his hand, and the bay between his legs responded with new vigor.

With a glance back at the gelding receding in the hanging alkali, Clay patted his saddle pony's foamy neck and encouraged it to greater speed. He hated to leave the gray, but a man on the verge of losing his life had bigger worries.

When the trace skirted another sharp bend, Clay checked over his shoulder and thought he could make out riders at the base of the drifting cloud. They were there and then they weren't, the swirls kicking ever higher as they closed on him.

A desperate mile raced by, and then another and another as the cadence of the bay's hoofs began to slow. Its breaths were labored, its heart pounding against Clay's leg. It was a ride that tested the horse's mettle, but the situation also was taking Clay's measure as a man, and he didn't like what it showed. From the moment he had left San Saba, he had realized what waited at trail's end, and he didn't know if he could find the courage for this day or any other.

With his own dust obscuring the country ahead, Clay never noticed the prairie schooner until he was within a few hundred yards of it. But there it was across the river, the wagon sheet shining white at ten o'clock, the only thing of any height as far as he could see. For a man fast losing hope, it buoyed his spirits even though an impassable stream kept him from it.

Then the Pecos veered away and came back again three times, caught up in a snake-track dance, and when Clay negotiated a final twist, he found the fourteen-foot schooner broadside before him on his side of the river. It was stationary, its tongue on the ground at the narrow mouth of a horseshoe bend. The distance from bank to bank couldn't have been more than twenty yards, creating an effective gate to a one-acre natural trap grazed by six or eight mules.

Clay threw dust against the sideboard as he drew rein so sharply that the bay almost sat on its haunches.

"Anybody here?" he shouted.

For a moment there was only the screech of the grease bucket as it swung under the rear axle. Then a figure burst around the jockey box suspended over the tongue, and Clay looked into the pinched eyes of a girl of maybe twenty in a spotted calico sunbonnet. A matching but soiled dress, long-sleeved and high-necked, was so loose-fitting that she held it at her knee to keep the wind from showing more than her front-laced shoes and a glimpse of a ruffled petticoat.

Clay frantically scanned the grazing mules beyond her. "How many men?" he pressed.

She shrank a step, drawing his attention. As he read the confusion in her shaded face, he could only imagine Molly's alarm under similar circumstances.

He threw an arm back up-trail. "They're comin'! Where's your men?"

She whirled in the direction he pointed and must have seen the dust, for when she turned back, her flushed features showed a person overwhelmed.

"Miss? You got to talk to me!"

"There's just Mr. Casner. He's out scouting."

"You by yourself?" Clay wanted to ask who would leave a girl alone in a place like this, but now wasn't the time. Dismounting with his Colt, he hurriedly secured the bay to the front wheel and stepped over the tongue. With a glance back at the rising plume, he wished he hadn't been so spooked by the thought of exhuming a body.

"Not even a full load!" he told her. "You got a gun?"

The girl's second glance at the cloud seemed to release her from her shock.

"There's a double-barrel!" She ran for the rear of the wagon, the wind whipping her dress and petticoat.

"Shot and powder!" he shouted as he chased after her.

Around a yellow-spoked wheel as tall as Clay, she mounted a crate with weathered slats below the open end gate and climbed up. Wood creaked as she parted the flap and stepped inside a wagon bed four and a half feet wide, a confining space cluttered with chests, a barrel of coal oil, quilts, and a spare wheel. Garments of calico, duck, and hickory dangled from the exposed bows and brushed her bonnet as she crawled into the shadows.

As she rummaged, Clay peered around the schooner's outside corner and found a dozen ghostly horsemen taking shape against whorls of alkali downriver. When the riders reached a point just outside of rifle range, the dust overtook and concealed them, and as the haze dissipated he understood why. They had held their ponies, maybe to assess the situation, and now they merged into a single unit of horseflesh, buckskin, and waving feathers.

If Clay had held out hope these might be white men, reality had dealt him a terrible blow in a fight that was his first and maybe his last. But experience hadn't helped his father, a veteran Indian fighter who had served with the Texas Rangers. Clay didn't remember that long-ago raid on the San Saba, although he seemed to recall a big man telling him to stay put beside his baby sister in their mother's arms. Still, the tombstone with the inscription "Killed By Indians" had been a part of Clay's life ever since.

As a teenager, he once had pressed his mother for details of the attack, but she had reacted with such emotion that he had never broached the subject again. A couple of years later, Clay had set a second tombstone, and then it had been up to him alone to fend for his sister.

"You got to hurry!" he shouted back to the girl.

Hoofs began to thunder, and Clay faced a charge that threatened to earn him an epitaph like his father's.

Lifting his .44, he considered how to measure out four pistol balls against a force so large. What was the use? Even if the girl came up with a shotgun, even if he could steady his trembling hand and shoot straight for once, what chance would the two of them have?

It was a hell of a thing, waiting to die. Clay wondered what had passed through Molly's mind as she had lain on that patchwork quilt and bled out. Had she too dwelled on what it would be like in that final moment when the world drifted away? How had she found the courage to face it alone, when he couldn't even muster an ounce of what it must take? His dry mouth, his pounding pulse, the heave of his lungs — he was a damned coward compared to her.

They came at him in a compact wedge, a seeming horde of shrieking devils straight out of hell. They were a squat people with low centers of gravity, their figures conforming gracefully with the motion of their bareback ponies. Clay wasn't sure if they were Comanches or Kiowas; all he knew was that each of them seemed joined to his horse, a single fierce fighter intent on killing.

"They're on us!" he shouted, cocking the revolver.

He could see sunlight glinting from bits of metal and shell on the fringe of their buckskin leggings.

Wait till they're in range! he told himself.

He distinguished individual warriors, each with an eagle feather in coal-black hair with long braids on either side.

Wait! You've got to wait!

He saw hideously painted faces — one black down the left side, a second black down the right, others streaked dark above plucked eyebrows or across coppery-brown cheeks.

Just a little longer!

He saw the lead warrior slide away from

his paint's withers, maintaining only the crook of his leg across the shielding animal, and reemerge under the pony's neck with a bent bow and a nocked arrow.

Now!

Clay took aim and fired, because it was the only thing left to do.

The ball kicked up dirt beside unshod hoofs, but the paint shied at the roar and the arrow thudded off-target into the sideboard at Clay's elbow. Suddenly warrior and animal were down in an awful wreck, a shotgun blast reverberating in Clay's ears. The arrow shaft still quivered as he looked down the sideboard to find a smoking muzzle poking out under the wagon cover.

Still, the Indians surged at him, their unearthly war whoops icing his blood. He fired a second shot that staggered a roan as more arrows came flying, ripping through the wagon cover, driving into the sideboard, imbedding in the crate at Clay's boot.

He squeezed off his last two rounds in quick succession and a warrior tumbled off a bay with a skunk pelt in its tail. The lucky shot broke the wedge at the last instant, but warrior after warrior now veered for the wagon tongue. They seemed intent on wheeling around the schooner in order to press the attack, but they didn't reckon with so narrow a space between schooner and bank. It forced the foremost rider within deadly range of the shotgun, and when the second barrel boomed, the warrior's squealing animal dropped and drove him head over heels through raging dust.

Clay knew there were no more loads to fire, but threat worked where gunpowder couldn't. Horsemen swooped in, two abreast, and scooped up their fallen, and then the band wheeled and raced into the dusk.

It was a reprieve, but a tenuous one. A second wave in the next minute or two would catch Clay and the girl defenseless, and he feared that at any moment the disappearing hostiles would spin and come at them again.

"They'll be back!" he warned.

He turned to the schooner bed and found the girl framed by the flaps as she poured gunpowder in her palm. She was a wisp of a person, and the standing twelve-gauge with the walnut stock and twenty-inch barrels seemed daunting for one her size. He started to offer his help, but she seemed as proficient at loading as she was at shooting.

He checked for Indians again, but found only a haze settling across the barrens.

"Any forty-four balls?" he asked.

When she didn't answer, Clay took it for a no and didn't ask again. Time was critical, and he couldn't afford to distract her. Loading through the muzzle was a multistep process — pour in a measured powder charge and slap the barrel to settle it, tap in a wad and the shot and a second wad, and then seat the load with a ramrod. Even under ideal conditions, nearly a minute would pass before a shooter could reach the point of priming a gun with a percussion cap, and this girl had two barrels to load under desperate circumstances.

But what kind of deterrent could a couple of volleys be? The two of them had fired three times that many before the Indians had turned, and next time his .44 would snap against empty chambers.

Unless . . .

Clay laid aside the Colt and hastily retrieved the leather pouch from his pocket. The rotted drawstring broke as he tried to untie it, but he spread the opening and shook four or five rough-edged rocks into his hand. The largest was the size of a robin's egg, and together they were as heavy as an equal amount of lead.

But pistol balls, they weren't. He started to discard them but decided the pouch was their rightful place. They had meant enough

24

to somebody to conceal in a boot, and respecting them was like safeguarding Molly's locket.

But now Clay noticed something handwritten inside — paper folded into a wad. He dug it out, still hoping for a cache of .44 balls, and found a sheet so brittle that it tore to his handling. It was obviously a letter, nothing more, but a glimpse of a sketch kept him working until the triangular fragment was fully open. Between the fading light and the whipping wind, he couldn't tell much, but he saw that it was an ink-blotted map instead of a letter.

Returning the items to the pouch and pocketing it, Clay scanned for hostiles past the dead horses and weighed his options. There would be no moon tonight, just a steady dark as black as his hopes. If those Indians didn't storm the wagon before nightfall, they were sure to do it afterward.

Clay turned to the schooner's interior and found the girl ramming in a charge.

"When's he supposed to be back?" he asked. "The man you said was with you?"

She glanced up but the rod continued its short strokes.

Now Clay pressed for an answer. "What kind of gun he got? If we don't get some help . . ."

The girl made eye contact. "Won't do much good with a shovel. That's all he took."

"In Indian country? What's the matter with him? And leavin' you by yourself?"

Both barrels evidently ready, she leaned the shotgun against the upright spare wheel beside her.

"A body gets used to it," she said.

Clay continued to focus on the wheel. It was a smaller one, designed for the front axle, but it still had a diameter of almost five feet.

"Listen, miss," he said, studying the wheel spokes and its heavy iron tire. "They're comin' back for the horse and mules. If they'll just wait till after dark, maybe we got a chance."

The moment he said it, he wondered if Molly was counting down his final moments from that shaded grave on the San Saba.

CHAPTER 2

Inside the schooner, Lil Casner waited and thought.

She was only twenty, but she had seen enough of life not to care much if she never saw another sunrise. She remembered a hardscrabble farm near Red Hill in East Texas, and a two-room house as cramped as the schooner. Constructed of oak logs, the dwelling couldn't have been anything but confining, considering that she had vied for space with five younger siblings.

She supposed that her mother had been caring enough, or at least as much as possible when her attention had been so divided. Lil reckoned that even her father had cared, although he had always seemed more invested in his cotton fields and a sandy patch of subsistence crops. "One step from the poor farm," he had often said with truth.

But Lil's worst memory was of a day six years ago when a disgusting, middle-aged man named Casner had pulled his wagon to a stop outside their home. Her father seemed to know him, but Lil scarcely would have paid Casner any mind if he hadn't reeked so much. Then Casner gave her father some money, her mother bundled together a few items for her, and the next thing Lil knew, Casner wagoned her away as his bride. By nightfall, a filthy man three times her age had been clinging to her and grunting.

No matter what these Indians might do, Lil knew it couldn't be worse than what had happened at age fourteen when her innocence and life had both been stolen away.

Over the years, Lil had suffered all kinds of abuse at the hands of this controlling man who denied her any friends and dictated her every action. Her life had revolved around Casner's needs and his alone, and she hadn't even received a constant roof overhead in return.

For the last six weeks, they had been on the trail, all the way from Fort Griffin on the Clear Fork of the Brazos. Early on, they had fallen in with freighters bound for Fort Stockton. The wagons had crossed the Pecos at Horsehead Crossing, but despite Indian sign and warnings from the freighters, Casner had held to the river's near side and turned upstream alone. Common sense couldn't prevail with a man obsessed, and when he and Lil hadn't been wagoning slowly along, Casner had been off chasing a fool story that had dominated his talk for as long as Lil could remember.

But maybe not all men were fools. This lean stranger with the boyish looks and intelligent blue eyes had joined her in the gloomy schooner and seemed to have a plan. He had fetched his lariat, and now he ran his hand along the spare wheel's iron rim.

"Just five minutes!" he whispered. "That's all we need, five minutes after good dark!"

She couldn't imagine what he had in mind, but she was conditioned not to question. The back of Casner's hand had taught her well.

Taking the wheel in hand, the stranger carried it out and lowered it off the end gate. The open flaps framed him as he turned.

"Ma'am, I'm sorry I can't do more to help you except be here. A girl deserves to have somebody there for her, especially when she's dyin'."

He was only a silhouette as he lowered his head and shook it. When he looked up, he removed his hat and held it at his waist.

"I'm sorry, miss." His voice was even quieter. "I'm still plannin' on us gettin' out of this fix." He glanced outside. "Name's Clay Andrews, out from the San Saba country. What they call you, if you don't mind me askin'?"

"Lilly Casner. Lil."

"Pleased to meet you, Miss Lil. I just don't like the circumstances."

Lil had forgotten what kindness in a man was like, and it lifted her spirits even as she realized this might be the last moment of her life.

"If you'll hand me the shotgun," said Clay, slipping on his hat, "I'll keep watch."

When she extended the weapon, his hand brushed hers, and she strangely wished that his touch could linger. "I'll pray on things, Mr. Andrews."

"You do that, ma'am."

The crate outside creaked as he stepped down, and then he turned back a moment.

"Keep your chin up, Miss Lil. No reason for somebody so young not to have her whole life ahead of her."

His voice choked a little, but Lil was beyond emotion; he couldn't have known that she had no future even if she lived.

A gloom slowly crept over everything — the river bend between the flaps, the inside of the schooner, the innermost part of her that could only wait for the end. In her loneliness, she found herself longing for Clay's company, his encouragement, but what would it serve when she would never have a tomorrow?

As hard dark fell, adding to her despair, she heard Clay's urgent whisper.

"We got to go, Miss Lil!"

His voice inspired confidence even when her hopes were lowest, and she scrambled across the wagon bed and found him waiting.

"Like a church mouse!" he implored as he gave her the shotgun and helped her down.

It was as dark a cloudless night as Lil could remember, and she brushed back her bonnet to let it dangle so she could catch more starlight. Clay stooped beside the right rear wheel and she went closer, clueless as to what this was about. He seemed to do something with his catch rope, but all she knew for sure was that she felt so much more vulnerable out here in the open.

The spare wheel stood against the end gate's corner, and it rocked a little as she bumped it. Then Clay rose, took the wheel under his arm, and started toward the hidden river. He carried something else as well, and as Lil followed she saw that it was his coiled lariat. He seemed to be playing it out behind, for what purpose she had no idea.

When they reached the riverbank, Clay leaned the wheel into her shoulder, an unspoken indication that he wanted her to support it. She obliged, leaving him free to kneel and stretch the lariat taut. The way it lay flush on the ground, she realized that he had secured it to the base of the schooner's rear wheel.

She was still as curious as ever when he pivoted to the river and threw the coil over the drop-off. Could this stranger be crazier than her husband?

She watched with hopelessness as Clay peered into what she knew were deadly waters a dozen feet straight down. But when he retrieved the rope, she understood now that he had measured it, for at a specific point in the strands, he tied it around the wheel's rim, leaving several feet trailing.

As the purpose dawned on her, Lil whirled at the call of a night bird unlike anything she had heard on the river.

She felt the brush of Clay's bristly cheek. "Now, Miss Lil!"

He lowered the wheel over the edge, and when he seized the gun she went to her stomach at the bluff with the river behind her. Working her hands under the rope, she slid her legs over the drop-off. Clay took her wrists as she kicked for support below, and only her forearms were still on the crest when her shoes found the narrow wheel rim. A long step took her on down to the hub.

She could taste the briny earthen wall as she looked up, her hands aching from her grip on the rope. Clay's hold slipped away as she dropped farther, searching blindly between angling spokes until her toes found the lower section of rim.

Clay's boot brushed her face, and she moved aside to let him slide down. The rope groaned and the wheel swung alarmingly, but he quickly found footing beside her. There was no place for her head except the hollow of his neck, a position she had never been in with any man except Casner. She could smell Clay's trail dust and sweat, but it was nothing like the reek to which she was accustomed.

Tense minutes passed before the night bird called again, and then the night exploded.

First came hoofbeats, rising up from deep in the bend. In moments they were overhead, trapping her between a quaking bank and an echo from the bluff across the river. Then the damned in hell seemed to cry out

— piercing cries that shook Lil to the core — and she knew that Indians not only had crept past the schooner and stampeded the mules, but now stormed the camp.

Lil's fragile holds began to give, her toes and hands screaming *no more, no more!* Clay must have felt her struggling, for he fed the loose end of the rope into her hand and twisted it around her wrist. For an eternity she fought to cling there, strangely wanting to live now that she might not. Then there was a bang, a snap, a screech of wood as if a warhorse had bumped the hidden schooner. The next instant, rubble showered her and the bank surged skyward as the wheel dropped.

It came to a wrenching stop that jarred her loose, and the world became nothing but putrid water that blinded and choked and muffled her cry.

For a moment she was helpless in a raging river, but then a force equally powerful yanked her in the opposite direction as the rope cut into her wrist. The stars came out, disappeared, and came out again. The vicious cycle continued, teasing her with air only to deny it, even as she realized that the schooner had rolled a few feet toward the bank and trapped her between a taut rope and a treacherous current.

Lil was drowning by evil degrees, but something just as wicked was happening around her. Through swamping waters burst an eerie glow, and when she popped up again, the world seemed on fire. The far bank's upper reaches burned with a strange flicker, and so did the reflecting waters before her.

When Lil went under once more, she wondered if this was perdition. But now the force through the rope grew stronger and she began to move against the current. She surfaced to find Clay and the wheel in witch fire right above the waterline. He reached for her with an arm twisted in the rope, and as the river sucked her under again she felt the clamp of his hand on her wrist.

She came up to stay, gasping and choking in a twilight where only night should have been. She was as weak as a newborn foal as she seized the rim, and only Clay's grip kept the rushing waters from sweeping her away. Looking into his face, illuminated as if by lamplight, she saw him mouth a desperate word — *Quiet!*

From somewhere above, the night crackled and popped and roared as the flickering twilight persisted. Perdition, it wasn't, but she realized it might be a jumping-off place to it. The Indians must have splashed the schooner with coal oil and torched it, and now the vehicle blazed in the gloom and sent smoke boiling against the stars. She could smell it and taste it, thick and oily in her throat.

She froze, muting her gasps. But even if she kept silent, what could keep those Indians from seeing the rope on the ground?

Lil lifted her gaze in terror, expecting a demon's painted face to burst over the summit. Then the wheel slipped hub-deep in the river, forcing her to find new handholds on upper spokes that twisted with the currents.

Clay was up to his thighs in water as he looked up at a rope still sliding inch by inch. "We got to take a chance!" he whispered.

But Lil already knew it. The fire was consuming the schooner, burning the wood right off the iron, and any moment it would work its way down to the knotted rope and give them up to a river that had no escape.

With Clay's help, Lil gained the hub and then the iron rim above it. Looking up, she gripped the rope overhead, but the prospect of climbing out seemed impossible for someone who had left her strength in the river.

"You can do this!" Clay said in her ear.

But even with his boosting arm and her

wild kicks against the bluff, she couldn't pull herself up more than a few inches. As she slid back to the wheel, she knew that this stranger was about to abandon her just as her family had.

Clay must have read the surrender in her face. "I'm not leavin' you!" He twisted about. "Put your arms around my neck — get on my back!"

With no room to maneuver, even that seemed unlikely, but he had given her something she had never had before — hope. As she wrapped arms about him, he hoisted her and she managed the rest.

He worked the shotgun between her hand and his chest, and the wall began to move. The lariat continued to slip, but he redoubled his efforts as his boots slapped the bank. It was more than anyone could expect of a man, and she couldn't believe that this stranger would risk his life for somebody who had been cast away by even her own parents.

As Clay hooked a forearm over the crest, the rope gave way with a sharp *pop!* Suddenly they were swinging pendulum-like against the wall, and all Lil could do was muffle a startled cry.

For a split second she imagined that she was already down in those awful waters again, but Clay grimly held on as he clawed at the bluff and dug for a foothold. She didn't know where he found the will, much less the strength, but he kept at it until he managed a second handhold on top. Still, it seemed impossible to drag the two of them up, but seconds later she peered across the flat at a scene out of hell.

CHAPTER 3

Beyond exhaustion, Clay clung to the crest with the girl on his back and saw the fire burning against the night.

It devoured the schooner with a distant roar, the wind whipping yellow flames that threw off a swirling smoke blacker than midnight. Even at ground level, the residue burned Clay's sinuses and stung his eyes, but he kept them open as he winced to the searing heat.

Had he seen Indians, he wouldn't have known what to do, other than release his hold and accept a death more merciful than anything those sons of hell would offer. But as he quickly scanned the bend and floodplain — at least to the extent the blinding light allowed — he found only ominous desolation.

All the way up the bluff, Molly had been powerful in his mind, a motivating force pushing him to the limit and beyond.

Nevertheless, it seemed impossible to achieve the last step. But when he threw a leg over the crest and he and Lil rolled to safety, he felt almost a sense of absolution for accomplishing for her what he hadn't been able to for Molly.

Clay was too spent to do anything but lie on his side, searching for air while his pumping heart tried to break through his chest. Between him and the fire, the girl was trying to rise.

No!

He threw out an arm and dragged her flush against the ground. Her face was toward him now, a dark shadow as he looked toward the fire, but he knew it held confusion.

"They'll see us!" he whispered. Indeed, against a fire in a country this flat, a silhouette would stand out from a mile away.

But as Clay watched and waited, expecting the worst and knowing he had no option except to let it happen, he saw only the same kind of inferno that had raged inside him for all these months.

Terrible hours followed, punctuated by the faraway howl of wolves and the constant shifting of the choking smoke. Never was a night so long, except the one after he had found Molly, but day finally broke across a monument of blackened wagon irons rising from the smoldering ashes.

His face felt flushed and drawn, as if chapped by the fire's heat, and he could see the hint of such in the girl's complexion as she slept an arm's length away. Her clothes also told a story; they were as mud-caked as his.

Clay cautiously rose to an elbow. The floodplain stretched empty, except for a distant figure against a sky streaked red ahead of sunrise. It gave him enough pause to take up the shotgun, but he soon decided that it was only a yucca.

He stood, still scouting, and dwelled on the events of the evening before. Until now, he had always been sheltered from violence, at least within memory, and his emotions were still raw. Fear, excitement, and anticipation still pounded in every artery, and he considered how lucky the two of them had been. The stretched lariat should have been obvious in the firelight, but the Indians evidently had fled after torching the schooner.

"Is it safe, Mr. Andrews?"

He found the girl rising to her elbow.

"Just 'Clay,' ma'am. Two people go through what we did, I expect they're on a first-name basis." Indeed, he felt a strange union with her.

He took her arm as a courtesy. As he escorted her up, she gave him a peculiar look, as if unaccustomed to such a gesture. Then her gaze fixed on something behind him, and he turned to stare with her at the coals glowing through the wagon irons.

"Everything I had was in there," she said.

Clay felt for her, but when he checked her face it was emotionless.

"Not ever'thing, Miss Lil. You still got your life."

But as forlorn as her eyes were, he wondered if she had lost that too somewhere along the way.

"Ma'am, we's still in a fix. I don't know what happened to the man that's with you, but we can't just stay here hopin' he'll show up."

She only looked at him.

"Wherever he is," Clay went on, "he'll have to fend for himself, 'cause that's what we got to do." He nodded upriver. "There's a cattle outfit up that way somewhere. We got to try for it."

They started upstream at sunrise, two figures adrift in a wasteland with threats real or imagined on all fronts. As they fell into the windswept wagon ruts that Clay had followed since Fort Concho, he pondered what would be waiting for him ahead. Justice? Retribution? Or more questions for which he would never know the answers?

But maybe his journey through Indian country would end much sooner than he wanted.

"I'm grateful for the way you helped me." Lil's voice had a lilt like Molly's. "You could've left me in the river."

"Where I come from, a man don't do that to a girl."

The moment Clay said it, Molly's hasty handwriting rose up out of his memory. *A man wouldn't, all right,* he thought, *but a bastard out of hell might do anything.*

"I guess you come from a better place than me," she said.

"Where would that be for you, Miss Lil?"

She hung her head, a portrait of unhappiness against a sweeping desert that had no joy to offer.

"That schooner most of the time. Since I was fourteen, anyhow."

Clay wondered what had changed things all those years ago. "I guess you did lose a lot in the fire, then. When somethin's your whole home thataway —"

"Wasn't ever a home to me."

As Lil interrupted, she lifted strangely bitter eyes. But she wasn't finished. "Wish it'd

43

burned up a long time ago."

Clay didn't know how to respond, so he kept quiet. He had been so caught up in his own affairs, he hadn't considered that maybe he wasn't the only one with troubles.

For a couple of miles they trudged in silence beside their elongated shadows, stark against the same alkali that powdered Clay's boots. During the night, the soil had agitated his skin right through his clothes. The worst itch was on the inside of his thighs, but with a lady present, all he could do was push up his sleeves and rub the welts on his arms.

"Coal oil's good for your breaking out," said Lil.

"Yes, ma'am. Don't expect to be seein' any for a while, though."

"Nobody ever called me 'ma'am' before."

Clay couldn't imagine. *Even if she's a whore,* the saying among cowhands went, *you still respect her 'cause she's a woman.*

Clay stopped, and when Lil halted as well, he faced her and reverently removed his hat. "Nobody? Miss, they sure ought to have."

She studied him for so long that Clay pondered whether he had said something wrong.

"I never met anybody like you," she said. "Never met anybody really, last six years."

"I know what lonely country a place like this has got to be for you."

She only lowered her head again.

"Ma'am, don't get down about all this. We's in a lot better place than we was last night."

"I guess."

"Bet we's the only ones ever shared a porch swing down inside those banks that-away."

Now her gaze came up. "Mama made us kids a swing under a sweet gum once."

"I imagine y'all had a little more fun than we did."

"I used to spend hours pushing my brothers and sisters."

"Well, we got somethin' in common then. I rigged one up for my own . . ."

For a moment, the memories cut deeply, and he had a hard time getting the word out.

". . . sister. I — I guess that's been a long time ago."

Clay didn't know if his sadness was contagious, but something brought Lil's chin down again.

"Long time for me," she whispered.

He checked their surroundings. "We better keep movin'. Least in this country, we can see Indian sign a long way off." He squinted upriver at something just above the horizon. "See that yonder? What do you figure . . ."

Whatever it was, it swirled in place, a dark blight in which he could almost make out individual specks.

"Not colored like dirt," said Lil, shading her eyes as she peered.

"No, guess it's buzzards."

"Barely a jackrabbit here. Wonder what they're after."

Clay looked at Lil and found her looking back, and he knew that they shared the same awful thought.

In all the twists of the river during the next hour, Clay couldn't decide which bank the vultures guarded. Then he and the girl broke around a final coil and he found the buzzards wheeling over a location on the near side not two hundred yards away. On the ground gathered more buzzards, stalking about with spread wings.

Clay froze, and when he put his arm across the girl's path, she stopped with him. Maybe it was merely the carcass of an animal in that bleak and despairing bend, or maybe it was something more that threw the scent of death on the currents. All he knew was that he hadn't felt this way since he had stood in the doorway of Molly's room and stared in at hell.

"You need to stay here, Miss Lil," he said hoarsely. "One way or another, you need to stay here."

The girl didn't respond, but she didn't advance as he started for the vultures. With every hesitant step, Clay relived that walk across Molly's room — the hollow strike of his boot heels, the jingle of his spurs, the buzz of flies that swarmed in his face.

Molly! Molly!

He recalled the vacant sound of his cry too. But more than anything, he remembered the stunning disbelief that set him reeling toward the dark stains. Suddenly he was there, reaching for Molly's pale features in memory and scattering a host of hook-beaked scavengers in reality.

As the broad wings flapped and their shadow trails raced across the barren flat, the face-down body of a man burst into view. The talons and beaks had been effective, shredding the clothes and carving away at tissue and cartilage. But it was the crown of the head that was most ghastly, for a large section of scalp and hair was gone, baring a bloody skull for the flies.

All around, disturbed ground and dark splotches told a story of a man thrashing as his life had bled out, and the feathered arrow projecting from his shoulder blade explained why. But there was another striking detail as well. Something beneath the body elevated it a few inches, and a glint of sunlight in the far hollow of the neck offered a clue.

For two days, Clay had marched from one dead man to another, pausing only long enough to try to keep from joining them. He didn't want to touch the body, didn't want to do anything but back away from the raw flesh and the stench that churned his insides. But the girl deserved to know, and he had to be able to tell her something.

Kneeling, Clay laid the shotgun on the ground, took hold of a body as stiff as Molly's, and turned it.

It was a man, all right, with the scraggly gray whiskers of someone in his fifties. Out of a deeply scored face frozen in a grimace, glassy and dilated eyes looked up at Clay just as his sister's had.

Molly! Molly!

Clay's cry still echoed through his mind, stirring more memories. That single page so stained by blood. Those scribbled words that had been her last thoughts. That maddening phrase that had tortured him day and night. Would whatever he found at trail's end bring him peace?

If Clay had harbored any doubt about the old man's identity, the shovel blade reflecting sunlight beside the shoulder erased them.

"Had it coming."

Startled by a voice from behind, Clay seized the shotgun and spun. Only feet away, Lil stood framed against the sky as she stared down at the body. Springing to his feet, Clay did something that defied propriety — he embraced the girl so that his shoulder shielded her from the gruesome sight.

"Should've stayed back, Miss Lil. Should've stayed back."

With pressure from his arms, Clay turned her from the scene and escorted her away. He kept a hand on her upper arm and was surprised that he didn't feel a tremble. Only then did he realize what she had said, and he wondered if he had heard right.

But maybe the girl was stunned. Who wouldn't be? Anyway, who was to judge how a person should act at a time like this? He just wished he had been able to spare her the same kind of memories that would follow him all the way to his grave.

When they had walked fifty paces, Clay stopped and faced her so that her back was to the body. Her eyes showed nothing — neither horror nor grief nor fear — but he knew that all those emotions, and more, must be locked inside, waiting to break out.

"Miss Lil." Clay found a knot in his throat. "I'm goin' over and buryin' him. You've got to promise me you won't look back no more."

She only stared at him without emotion. He wanted to leave her the shotgun so she could stand guard while he was distracted, but he was afraid what someone in her frame of mind might do. He gave a hard look left and right, finding only dust devils crawling under a sky so low on all sides that it seemed ready to swallow him.

"You see somethin', you let me know," he said, starting away.

The buzzards had returned, but Clay quickened his pace and they took flight once more. Upon reaching the remains, he worked diligently, digging again that lonely grave under the San Saba live oak even as the Pecos alkali flew from the shovel.

But he also dwelled on the dead man at his feet. Given his age and name, this was obviously the girl's father, but Clay couldn't imagine anyone irresponsible enough to leave his daughter out here and traipse off with only a shovel.

After closing the grave, he left the shovel upright at the head as a marker and struck out for the girl. During the burial, he had glanced at her a few times, always finding her obediently turned away, and she still studied the distance as he came up at her shoulder.

Clay didn't know the proper thing to say at a time like this, but he knew the right thing to do. He took off his hat and held it with both hands.

"Miss Lil."

She turned, but now he had a hard time looking at her. "Miss Lil, I'm done if you want to say a few words over his grave."

She glanced over her shoulder. "Why would I want to do that?"

"I just thought . . ." Clay groped for words. "I'm awful sorry, ma'am, you losin' him thataway."

When her expected response never came, Clay looked back at the fresh mound stirring in the wind. He had said a few things over Molly's grave, all right, but all of them had been cries for answers.

Once more, he faced her. "Before we move on, you sure you don't want to go over? I can just imagine what it must be like to go off and leave your father in a place like this."

She gave him the strangest look, and then

her face blanched and her eyes seemed crestfallen. "Papa's got his share of blame," she muttered as she looked away. "That and his thirty pieces of silver."

Clay couldn't have been more confused. "His what?" He glanced at the grave. "I checked his pockets. They must've took what he had."

"Nothing like what got took from me."

Clay supposed she meant her father, but she was so mysterious about it that he wondered.

CHAPTER 4

Twenty-four-year-old Fin should have been riding up the Pecos, but instead he sat in the shade of his horse and twirled a salt-grass stem between his teeth. At daybreak the owner had sent him out from headquarters at the Narrows to join other hands in working the upriver reach of the Bar W range, but Fin seldom missed a chance to shirk a duty if he could get away with it.

Anyway, he didn't consider this loafing. The way the sun beat down, he figured it was just common sense to take advantage of the breeze on this thirty-foot ridge that overlooked the Pecos lowlands and a wilderness without natural shade for a hundred miles.

Besides, Fin had some daydreaming to do. For a while, he had contemplated his new-found nickname, but now the bluish escarpment low on the northwest horizon seized his fancy. Gilded mountains lay across the river, or so he had been told. Of course, "across the river" was a pretty vague description in these parts. In any one-mile stretch, the Pecos ran in every direction, perplexing enough to confound even the North Star.

Right now, Fin wished for a pointer star to that mother lode he had heard about ever since coming out from San Saba three months ago. In a country without women, it was the favorite topic in Bar W cow camps, and whoever told the story invariably gestured to those far-off mountains. No two people told it the same; Fin didn't even know if the range was called the Guadalupe or the War-Loopy. But he had heard enough common elements to piece together a tale sure to fire the imagination of any six-bits-a-day cowboy.

Back in the fifties, a goateed man up in years had ridden into faraway Fort Chadbourne between the Colorado and North Concho rivers and held forth in a tavern. Old Ben Simkins, they called him, and as the whiskey flowed, he bragged that he was about to strike it rich in the far reaches of the US Army's Upper Road to El Paso. Patrons of the establishment greeted his big talk with derision — until he produced nuggets and flashed a map fragment that he claimed to have found in a cave west of the Pecos.

Here, the story got a little sketchy. Evidently, the map had been intact at first, caught in a pile of human skeletons. The exposed portion pinpointed Skeleton Cave's location — something he no longer needed directions to — but the remainder of the map promised more, much more. In the gloom, Simkins made out a reference to a fabulous gold mine deep in the nearby Guadalupe Mountains, and the fragile document was sure to point the way if he could only extract it.

Then Simkins heard Indians approach, and in his haste to escape, he pulled too strongly and the map tore. Leaving behind the secret to the Guadalupe's mother lode, he fled with tantalizing nuggets and a map fragment that would give rise to a legend.

Others told it differently, but everyone seemed to agree on one point. After being grubstaked at Fort Chadbourne, Simkins set out again for Skeleton Cave, only to disappear forever and leave his backers with nothing to show for their investment.

Fin looked at his hands. They had never held more than twenty or twenty-five dollars at any one time, and that had been once a month at payday. But the unwelcome calluses and a crooked finger or two were there every day, constant reminders that it was folly to hope he would ever strike it rich as a cowhand.

Any chance of stumbling onto treasure in that Apache stronghold seemed remote at best, but Fin had ideas. He had suggested a joint venture to a few other Bar W hands at headquarters, but so far no one had been willing to give up a sure six bits a day for a wild-goose chase that could cost a man his life.

From his lofty vantage point this morning, Fin looked upriver, finding scattered beeves grazing the floodplain. Pope's Crossing was at the Bar W's distant upper limits, and he wondered if those bog riders he was supposed to meet downstream of it were as tired of work as he. If so, they might be ready to ford the Pecos with him and scour the hills for a cave of skeletons.

"Thought I made myself clear."

Fin almost shed his skin at the gruff voice from behind. He turned so quickly that the horse above him shied and jerked the reins from his hand. Through the pony's shifting legs he glimpsed an appaloosa, and as his own horse trotted away, he saw a dour-faced rider against the sky.

Fin scrambled to his feet as the man

gigged his mount after the runaway. Fin would almost have rather faced a Comanche than old man Brehmer, owner of the Bar W herd. Fifty or so, the heavyset cowman with the gray mustache was a no-nonsense sort who already had warned him about not pulling his weight. A Brazos country native, so Fin had heard, Edward Brehmer had come out only six months before and turned loose the first herd on the Pecos. He had fought a relentless sun, precipitous banks that forced cattle to search out watering places, and quicksand that seized even the stoutest steer. Fin supposed Brehmer had every right to be ornery; he just didn't want the old coot chewing him out again.

Fortunately, Fin had a few seconds to think up an excuse, and when Brehmer came riding back with the horse in tow, the young cowhand was on his feet and taking the offensive.

"Seen Indian sign, Mr. Brehmer," he said. He gestured upriver. "Up yonder, bunch of dust. I decided to keep a eye on it, see if they's comin' down toward headquarters."

Brehmer's profile became silhouetted against the sun as he pulled rein and looked upstream.

"Indians hadn't bothered us yet," said Brehmer. "Whirlwind's all I see."

Fin knew he had some persuading to do. "Yes, sir, the dust died down a little bit ago. Think they was mustangs, is all. I was just fixin' to start on upriver."

Brehmer's mustache twitched as he turned probing blue eyes to him. "Not lying to me, are you, Fin?"

Fin must have been losing his touch. There had been a time when he could have lied convincingly.

"No sir, sure seen somethin' that made me leery for a while. Be on my way now."

Fin took the reins of his horse from Brehmer and swung up into the saddle. Squeezing the animal with his thighs, he started away, but he still seemed to feel the owner's stare against his shoulder blades.

For anxious moments, Fin expected Brehmer to call after him, but when no words came, he congratulated himself. He hadn't lost his touch after all, the way the cowman had bought his story hook, line, and sinker. Now, if Fin was of a mind, he could daydream all the way to upper headquarters about interesting those river riders in chasing after a golden hoard.

That is, if the dark man inside him would let him.

After six hard years, Lil had escaped purgatory, but she couldn't understand what she had ever done to demand such penance in the first place.

With the freedom and all the questions came fear and loneliness. She had hated Casner, but she also had been dependent on him. From the time she had been fourteen, he had told her what to do and when to do it. He had never let her think for herself, and now that she was forced to, she felt lost.

She found herself longing for her parents in a way that she hadn't since those first few months after Casner had taken her away. Were they still in that same ramshackle house beside those cotton fields blowing sand? Were her brothers and sisters still there, or had they too been shuffled off to the highest bidder like milk-pen calves? Were any of them — mother, father, brothers, sisters — still alive?

Lil didn't know, and maybe none of her questions mattered anymore. That stage of her life had long since ended, snuffed out by the very parents she now wished for, and there could be no turning back. Her very soul had been taken from her, and her mother and father were more to blame than even Casner.

For wearisome hours Lil trudged with

Clay under a firebrand sun. Her dry throat burned, but not until they came upon a game trail angling down inside the river's bank did the two of them quench their thirst. It was the same as drinking putrid pickle juice, but at least the brine would keep her going.

That is, if she could keep it down. Within moments, the Pecos potion tied her stomach in knots.

The road continued straight whenever the river veered sharply, and for brutal miles Lil watched her shoes reach out mechanically across a country with almost more cow skulls than grass clumps. She and Clay came upon live cattle as well, W Bar–branded longhorns that crossed the road as they ambled in for water or headed back out for better grazing. Clay told her it was a good sign, for cattle meant that a cow camp was ahead.

Lil wished that somebody could tell her as easily what all of life's struggles meant.

"Why you suppose things happen like they do?"

Lil surprised herself by vocalizing what she pondered, and the question seemed to impact Clay in a way she wouldn't have expected. He twitched and his face went white.

60

"Not any reason. Life kicks you in the stomach ever' chance it gets."

He started to say more, but abruptly he appeared startled by what he had blurted. He looked at her with pity and regret, and his blue eyes seemed to open a window to a lot of buried sorrow.

"Miss Lil," he said as they stopped and faced one another, "I know what you just lost. I didn't have no business sayin' somethin' like that. I know you're feelin' all kinds of hurt, and I'm sorry if I made you feel any worse."

His voice was choked, his eyes on the verge of tearing — this man who had confronted all those attacking Indians without blinking. Sensitivity in a man was as foreign to Lil's experience as Clay's quiet strength, and she was struck again by how different he was from Casner and her father.

"I'd rather somebody tell me the truth and it hurt," she said, "than hear a lie that's supposed to make me feel better."

She remembered her mother walking her out to Casner's wagon with her belongings and telling her how happy she would be — the last words her mother had ever said to her.

"Better sometimes if a body don't say nothin' at all," said Clay. "Life throws enough at a person without havin' to be reminded of it."

"So is that all we can do, Mr. Andrews? Just take what's dished out?"

He turned bitter eyes to the bleak horizon down-trail. "Maybe it's the ones that die that's the lucky ones. Get left here and you got to deal with it all."

"You think He ever hears us?"

"Who?" Clay looked at her.

"When you pray, you suppose He listens?"

Clay breathed sharply. "I expect He's got better things to do. He sure don't do nothin' to help anybody."

"He helped us, Mr. Andrews."

Clay only looked at her.

"Yesterday evening, last night," she went on. "He got us through all of that."

He gave a half laugh of disgust. "I hate to tell you this, miss, but wasn't no God did that. What I didn't do, pure luck took care of."

Again, he seemed to realize that he had violated propriety, and all the caked dust couldn't hide his regret. "Ma'am, I didn't have no right. If it makes you feel better thinkin' somebody up in the clouds is lookin' after you, you go right ahead thinkin' that."

Lil didn't know what to think, and six

years of memories didn't help any. Maybe that's why she began dwelling on Clay instead of herself, and when she did, she saw a person crushed by some burden maybe as big as her own.

"Think anybody can be happy, Mr. Andrews? With all life hands us?"

Clay hesitated a moment. "Guess I won't know till it's over and done with. Never knowed whether I was happy or not till . . ." Emotion cut his words short. "By then it was too late. Don't expect I'll ever feel that way no more."

Now his eyes did glisten. "Miss, dwellin' on things — for either one of us — ain't goin' to help any."

Maybe not, thought Lil. But it had been the first conversation of substance she'd had in six years, and there was a measure of comfort in realizing that she wasn't alone in not understanding so many things.

Late in the day they intersected a beaten road stretching across their own. Out of a yucca-dotted rise two miles to their right, a dry wind carried the loose dust of the wagon ruts toward the Pecos. Lil couldn't tell where the road met the river, for a couple of hundred yards distant the trace angled away and disappeared in the coils.

"We's in luck, Miss Lil," said Clay. "It's

got to lead down to the water, and I expect you're as dry as me."

She was more than thirsty. The dehydrating sun had cracked her lips and robbed her of spittle, and the ground had begun to swim with her every step.

As she anticipated the bitter waters, she followed Clay's lead toward the stream. The suspended alkali curled around her ankles as the two of them dropped into the ruts, but Lil had taken only a few steps before Clay hesitated and threw an arm across her path. She read alarm in his face as his shotgun barrel traced the imprint beside his boot, one of a series of horse tracks scoring the road.

Quickly he pulled her down with him in a crouch and yanked off his hat. The two fingers that he flashed as he scanned downroad told her everything he knew: Two riders had come this way, and it hadn't been long ago, judging by how distinct the tracks were.

Lil knew enough about Indians now to realize that this was no place to make a stand. Even with only a pair of riders ahead, a double-barreled shotgun rammed full didn't leave any margin for error.

When Clay tugged her arm, she abandoned the wagon ruts and ran upstream with him. She mirrored his low profile for a hundred demanding yards, and another fifty yards as he veered for a bulge in the river. Lil was heartened by the knowledge that here, away from both trails, they could flatten themselves among the saltgrass clumps and maybe avoid detection.

But Clay evidently had other ideas. They were within forty-five yards of the riverbank now, and after motioning for her to lie down, he continued on alone. As he closed within thirty feet of the precipice, he dropped to his stomach, the shotgun crossways before him as he squirmed the rest of the way.

As Clay peered over the edge, Lil could see his entire body relax. He came to his feet, his attention still directed downstream.

"Halloo!" he shouted.

He waved the shining shotgun against the sky, and Lil thought she could hear an answering voice.

"We's comin' down!" Clay added.

Lil rose anxiously on burning feet as he returned in a brisk walk.

"Bog riders down at the crossin'," he said.

She reeled a little to dehydration and exhaustion, and Clay must have noticed, for he took her arm.

"You be able to make it, Miss Lil?"

Casner never would have asked, or steadied her either. Had she fallen, the old devil would have left her to fend for herself.

"I'm not used to anybody caring," she said.

"Sure can't figure that. If you don't mind, ma'am, I'll keep a-hold of your arm. You're kind of unsteady on your feet."

She didn't resist, although she still couldn't help but wonder when something might trigger the back of his hand against her face. Casner had conditioned her all too well.

Five minutes later, an eroded cut in the bank yawned open, revealing an easy approach to the kind of rushing red waters that had almost claimed Lil the evening before. The sun danced in the riffles and glinted off salt residue in a matching cut across the river. As Clay helped her down the gentle grade, she found the white splotches equally widespread under her shoes.

The water at this crossing was unusually shallow, not even stretching bank to bank. Immediately upstream on the near side, the two bog riders were afoot beside a speckled longhorn mired up to its rib cage in dark mud. The men were turned away, their pants legs rolled up to their knees as they worked to extricate the steer. A catch rope stretched from the animal's mossy horns to a bay horse under the sheer bank, while a dapple gray was secured to a nearby boulder that supported worn boots and threadbare socks.

Before the bovine, the younger cowhand stood with a two-handed grip on the widespread horns that could disembowel. Still, the wild steer slung its head a little, doing its best to hook the chisel-jawed older man who stamped around its foreleg.

"See here, Pate?" asked the latter. "You got to tromp him out. You got to break that suction down around his hoof."

"Looks like you could use a hand," said Clay.

The two men looked around. Lil saw them plainly now: the chisel-jawed cowhand with a lot of weathering in his late-thirties face, and his fair-complected young companion with a schoolteacher look about his squinting eyes. He gave all appearances of being nearsighted, but he must have made Lil out all right, for he removed a hand from the steer's horns and started to tip his hat.

It was all the distraction the longhorn needed. The animal's raw strength overpowered his tenuous hold, and two and a half feet of curved horn swept around with a glancing blow that threw the older man off-balance.

The latter howled in inappropriate laughter as he plopped on the seat of his britches. But the studious-looking cowhand had even less to laugh about, faced as he was with free-swinging horns. He tried to shrink back, but his feet were planted in the mud. Then a wicked point hooked his shirt and drew him in against the animal's head, right between the raging horns.

Simultaneously, the geldings went wild, spooked by the melee. With the roping horse shying, the lariat snapped taut, pinning the young man's hand against horn.

Clay shouted a too-late warning and sprang toward the horse. Even out of the quicksand, footing was soft, limiting the horse's shifting, and within seconds Clay seized the bridle and relaxed the tension on the rope. The injured cowboy, free now, pulled back out of harm's way to stand rubbing the back of his hand.

"Told you to watch them horns," chastised the sprawled figure with a grin. "Got any fingers left?"

His grimacing partner studied his hand. "My Lord, I could have *lost* them." He turned to Clay. "I'm really grateful, mister. I guess I'm out of my element."

"Let's try it a different way," said Clay. "You step over and let Miss Lil tend you." He tilted his head toward her and climbed into the saddle.

Lil didn't realize that she was almost as tall as the tawny-haired young man until he approached, but that didn't mean she was any less intimidated. She had barely interacted with anyone other than Casner for six years, and she was about to do so with two different individuals in less than twenty-four hours.

"My name's Pate, miss," said the cowhand, successfully tipping his hat this time as he proffered his injured hand. "That's Green still laughing down there in the mud. Everything's always humorous to him, unless it's Indians. We ride for the Bar W's, or at least Green does. My father's the owner."

It was more information than Lil had expected, but it didn't ease her apprehension as she took Pate's hand in both of hers. The palm was too soft for a cowboy's, and so was the skin on the back of the fingers that bore a reddish rope burn.

"You move your fingers all right, Mr. Pate?"

"Pate's my Christian name."

"Go ahead and try to bend them."

When she withdrew a little, he flexed his

fingers gingerly.

"You don't think they're broken, do you?" he asked. "I'll still be able to hold a pen, won't I?" His voice had the tone of a worried youngster, even though they were about the same age.

"They don't feel apart none, but if they go to swelling on you, they might need a splint."

"Feel these two knuckles here," pressed Pate. "You don't think maybe . . ."

Lil inspected the joints front and back, her fingers gently testing, and even after she released her hold, his hand lingered before her as if begging for another touch.

"What you waitin' on there, Pate?" teased Green, who had gained his feet. "Want her to put a mud poultice on that?"

Shaken into awareness, Pate flushed like a smitten adolescent and dropped his hand. Lil was surprised that anyone could be more ill at ease than she, but she spared him further embarrassment by going to the river's muddy edge and cupping up water with her hand. She was downstream of the bogged steer, and the brine was as strong as ever, but no one with her degree of thirst was in a position to complain. She drank until she felt bloated, and finished by splashing her burning face.

Retreating to solid footing, she noted Clay's know-how astride the bay as he helped with the steer. It was a team effort, with Green tramping the mud and breaking the suction around first one hoof and then another. Clay, meanwhile, kept the lariat taut, denying the steer an opportunity to wield those horns again. Green issued instructions on when and how much to pull, and Clay and the bay responded with appropriate force.

Each time a hoof worked free, Green tied the leg to the steer's torso to prevent the steer from bogging it again. As he secured the last hoof, the steer rolled to its side, a position from which it was easy for Clay's mount to drag the animal to firmer ground. Even then, the steer remained dangerous as Green slipped the loop off its horns and set about releasing its legs. The Bar W cowhand saved a rear hoof for last, untying it only after gripping the bovine's tail near its base.

"See what I'm a-doin', Pate?" Green asked. "Soon's he gets up, he'll go to flashin' them horns. You got to twist that tail one way and then another to keep him off of you."

Sure enough, the steer scrambled up, angry and ready for battle, and the cowhand deftly fended it off until the animal went on its way.

Clay dismounted and handed Green the reins.

"How many in your party, mister?" asked Pate.

"Just us." Clay started for the stream.

"I'll be durned," said Green, flashing that toothy grin. "Just one wagon?"

Clay knelt at river's edge. "Not even that." He scooped up water in his hand and drank. "Been on foot all day."

Pate looked concerned as he turned to Lil. "There's Comanches out here, miss. We've been seeing fresh sign all week."

Clay overheard. "We found more than that. Or they found us, is more like it."

"Attacked you?" asked Green, his smile fading.

"About as bad as it could get. I'm glad we found the two of you, 'stead of them findin' *us* again."

Pate wheeled one way and then another. "Hadn't we ought to start back for headquarters, Green?"

"Dark's liable to catch us, all right, with some of us walkin'." Green took his own careful survey of the banks. "Ol' bay horse of mine's gettin' a sore foot, too. Let's get our boots on and get out of here."

Clay drank again before standing and nodding to the footwear. "This river seems to collect boots. Found one just yesterday, sticking out of the ground."

Lil flinched. "A grave, Mr. Andrews?"

He turned. "Yes, ma'am. I guess there's shallow graves all up and down this —"

Clay seemed to catch himself, and he lowered his head. Lil supposed he didn't want to be insensitive about the burial earlier in the day, but Lil's reaction was for another reason entirely.

Casner's obsession with a grave on the Pecos had known no bounds, and he had died in search of what Clay may have stumbled across.

CHAPTER 5

As the sun began to sink across the river, they struck out upstream with urgency, with Pate on the dapple gray and Lil in an unladylike position astride the bay, her dress draped on either side.

After a formal introduction, Green had done his best to get Clay to ride the gray — "You know you's wore out," Green said — but Clay didn't think it was right to make both their rescuers walk. Green, in turn, was stubborn enough to refuse to ride as well, leaving Pate to swing astride the animal.

Clay quickly noted that the young man was far from proficient on a horse. He seemed uncomfortable and kept a full-fisted grip on the reins. He rode too deeply in the saddle rather than support part of his weight in the stirrups, and the concept of letting his body work in concert with the horse's gait, rather than fight against it, seemed foreign to him.

But as Clay found out in listening to Pate's conversation with Lil, this son of the Bar W owner had the advantage over all of them when it came to book learning.

"So with Mother from a well-to-do family in Virginia, she taught me to read when I was four," Pate was saying. "A few years ago, she insisted they send me away to school in Richmond. As soon as I graduated and returned to Texas, Father brought me out here to the Narrows with him. He's determined to make his cattle business a success."

Pate looked at Lil, as if expecting a response, but she kept her silence. "I've been doing Father's bookkeeping," Pate went on. "But he wants me to learn the business from the ground up so I can take over someday, whether I want to or not. That's why he paired me up with Green."

Now Lil did speak, quietly and with a reflective stare down at her saddle horn. "It's good you got parents that care."

"I'd like it a lot better," said Pate, "if I got more say in the matter. My idea's to go back to Virginia and apprentice with a newspaper and become a writer."

Green chuckled; the topic wasn't Indians. "Tell her what your pa had to say when you brought it up to him."

Pate sank even lower in the saddle. "He gave me a look that could kill a mesquite tree and informed me I was like the rest of my generation, that I wanted to make a living without having to work for it."

Green laughed so hard that Clay hoped those Comanches weren't in earshot.

"Your pa's like a lot of us ol' boys," Green said as soon as he regained control. "If it ain't somethin' you do with your hands, it ain't work. Book says, 'Whatsoever thy hand findeth to do, do it with thy might.' "

"How do you think words get written down?" Pate challenged.

"Try tellin' that to your pa."

"I did. That's how I ended up out here with you."

Green gave another hearty laugh. "Trouble with them teachers of yours, they never learned how to do nothin', so how they goin' to teach it? Me, now, I know my cow business, 'cause that's all I done growin' up. I seen it all and done it all, like that bogged steer back there. 'Less you tromp 'em out, you could pull an ol' cow's head off 'fore you'd budge her. I didn't learn that in any ol' schoolbook."

"Don't sell books short," said Pate.

"I sure don't sell the Good Book short,

young'n. But makin' up stuff in your head, the way a writer does, ain't nothin' but a growed-up man a-playin'. You stick with me, Pate, and I'll give you the kind of education your pa will be proud of."

Pate continued to ride short in the saddle. "He's sure not keen on my pursuit of literature."

"At least," muttered Lil, "he never sold you off."

Clay watched her move against the sky's fading light as her horse nodded along. "Never done what, Miss Lil?"

Lil looked at him, almost as if she hadn't realized she had spoken aloud. It wasn't the first time Clay had heard her say something mysterious.

"I just wish," said Pate, "that my father could understand the power of the written word."

Clay shuddered. A few scribbled words could have a devastating impact, all right, enough to torture a man and drive him to this forsaken land in search of answers. He had been waiting for an opportunity to ply the Bar W hands for information, but now the question rose up so powerfully from inside that he interrupted Pate to ask it.

"A fellow by the name of Cox sign on with the Bar W's a few months back? Lucius

Cox?" Anticipating, Clay looked from one man to the other.

"Out here's the kinda place a man comes to get away from names," said Green. "Like as not, he goes by somethin' like Pie Face or Slew Foot. Ain't that right, bookkeep Pate?"

"My father says he's not a census taker," said Pate. "If a man doesn't want to give anything but a nickname, he doesn't press the issue. He says all he asks of a hand is responsibility and a hard day's work."

Trudging onward to the slow drum of the horses' hoofs, Clay looked down and racked his brain for a nickname Lucius might have used. There seemed to have been something, all right, back in their boyhood when young Molly had accompanied them to a fishing hole on the San Saba River. But for the life of him, Clay couldn't remember what it was.

"You got a friend out here, Mr. Andrews?" asked Lil.

As Clay raised his head, he didn't know how to answer; sometimes the only difference between a friend and an enemy were a few hastily written words. So he replied the only way he knew how.

"Well, Miss Lil, I'm sure pleased the two of *us* is friends now."

She blushed through all the caked dust

and turned away, and once again Clay regretted crossing the line into impropriety. She had just lost everything in the world, for God's sake.

Pate looked at Lil. "I thought the two of you were traveling together."

When Lil didn't say anything, Clay did. He knew there were some things a person in grief didn't want to dwell on.

"We met up yesterday, right before the Indians attacked. We just buried her father this mornin'."

Lil turned with a creak of leather. "He was my *husband,* Mr. Andrews."

Clay couldn't see his own jaw drop, but it must have. "I thought —"

Green, evidently accustomed to keeping a sharp lookout, was the first to see trouble. "Looka yonder!" he exclaimed, throwing an arm to their right.

Three quarters of a mile away, a red-hued promontory rose fifty feet, the endmost point of a bordering ridge that unfurled as far upstream as Clay could see. There seemed to be something against the dusky sky, all right. Clay started to suggest that it was a Spanish dagger, but then the figure moved and disappeared behind the rise.

"I don't see anything," said Pate, still looking.

"And you on top of a horse," said Green. "Didn't squint them eyes enough, 'cause he was sure there."

"A Indian?" asked Lil.

"Yes, ma'am," said Clay, still reconnoitering, "and I expect he finds us pretty easy pickin's."

Pate blanched. "You think he'll go after more, Green? What do we have that they would want?"

Clay glanced at Lil and wished Pate hadn't asked; a couple of horses were inviting enough, but there was more to be concerned about.

Clay checked the older cowhand's profile. "We anywhere close to headquarters? How far?"

"Four or five mile."

"Climb on!" said Pate.

Clay considered their chances. If it came down to a horse race, he wouldn't have bet a plug of tobacco on a pair of animals carrying double, especially when one had a sore foot.

He made eye contact with Lil. "Miss, you and Pate got to ride on. Me and Green will make a stand if we have to." He looked at Green. "You up to it?"

In answer, Green slapped the dapple gray's hindquarter and urged it into a trot.

"You got you a revolver, young'n — use it if you got to!"

"But —" protested Pate with a glance back.

"You ride too, Miss Lil!" said Clay, giving her bay a similar swat.

The surge of her horse seemed to startle her, and she seemed so vulnerable as she looked back at Clay.

"You'll catch up with me, won't you, Mr. Andrews?"

Clay didn't answer because the oncoming night made him wonder if more than day was ending. But there was something in the way she asked it that made him hope that they hadn't seen the last of one another.

Dark began to settle over the land like a veil growing thicker. Four or five miles should have been no distance at all for a horse, which, even in a jog trot, normally could travel seven miles in an hour. But the gait of Lil's bay wasn't smooth, as if the animal indeed was going lame.

The dapple gray with Pate in the stirrups began to pull away in a measured lope, but Lil had never whimpered in all the times Casner had left her, and she wouldn't start now. Still, she couldn't help remembering the way Clay had stood by her all through their ordeal — and how even now he might be making the ultimate sacrifice to give her this chance.

As Pate gradually stretched his lead to fifty yards, he repeatedly glanced to his right, no doubt scanning the ridge. Lil, however, already knew what a Comanche charge looked like, and she didn't care to see another. But when the young man's dapple gray broke into a gallop with too many miles left to go, she turned to find dust billowing from the ridge a mere half mile away. Riders poured down the slope and veered toward her, and she knew that they were intent on taking away her tomorrows — or giving her one that would be worse than those frightful years with Casner.

Slapping stirrups against the bay's rib cage, she urged the struggling animal into a run. She knew that this was a bronc rigged for cowhands, not for a woman who knew nothing but a sidesaddle. But she was so slight in build that maybe even a sore-footed bay could hold a lead.

The trail swung close to the ridge with its deep-set gulches and angling folds. The dust swept into the dark recesses, hiding their secrets, and as the road bent with the ridge's base, she looked back and found a rise concealing the Indians. They reappeared in moments, or at least their dust did. Then she passed another gulch and broke around another rise, and the next time that she could see behind, the Comanches had gained on her.

The pattern repeated, too many times to count, with her pursuers steadily overtaking her. Lil knew what was about to happen, and she was as powerless to stop it as she was the oncoming night.

But maybe in those imminent shadows lay the only chance she had. At the next shadowy gulch, she reined up hard and slid off the bay. It was less a controlled dismount than a fall, but she pulled herself up by the stirrup and struck the animal on the rump, sending it trotting on into the dusk. Whirling to the narrow canyon, she bolted up it with another image of the stranger who somehow had reignited in her the will to live.

Lil managed only twenty-five or thirty yards before the muffled sound of hoofs exploded into a din. They were upon her, and all she could do was flatten herself in the rocks and pray that her ruse would buy her time.

The rumble grew fainter as her pursuers evidently continued down-trail, and she scrambled up and stumbled on. Soon they would catch up with the bay, and when they found it without a rider they would start back in search. If she didn't find a hiding place in a minute or two, the best she would be able to hope for would be a quick end.

At the head of the gulch she came upon a dark overhang or cave. Left and right, the gorge walls looked unscalable, but she also knew this for snake country. Rattlers had slithered under the wagon wheels more than once, alarming the mules, and Lil didn't relish the idea of entering a possible den.

It was a frightful place, this pitch-black hole. But with hoofbeats rising in her ears, she stooped and plunged inside.

From behind came voices in a strange tongue, and she pivoted on the powdery floor in search of an inner refuge. The grotto reeked with animal feces and an almost metallic odor that burned her sinuses. Twenty feet ahead shined a strange keyhole of muted light, the only thing she could see. As the gulch behind echoed with approaching footsteps, she desperately felt her way deeper, terrified that her next step would land her in a tangle of rattlers. She could imagine those demon eyes watching and waiting, but there were eyes of fiends behind her as well.

It was a terrifying few steps of blind groping underneath low-hanging rock that peeled her scalp, but Lil finally bumped into a wall. At arm's length above her, a shelf of rock lay in twilight. Directly over it a few feet was the keyhole-shaped opening, which might have measured fifteen or sixteen inches at its widest.

A pair of eyes suddenly stared down from the ledge, the orbs glowing like distant green lanterns. Then a shadow moved against the opening above, and the ghost of an animal disappeared into the desert shadows outside.

Lil shrank back, but as she did a maraca-like vibration chilled her.

Rattlesnake!

It came from somewhere around her feet, and she reached for the shelf and dug for a foothold. For harried moments, it was one step up and two steps back, but eventually she rolled into the lair.

The next instant, a voice sounded.

Lil froze, finding silhouettes stirring against the main entrance. She heard more words in the same unfamiliar language, and then a second voice called out in Spanish.

Through Casner, Lil had learned many of man's vilest attributes, but she had also learned that Spanish was the trade language of Comanches. They were there, yards away, scourges who would make Casner seem holy. They were asking if anyone was inside, and Lil fought to silence her shallow breathing.

In moments they would be across the grotto and reaching for her. But now a second set of rattles began to sing, and with an exchange of words in that strange tongue, the silhouettes withdrew.

Still, Lil didn't dare move. Maybe they were lingering, baiting her into stirring against the keyhole of starlight. Here, at least, she was above the snakes, and their continued buzz was a buffer against blind search. If she could stay motionless long enough — if she could endure the thought of the bobcat or wolf or cougar returning — maybe she would have a chance.

Lil didn't think she had that kind of willpower, but she grimly waited as the grotto fell silent and hoofbeats rose and died away. Now the night held no other sounds except the *yip-yip* of coyotes.

Then a wind began whistling through the keyhole, and she looked up at the twinkling lights in the black sky and wondered if a God in charge of all of that could really care about anybody down here. Clay didn't seem to think so, and her life for the past six years hadn't been much evidence to the contrary.

Nevertheless, for the second time in as many nights, she had survived when things had seemed hopeless.

Lil wished Clay could tell her what to do next. She hadn't been allowed to make a decision for so long — her entire life, really — that she didn't know how. With Indians about in the night, she could stay hidden here until sunup before setting out for Bar W headquarters. But she also realized that traipsing this barren country by daylight would leave her exposed and vulnerable.

Out of the sky that stared down, a decision came to her. The stars spoke of Heaven and its angels, and this frightening hole was all too much like hell.

Lil came to a crouch and squirmed up through the constricting keyhole that opened to the night.

Chapter 6

With attack maybe imminent, Clay's shotgun and Green's 1858 Remington revolver
weren't enough to inspire confidence as the
two men fell back toward the Pecos. Still,
Clay felt oddly comforted knowing that he
had done all he could for Lil.

She seemed with him even now, so powerfully had the events of the last twenty-four
hours branded her in his thoughts. But that
didn't keep him from worrying about her
sore-footed horse, or the consequences of
Comanches overtaking it. Too, Lil's lot in
life troubled him, especially in regard to the
body he had buried. How had she come to
marry a grizzled old man so irresponsible
with respect to her welfare?

None of these concerns explained why he
should be so protective of the girl, but then
the answer came to him with all the clarity
of Molly's name etched in a tombstone.

Clay followed Green into a dry pond and

flopped down just inside the white-crusted bed, a depression only a foot deep with a thick odor of salt. Clay couldn't imagine a much worse place to make a stand, but the floodplain didn't offer anything better. Squirming up against the low bank, he peered between saltgrass pedestals and saw Pate's loping gray pulling away from Lil.

"He's runnin' off and leavin' her!" he exclaimed. "Don't he know her horse is crippled?"

For long seconds, the Bar W hand lying beside Clay didn't say anything. What *was* there to say, considering how the dapple gray steadily increased its lead?

"Young'n means well," Green finally muttered. "He just don't know no better."

Clay watched in frustration as the minutes passed, and he didn't like what he saw when even greater dust began to fly from Pate's horse.

"Should've give *her* the gun! Look at him — he's got that horse in a run!"

"Got reason to. Look comin' over the hill!"

But Clay had discovered the dust pouring off the ridge, and he felt the same helplessness as he had in finding Molly's eyes frozen in a lifeless stare. If a woman was in trouble, a man was supposed to do something.

Damn it, it was his *duty,* come hell or high water. But as a determined horde burst out of the dust at the ridge's base and veered for Lil and the bay, options seemed so very few.

Clay sprang to his feet without realizing it, and in another moment he was running toward the scene and waving the shotgun overhead.

"Here!" he shouted at the top of his lungs. "We's over here!"

When the war ponies continued on for Lil, Clay cocked a hammer and fired into the air. The roar set his ears ringing as he rocked to the recoil. But pounding hoofs must have drowned out what the distance hadn't muffled, for the war party stayed on its hell-bent course.

Clay already had his thumb on the second hammer when something hit him hard from behind and the ground flew up into his face. The gun stock caught between his midriff and the hard-packed alkali, sucking all the air from his lungs. He rolled around in the dirt as he fought for breath, and then firm pressure on his shoulders stilled him against his will.

"Quit your movin' and lay low!" said Green, flush on the ground beside him. "Keep that other load in your pocket —

we's liable to need it!"

Clay looked up through waving saltgrass and saw the receding sets of shadowy riders framed against the ridge. The gap between Lil and the Comanches was closing fast, and Clay was just lying there letting it happen.

He whirled on Green. He could hardly find air for words, but somehow he forced them out. "I could've turned them, you SOB!"

Green stayed composed as he studied the distance. "No, you couldn't've, and I reckon you know it. I sure gotta give you credit for gall, but your smarts is somethin' else."

Green was right, but that didn't make the Bar W hand's interference acceptable. Even now, Clay wanted to clamber up and do all in his power to divert the Indians' attention, but they were already disappearing into the dusk.

"We never should've separated!" he muttered between heaving breaths. "If we'd stayed together, we might could've fought them off!"

"I don't like it neither. I think the world of that young'n, but we give them the best chance they was."

"Yeah? Look at us! *We's* the ones layin' here free and clear. If you and me had took the horses, we could've led those devils away from her!"

Green came to his feet and began to reconnoiter in all directions. "You can keep layin' there second-guessin' yourself, but that ain't helpin' them or us neither one. Get yourself up. We got some miles to make."

Clay followed after him, overcome by helplessness and seething with anger at this man who had denied him the chance to do everything he could.

"Don't be layin' your hands on me no more." Clay heard his own voice quake. "You understand me? Not another time more!"

Green wheeled and faced him, and it seemed like a long time since the Bar W hand had smiled. "I hear you. And while we's gettin' things out in the open, I don't appreciate you disrespectin' my godly ol' mother thataway. She deserves better."

"What are you talkin' about?"

"That 'SOB' you called me. A man can call me anything he wants, and maybe I deserve it sometimes. But I draw the line when he talks about the sweet ol' lady that raised me."

Clay certainly hadn't meant it that way. In fact, the term was so common among cowhands that he had never considered its literal meaning. Now that he did, he regretted all the times he had used it, considering his level of respect for every woman.

Green continued upriver through the falling night, and as Clay fell in behind, he not only began to mellow toward this cowhand, but have real respect for him. If a man treated his parents and horses well, it said a lot about what was inside him. Still, the two of them trudged in silence for a long time before Clay managed to say what he knew he should.

"I want you to know I was just worried about the girl," he said in a hushed voice. "Maybe I was a fool, tryin' to draw those Indians over here. Maybe I was a hothead callin' you what I did, seein' how you took it."

"Tell me somethin' I don't know already," Green responded, but Clay didn't know for which of his offenses he meant it. Both, Clay supposed.

"Don't think you's the only one upset over all this," the Bar W hand added as he kept up his brisk pace. "I treat that young'n like he's my own. You think I want to go traipsin' in without a mark on me and look his daddy in the face and tell him I let him get killed? You think you got guilt, mister, but you don't know the half of it. I'd rather be hacked up and scalped myself than have somethin' happen to him."

The image was a terrible one, and a hazy memory of the night Clay's father had died flashed through Clay's mind.

"Only somethin' out of hell would do the things they do," he said.

"Pretty hard to argue they's fightin' for their home, when they take to the war trail just to go make trouble. Even the Apaches out in the Guadalupe country stay out of their way."

A crushing burden seemed to settle even more over Clay's shoulders. "I . . . I can't stand the thought of what they might be doin' to her. If what she's been through since yesterday's not hell, I don't know what it is."

But Clay did know, for he had walked through that San Saba door.

Green stopped and faced him in the dark. "You might be headstrong, but you's showin' me some things that can't be taught, like Mr. Brehmer's always sayin'."

Clay couldn't imagine what, and he couldn't read any clues in the Bar W hand's shadowy face.

"Just met up with that girl, did you?" verified Green.

Clay's guilt wasn't getting any better. "I . . . I guess I led those Indians right to her camp."

"Providence has got His ways, and we sure can't figure 'em sometimes. All I know is, not many men would step in as responsible-like for somebody they don't hardly know."

Clay wasn't sure about that, considering all the cow herders he had worked with — except for one maybe. But a pat on the back wouldn't help when he had failed her so.

Green, meanwhile, was showing something of his own character. For all his talk about foolish bravado, the Bar W hand had led them straight across the floodplain to the location under the ridge where the Comanches had fallen in after Lil and Pate. Clay had intended to follow after Lil alone, if necessary, but he was glad that he had happened upon someone as responsible as Green.

Tracing the road, they went on, silenced by a threat they wouldn't be able to see. But Clay also wouldn't be able to see a body easily in the starlight, although that didn't keep him from scanning for an ominous shadow on the ground.

With a twitch in his cheek, Clay wondered if it would be better for Lil if they did find her already dead. At least that way it would be over for her — an end too awful for any man to understand — while otherwise she might have been spirited away into an ordeal that would go on and on.

There was a third alternative, of course: that she had escaped. But as he and Green skirted gulch after dark gulch until Clay was certain they had passed the point where Lil and her pursuers had disappeared, that likelihood seemed distressingly more remote.

From out of the night dead ahead came a suggestion of movement, shadows against shadows. Clay, lagging only a step, seized Green's shoulder and the two of them froze. Now that the jingle of their spurs had ended, Clay could hear a slight wind, the nearby hoot of an owl, the distant wail of a lobo — and something that was like the low vibration of an earthen drum.

Green must have heard as well, for the two of them abandoned the road together. They crept toward the hidden river before crouching in mesquite chaparral that greeted Clay with a thorn in his cheek. The rumble had grown louder, and now he could distinguish the individual hoofbeats of several horses.

As dark as it was, the odds were that the horsemen would ride on by, but that wasn't reassuring enough to keep Clay from mentally weighing a single shotgun load and a half dozen more from a Remington .44 against a party of that size. He had heard that Comanches usually attacked only when they had a tactical advantage. If the worst were to happen, he could only hope that a quick fusillade out of the gloom would discourage the warriors from engaging an enemy they wouldn't be able to see.

Through his boots, Clay felt the rising impact of hoofs as the shadows approached along the road. Voices began to murmur. As the party came abreast, almost within spitting distance, Clay tensed his thumb against a hammer and hoped he never had to cock it.

Then came more quiet words: Comanche or Spanish or —

"Over here!"

At Green's hail, Clay flinched and cocked the hammer involuntarily. Thorns strafed his hand as he swung the muzzle toward shadows that abruptly grew still. His twitching finger almost squeezed the trigger before three or four voices blurted simultaneously from the road.

One was deeper and louder than the rest. "Green? That you?"

"Yes, sir, Mr. Brehmer. Pate there?"

"I'm here, Green, with my father and five others," came Pate's voice. "I made it to headquarters and they saddled up and we —"

"The girl!" interrupted Clay. He lowered the shotgun and broke through the clawing mesquites in a panic. "She with you? She make it all right?"

"You that stranger?" asked the authoritarian voice that Green had identified as Brehmer's.

"Somebody answer me!" cried Clay, running the last few steps into the road.

The shadows began to swim. "Settle down, mister; you're spooking the horses," said Brehmer. "She and you two's the ones we came looking for."

Clay's fear turned to rage as the riders' dark outlines rose up before him. "Which one of you's Pate?" he demanded.

"Why, right here."

The young man's voice came from a nearby mounted figure silhouetted against the starlight above the ridge. Clay lunged toward him, surprising even himself.

"You run off and left her!" Clay cried, seizing Pate by the arm and dragging him from the saddle. "You had a gun and run off and left her!"

The horse shied as Pate hit the ground,

and a lot of shadows began to stir to a shifting of hoofs.

"Pate, what's happened there?" pressed Brehmer.

For a moment, the hard impact and the shock of Clay's action must have stolen away Pate's air.

"Pate?" repeated Brehmer.

"He . . . he pulled me off my mount, Father," Pate wheezed.

"I ought to do a hell of a lot more than that!" Clay railed on. "You was the only chance she had! Instead of usin' that revolver you —"

Out of the corner of his eye, Clay glimpsed a brute-like shape coming at him. The next instant, its overpowering force bowled him over. Even as he went down, hoofs began to paw the ground around him.

No sooner had Clay realized that a horse had run him over than he heard a revolver click to full cock directly overhead.

"Maybe you've got a legitimate complaint, and maybe not." Brehmer's powerful voice seemed to come out of the stars. "But my son will answer to me, not to some stranger."

Through the legs of Brehmer's horse, Clay saw a figure walk up.

"Man's plum' worried out of his mind,"

said Green. "But from what I seen of him, he'll do to ride the river with."

Everyone fell silent as Clay stood up and dusted himself off with his hat. Finally came the sound of the revolver hammer returning to the safe position.

"Mister," said Brehmer, "I've got a lot of respect for what Green has to say, so I'll overlook it this time. Tell me who you are."

The hard fall had jarred Clay back under self-control. "Clay Andrews, out from San Saba. There's a young woman out here, Lil Casner, unaccounted for. We got to find her."

"Just chance we stumbled on you two in the dark," said Brehmer. "We didn't find her between headquarters and here, and if you didn't come across her on down the line, then there's nothing we can do till daylight."

With a chill, Clay surveyed the dark beside the road. A body could have been ten feet away and no one would have seen it, all right. What first light would show, he didn't know.

But one thing was certain. Whichever way this played out — whether it be a body they found or a horse and rider they *didn't* find — the outlook couldn't have been direr for a girl who somehow had become important to him.

CHAPTER 7

Lil knew she couldn't be far from the Bar W headquarters, but the prospect of locating it by starlight was daunting. Even in daytime, this country offered few landmarks except for the Pecos, and even the river seemed lost the way it touched all points of the compass in its onward flow. But Lil's mother had taught her to find the North Star by means of the Big Dipper, and she set out with that flickering beacon and her best guess as guides.

Hidden thorns tugged at her dress and pricked her ankles as she crossed a broken tableland that demanded more than she had left. She stumbled in a daze, with images from split-second dreams darting in and out of the night. They were usually of Clay, glimpses that comforted and reassured, but sometimes the flashes showed Casner or faceless Comanches.

In a lucid moment, Lil found herself at

the ridge's rim, where the land fell away thirty or forty feet into a dark sea that must have been the floodplain. She stopped, wondering where her next step would come from, and saw a faint glow somewhere ahead along her general bearing. Perhaps originating at the base of the ridge, it was confined to a small area, the way a campfire would have been.

Somebody was there, with a light that pierced her gloomy world, but she had no idea whether it meant even greater danger.

With renewed alertness, Lil proceeded cautiously along a looping course that she hoped would bring her up over it from the elevated side. The glow proved more distant than she had anticipated, but she managed to stay clearheaded as she crossed a hundred-yard-wide drainage thick with scrub mesquite and eventually reached the head of a narrow gulch on her left. The night hid its depths, but the little canyon pointed toward a light source that originated somewhere over a nearby butte that must have marked a bend.

The glow brightened and dimmed rhythmically, drawing Lil closer along the gulch's farther rim, where travel seemed easier. She knew she was taking a chance, considering that a Comanche campfire could be ahead, but desperation overrode anything that common sense argued. She traced two doglegs, but when the gulch veered off-course dramatically, she continued straight for the glow across a flat covered with creosote and prickly pear.

Whatever the light's source, Lil was almost upon it now, and silence was critical. Yet never before had the rocking of her feet from heel to toe seemed to break the stillness of the night so much. She caught a faint whiff that reminded her of burning coal oil, and she dropped to her knees and crawled the last several yards to a drop-off.

Below, immediately shy of the canyon mouth, a lamp burned in the square gun port of an adobe house situated flush against the bluff. Abutting the house was a corral built in an elbow of the gulch so that a single adobe wall completed it. Several yards across the canyon, the twilight showed a half dugout carved in the opposite bluff. In the flickering shadows, it was difficult to distinguish native dirt from mud brick construction. Most notably, the roofs of both shelters seemed natural shelves between summits and canyon floor.

The horses must have sensed Lil's presence, for she could hear the rollers-like rattle in their nostrils as they pointed their ears toward her. The commotion evidently alarmed someone inside the house, for a rifle barrel poked through the gun port.

"Somethin's spookin' the horses!" warned a nasal voice.

The muzzle swung toward her, and the light went out, plunging everything into darkness.

Lil knew her life was on the line. She rolled away, an instant before a rifle boomed and the bluff's rim exploded in her face.

"Stop!"

Her frantic cry died in another echoing *crack!* that sprayed her legs with stinging gravel.

"Be certain what you're firing at!" shouted an authoritarian voice. "There's a woman unaccounted for!"

"Stop! Stop! Can't you hear me? Please stop!"

With the end of gunfire, Lil's cry broke through to the silhouettes converging in the canyon bottom.

"Good Lord! That ain't no Indian!" someone exclaimed. "Don't nobody shoot!"

The voices had all been unfamiliar to Lil, but then from the half dugout came one that made her question whether she was hearing it or dreaming it.

"It's Clay, Miss Lil! I'm comin' up for you!"

In the doorless entrance to the half dugout, Clay squatted with a morning cup of black coffee and reflected on things.

Glancing inside, he admired the ingenuity in this fourteen-foot-square shelter carved out of the bluff: the rock-lined walls, the ash-filled fireplace, the crisscrossed mesquite limbs that held back a dirt roof too thick for Indians to shoot through. He wondered if Lucius had ever slept in this *choza,* one of five that Green had said marked these bluffs at the Narrows on the Pecos. Rumor had placed Lucius on the Bar W's, all right, but sometimes rumor was about as reliable as wet gunpowder.

As Clay looked across the narrow canyon to the corral and adobe building that — to hear Green tell it — had once been a Butterfield Mail station, Clay strangely dwelled most on the young widow he had rescued from the overhanging bluff during the night. Given his long obsession, it confused him, but there was no denying that Lil somehow had become central to his thoughts.

Clay looked down at the steam rising from his cup, and he must have stared longer than he thought, for the next thing he knew, a long shadow covered him.

"Morning."

Clay knew the commanding voice as Brehmer's even before he looked up. The Bar W owner with the creased face and bushy, gray mustache stood with his back to another *choza* up the gulch.

"You didn't sleep long," Brehmer added.

"Helped, though. The coffee does too."

Squatting before a standing man was no way to carry on a conversation, so Clay stood as well. Brehmer got right to the point.

"My cows range from halfway to Horsehead Crossing up to the New Mexico line. That's a hundred miles of river, not even counting the bends, and it's full of Indians and wolves and quicksand. I can use every hand I can get. Pays six bits a day, and I expect a man to earn every cent of it. Are you looking?"

The offer caught Clay off guard, especially after he had dragged Brehmer's son off a horse a few hours before. Maybe Clay's search for Lucius had been secondary the last couple of days, but his need for answers burned as fiercely as ever. With cow herders strung out over such a wide swath, could there be any better way to check the Bar W hands one by one? As things stood now,

Clay didn't even have a horse, and he knew firsthand the pitfalls this river offered a man on foot.

"Well?" pressed Brehmer.

"Yes, sir," said Clay. "I'm interested."

"Good. I'll have Pate add you to the books. First thing I want you to do is ride with me to Horsehead Crossing and on over to Fort Stockton. I want to see if those Yankee soldiers will start patrolling my stretch of river better. You just had a bad couple of encounters with Comanches, and I want that commanding officer to hear it straight from you. I want to give you time to recuperate, so we'll leave day after tomorrow."

Clay glanced at the old mail station, its mud bricks delineated in the morning rays. "What about Mrs. Casner?"

Brehmer's mustache twitched, and with a sigh of resignation, he took his own look at the station.

"I expect she's still resting for now. But like I told her last night, this cow camp's no place for a woman. I'm not so sure it's fit for man or beast either. I've held out on bringing my own wife out, even though I've got a trunk of her clothes waiting on her. I told Mrs. Casner she can stay here till the next wagon company comes by, and if she doesn't have any kin, she needs to go on with them, California or someplace. A recent widow like her needs to be around other women."

An abrupt depression came over Clay as his gaze returned to his coffee. He had been so busy trying to keep the two of them alive that he had never considered Lil's future.

"You'll want to clean yourself up, with what you've been through," Brehmer continued. "There's a good bathing spot up the river a ways. Borrow some clothes and take your dirty ones to the house. I've already laid out some of my wife's for Mrs. Casner and told Pate to help with the hot water. I imagine she'll be glad to wash yours with hers."

Brehmer started away, and then hesitated. When Clay looked up, he found Brehmer's jaw hard-set.

"One more thing," said the older man. "My word's law out here, and you'll respect my son the same as you do me."

Clay watched him stride away and disappear around the butte at the canyon mouth. What the Bar W owner had said about respect was reasonable, and Clay was embarrassed that someone felt he had to be told such a thing. Still, he couldn't bring himself to regret pulling the young man from the saddle.

When Clay saw Green later that morning, he borrowed a change of clothes and a bar of lye soap and went to the river. Stripping, he gave himself a good scrubbing and then washed his woolen long johns. He wasn't sure of the propriety of asking Lil to do his washing, and he certainly wasn't going to let her address his underwear. But as filthy as his shirt and britches were, he knew that only hot water could do the job. Besides, delivering his clothes to Lil would give him an excuse to see her.

Wringing out his long johns and dressing, he bundled his dirty garments under his arm and returned to the dwellings. He draped his underwear over the corral fence to dry — hoping Lil wouldn't wander out and see — and turned to the mail station. It had no true windows, only the square gun port overlooking the corral, and the door was closed either for privacy or to guard against the rising heat.

Clay went to it and started to knock, only to hesitate. Considering what the two of them had been through together, he wouldn't have thought it possible to be nervous about seeing Lil. But after what Brehmer had told him, he didn't know what to say. A wagon party could happen by at any time and whisk her out of his life as quickly as she had come into it.

Summoning his courage, Clay knocked. As he waited, he remembered his hat and quickly removed it. At the last moment, he wished he had borrowed a straight razor, but all he could do now was watch the door creak inward.

Clay didn't know why he had expected Lil behind it, but he saw Pate instead, framed against the inside shadows. The young man fumbled nervously with a pencil and half-filled sheet of paper. Clay guessed that this was as awkward a moment for Pate as it was for him, but it was the owner's son who found words first.

"I added you to the books earlier," he said.

"Your father said you would." Over Pate's shoulder, Clay glimpsed movement. The young man checked as well, and then yielded the threshold as Lil came up.

"Miss Lil," said Clay.

"Mr. Andrews."

She seemed radiant with cleanliness: the short, brown hair parted in the middle, the face a little drawn from privation, the blue calico dress with a figured pattern and ruffles at the shoulders. Dark apparel and a black veil might have been more appropriate for one so recently widowed, and even in a cow camp, a man should have respected her need to grieve in private. But that didn't keep Pate from looking at her right now with the admiring eyes of an adolescent.

It was Pate who Clay addressed. "She's in mournin'," he reminded him.

Another uncomfortable silence ensued as the three traded glances.

"It's all right, Mr. Andrews," Lil finally said. "He's just been taking down what happened. He thinks it might make a good story someday."

Clay breathed sharply. "A story," he repeated doubtfully. When he looked again at Pate, the young man lowered his gaze and faded into the shadows.

"He warmed up some water for me earlier," Lil added.

It was clearly a defense of Pate, and considering what had happened the evening before, Clay didn't know what to make of it. Searching for words, he looked down at the bundle under his arm.

Lil obviously read more into his glance than he had intended. "He says he'll heat up some more so I can wash out some things," she said. "I'll bring yours over when they're dry."

"I hate askin' you to do that."

"I never was asked my whole life. I was

just told."

"I'd never just tell you somethin' like that and expect you to do it."

"I know, Mr. Andrews."

They stood there quietly for the longest time, Clay's gaze shifting from her eyes to his boots and back to her eyes. Unspoken words hung over them like a scythe, a powerful presence that neither seemed willing to bring to the forefront.

"Mr. Brehmer says I need to leave with the next wagon company," Lil said finally.

"He told me."

"He thinks I need to be around other women."

"Yes, ma'am."

Lil fell silent again, and the way she looked at him made Clay think that she expected him to say more. Plenty of things bounced around in his head, all right, but he couldn't vocalize what he couldn't digest.

"What do you think I should do, Mr. Andrews?"

"Start callin' me Clay, for one thing."

The moment he said it, Clay wanted to kick himself. From the way Brehmer had talked, she wasn't being given a choice about things. But she had nevertheless asked for Clay's advice, and the least he could have done was give her a straight answer and not a flippant one.

"You got anybody in Texas, Miss Lil?"

Clay wished he could understand what abruptly came over her face: the searching, the expectancy, the melancholy longing. But he supposed that a widow in mourning had every right to her private thoughts.

"Don't you have a family or somebody?" Clay pressed.

"Nobody that cares, I don't guess." She gave him a hard stare.

"Guess that's somethin' we got in common."

Even if Clay admitted to himself what he dared not — that he had feelings for this recent widow — the conventions of the day would never have let him act on it. After a year, maybe, or even six months, it might have been proper. But to pay court now would have been the height of disrespect, and were she to accept his attention, society would frown on her with the same disapproval it bestowed on a fallen woman.

Clay realized that he still hadn't tendered any advice. With things inside him tugging in all directions, all he could manage was another question.

"What is it you're inclined to do, Miss Lil?"

Her chin began to quiver, and Clay had

114

never seen anyone so forlorn and lost. He longed to put a compassionate hand on her shoulder, but that wouldn't have been appropriate.

"I know losin' somebody ain't easy," he said.

Her head went down. "If they're worth hanging on to." Her eyes came up again, as piercing as they were misty.

Clay didn't know what to make of her stare, much less her words, but he realized again that a grieving person didn't always act rationally.

"I expect you're wantin' to be around other women, like Brehmer said," Clay offered.

He hadn't intended it as advice, but her reaction indicated that she took it as such. Her face paling, she leaned out and looked toward the nearby Pecos. When Clay turned with her, he saw the wagon road along the stream's brink. Upstream for the next quarter mile, the road would squeeze between bluff and river, and beyond, it would carry a lonely person to another land.

And out of his life.

"I —" Clay knew what he wanted to say. Damn it, he knew what he *needed* to say, and the words started to well up out of his soul. *I don't want you to go!* They found their way to his lips, the kind of words that could grant new purpose, change a life, reshape a person's world.

But as he began to voice them, they died in a quick memory. Only the day before, he had buried Lil's husband. How callous and self-centered could he be, even to consider asking such a thing of her? Hadn't she answered his question about her inclinations with a stare at the road?

"Yes, Mr. Andrews?" Now she was looking at him again.

"Ma'am?"

"You started to say something."

"I . . . I'll be ridin' over to Fort Stockton day after tomorrow. Mr. Brehmer wants to talk with the soldiers about the Comanches."

"Oh."

Clay looked down and did his best to smooth out the alkali under his boots. If only Casner had been her father and not her husband. If only Brehmer hadn't all but ordered her to leave at the earliest opportunity. If only she had already served out her expected period of mourning.

If.

Were there any other word so filled with misery, Clay didn't know what it would be.

"Pate says you hired on."

Clay looked up at her words. "Yes, ma'am."

"You'll be needing these," she said, reaching for his dirty clothes.

He let them slide into her care. "I appreciate it, Miss Lil."

It was a simple expression of thanks, but somehow it seemed to strike her. Already, she had looked on him in ways he hadn't understood, and now she did so yet again.

"What you said yesterday," she began. "I never had anybody call me their friend before."

There was more to say, at least on Clay's part, but he couldn't formulate his thoughts, much less put them into words. He stammered a polite "Miss Lil," and then wandered away disheartened into the life that bound him as inescapably as a fore-footed gelding.

CHAPTER 8

As Clay pondered and regretted and wished throughout the rest of the day, he kept a sharp eye on the cowhands riding in by twos. Green had told him that eighteen or twenty men rode for Brehmer, including several at upper headquarters below Pope's Crossing near the New Mexico line. Sooner or later, Clay was sure to cross paths with Lucius if he was here.

He just didn't know how long it would take. According to Green, cowhands were spread far and wide across the Bar W's. This was open range, with natural boundaries on only two sides to keep the herd from drifting. The sharp banks and wicked currents of the Pecos did their job well, while to the east lay a hundred or more miles of arid terrain without a decent water hole. The stronger longhorns might venture twenty-five miles into it to graze, but they had to return twice a week for water. Still, that left the upstream and downstream extremes of the Bar W range for cowhands to contain, not to mention the necessity of constantly riding bog — duties that routinely kept pairs of men away from headquarters for days at a time.

As Brehmer had warned, this looked to be an outfit where a man earned his pay, all right. It made Clay question the rumors that had brought him here, for Lucius and hard work had never gotten along. From boyhood, Lucius had always been a loafer, never willing to fulfill a responsibility when he could shirk one.

Yet, Lucius had once been his best friend, or at least his closest. Growing up on adjacent homesteads had a way of ensuring that. Born only a month apart, they prowled the San Saba River together from earliest childhood and jointly ran a trapline in the live oak hills by age ten. Even early on, Lucius was more interested in finding the Lost San Saba Mine than in baiting and skinning. He was always a dreamer, relishing in fanciful talk rather than in productive labor.

Sometimes they let young Molly tag along, a kindly act to a kid sister by blood to Clay and by association to Lucius. Then Molly came of age, and it was no secret that

Lucius grew sweet on her. By that time, Clay was acutely aware of Lucius's war bag full of faults. Not only was he prone to fits, he was dissipated and self-centered, disloyal even to Clay and more likely to disrespect a good girl than treat her right.

Lucius was everything that no suitor of Molly's should have been, even if she hadn't realized it. But even after chasing Lucius all this way, Clay didn't know if a person so close would have been capable of the depths of dishonor that had made Molly's door a gateway to perdition.

Such thoughts went with Clay into dusk, and even after retiring for the night in his sun-dried long johns, he listened to Green snoring across the *choza* and reflected on Lucius and Molly and Lil. They were three separate individuals, but they were so entwined that they almost seemed one as he drifted toward oblivion.

At the last moment of consciousness, he heard a dull thud overhead. The next instant, something sprinkled his face.

Clay started and sat up. Checking the gloom above, he caught grit in his eye, as if the brush-and-earthen roof was disintegrating.

"Green!" he whispered.

The other man continued to snort in

undisturbed sleep, and Clay reached for his Colt and found Lil's shotgun instead. Fortunately, the Bar W's kept a store of powder and lead, so both chambers were rammed full of shot. Right now, though, that didn't seem much comfort against the dark unknown.

When Clay turned to the open doorway, he glimpsed a manlike figure dart across the canyon bottom. Simultaneously, more debris fell to a shuffling on the roof.

"Green!" he shouted.

He didn't take time to see if Green stirred. Cocking the shotgun, Clay burst to his feet and broke toward the glow of lamplight outside. He managed only a single step before a peculiar shadow flew at him from the doorway's upper reaches. Something with the texture of a flour sack slapped his face, but the portion that struck his shoulder squirmed as if alive. Even before it dropped at his feet, Clay heard a swift vibration like forks rattling in a dry washtub.

Rattlesnake!

Clay yelled involuntarily and shrank back from a threat he could hear but couldn't see.

"What in perdition!" exclaimed Green.

"The roof!" Clay warned, feeling more dirt fall.

Somebody was up there, retreating toward the bluff, and whoever it was had thrown a rattler inside by means of a linen sack. Now, Clay didn't know where to step, but he wasn't alone. From the *chozas* up-canyon, he heard repeated shouts of "Snake!" and "Watch out!"

If the raiders were intent only on stealing horses, Clay supposed it might be an acceptable loss. But he knew from experience that Comanches also wanted to strike fear when the odds were in their favor. They had scalped his father, one form of mutilation that served their purpose well, but violating a woman before killing her would magnify the terror tenfold. Whether or not these Indians suspected a woman was in camp, the most fortified structure was sure to draw the greatest attention of any warrior seeking to count coup.

So as Clay watched the dark figures not only descend on the corral across the narrow canyon from him, but also angle out of sight toward the station, it was rattler be damned.

"We got to stop them!" he cried as he bolted.

Clay made it to the doorway safely, but something — an arrow maybe — whirred by his ear before he had taken a half dozen steps outside. He didn't have time to react, for horses stampeded all around him as they raced from the breached corral gate. Dust rose from the pummeling hoofs, obscuring the night even more. An animal bumped him hard, but Clay managed to keep his feet and weave his way through the crush of brutes. Ahead, a wispy raider threw a shoulder into the secured station door, and when a second figure also applied force, wood splintered and the door flew inward.

A revolver exploded from inside with a muzzle flash that drove one raider back against the second. For a moment, the two figures were still upright before Clay, and then he shot from the hip and both dropped to the roar.

But nobody was out of the woods yet. Arrows were flying, and pistol balls too. Clay could hear the ping of projectiles striking adobe, and when an arrow imbedded in the door frame, he glanced around to see mounted silhouettes bearing down on him.

"I'm comin' in!" he shouted.

He stumbled over the two wounded raiders thrashing in the dirt and fell inside, a volley of gunfire following him. Lamplight flickered, a twilight that seemed to originate in another room. He rolled away from the door and somebody tried to shut it, but an outside arm lunged in at bottom and prevented it from closing fully.

"Need help here!"

The voice above him was Brehmer's, but Clay didn't take time to look through the acrid gun smoke. From where he lay on his hip, he pivoted with the shotgun stock and tried to bludgeon the pinned hand. He missed the first time, and the second as well, but on the third attempt he drove the butt hard against bone to a muffled cry. Quickly the arm wriggled back out of sight, allowing Brehmer to slam the door.

"We've got to hold it!" exclaimed the owner.

Clay scrambled up as the door gave a little, and then he was beside the older man, their backs flush against the heavy wood. For a moment Clay could feel resistance, but the two of them managed to seal the station against the night.

"There's a snake loose, Mr. Andrews!"

Only now did Clay hear the ominous vibration and see Lil standing in a chair beyond a table. The gun port in the room overlooking the corral was an advantage, but an opening large enough to accommodate a rifle barrel could also admit a rattler. He couldn't pinpoint the sound, for the way it bounced off the walls made it seem to come from everywhere.

But Clay had worries more pressing. With the jamb catch broken, there was no way to bolt the door. If three or four raiders joined efforts, they would be impossible to hold back.

He checked Lil's face, a portrait of hopelessness as she stood with her head near the crisscrossed brush of the ceiling.

"Miss Lil," he said, straining to project calm assurance, "I'm goin' to ask you to do something. I need you to get down off of that chair and drag the table over here."

She looked first at him, next at the cluttered table, and then at the floor. All the while, the snake kept up its numbing buzz.

"I know a rattler's in here," he told her. "But there's somethin' a lot worse right outside."

Her hesitation vanished. Stepping down, she rushed around the table and seized it with both hands. The floor was earthen, and dust rose from the grating legs as she dragged it toward him. In seconds she was against Clay, but through the door came sudden pressure that forced them even closer.

The devils were about to overpower them, and Brehmer must have known so as well.

"Get that table upside down!" he shouted.

During the time it took Lil to slide away and upend the table, Clay felt the door open and pop shut five or six times. Stemming the tide seemed hopeless, and Clay was already wondering how to ration a single buckshot load against a horde. Then the tabletop was against the floor, and he lifted it by a spindly leg so that the top angled on edge. But how to wedge it under the knob when he and Brehmer were in the way? To move even for a moment would be disastrous, for they were already losing the fight against strong and determined foes.

The outcome seemed certain, an end unlikely to be either quick or merciful. But Brehmer had other ideas. The nearer of the two to the door, he timed the assault from outside, and when the door popped open again he fired a revolver shot point-blank through the crack.

Clay heard a scream outside, and the pressure on the door relaxed.

"Now!" yelled Brehmer.

Both men slid aside as they dragged the table edge up under the knob, buttressing the door.

"It goin' to hold?" cried Clay.

Before he got the words out, the makeshift brace sustained its first test. The door quaked to a powerful blow, and then a second, but the bottom edge of the table only dug into the earth, securing it more firmly than ever.

"The back room!"

Lil's warning hadn't even registered on Clay before a rifle discharge shook the walls and lead whizzed through the room in ricochet. He instinctively dodged and cocked the shotgun as he brought it up in search. He saw gun smoke coming from the room on the corral side and bolted for it. With the change in angle, the interior doorway momentarily framed the gun port and a rifle muzzle as it withdrew into the night.

"Pate! Pate! Answer me!" called Brehmer.

But Clay could see for himself. Pate presented the mirror image of Lil's earlier pose; in the far-left corner, past a table with a coal-oil lamp, he stood trembling in a chair as gun smoke swirled around him. He held a revolver at his thigh, but the absence of color in his face and the way he pressed back against the wall told Clay that he had no intentions of fighting back.

"He . . . he's reloading!" Pate cried.

Clay already would have guessed as much, even if he hadn't heard the bang of the gun butt outside, the standard method of settling the powder. Taking up a position beside the doorway, Clay leaned around the jamb and looked down the barrel. He set the knob sight on the gun port and began to count, knowing it would take the Comanche more than a minute to reload. Clay maintained his focus as Brehmer and Pate exchanged words at the ten-second mark, and as Lil said something at the toll of thirty-seven. As Clay reached fifty, the knob continued to sway against nothing but black night, but he knew that the moment was imminent.

He could see it all in his mind's eye: the short, quick strokes of the rod as the shooter seated the load, the transfer of the percussion cap from fingers to nipple, the pull of the thumb as it set the hammer to full cock. He could picture the hands as they hoisted the weapon, the gun butt as it braced against a shoulder, the cheek that pressed against wood so that an eye could look down the sight and find —

Suddenly, it was there, thrusting through that square of black exactly as Clay had imagined: a muzzle ready to spit fire. But only Clay's finger squeezed a trigger.

The report rocked him and punished his ears, and abruptly smoke was everywhere, thick and pungent and choking. As it dissipated, he saw that the muzzle was gone and that the square of night was now an oval inside a frame of crumbling adobe. Whoever had been behind that muzzle had looked down his last gun sight.

"Tell me what happened!" Brehmer shouted from behind. "I can't leave the door!"

"Need powder and shot!" responded Clay.

"No buckshot here! Pate! Pate!"

But Brehmer's son stayed frozen, and now Clay saw one reason why. Under his chair, the rattlesnake was coiled in the strike position, its tail vibrating furiously.

Clay rushed closer, his eyes shifting from the rattler to the gun port and then to Pate. "Throw me that gun!"

But Pate seemed incapable of doing anything but muttering a few panicky words, even as Clay closed to within two arm lengths and stopped, just out of the diamondback's strike range.

"We've got to man the gun port!" Clay pleaded.

When the young man ignored the outstretched hand, Clay drove the shotgun butt down between the chair's front legs. He could feel the rattler's fangs strike the stock, but on his second try Clay caught the scaly body flush and disrupted its coil. It wasn't easy, fighting the chair's legs as much as the diamondback, but after a dozen thrusts he crushed the triangular head.

The rattler was still squirming as Clay dropped the shotgun and tore the revolver out of Pate's grasp. It was a .44 like his, and in seconds Clay had the eight-inch barrel through the gun port as he reconnoitered the night. The corral was cross-fenced against a raid such as this, and although the Indians had emptied the nearer section, the bulk of the remuda still crowded the farther.

Clay could hear hoofbeats punctuated by gunfire, but he couldn't see a soul, not even a body below the gun port. But that didn't mean a marksman wasn't targeting him this very moment, drawn to the light like a candle bug to a flame.

"Get that lamp out!" he yelled back.

Clay didn't know who was responsible, but somebody extinguished the lamp, casting a gloom that extended into the corral. Now the spooked remuda appeared only in shades of black, stirring against a bluff that loomed up against the stars.

From the other room, Brehmer continued to call for his son. Vigilance was too important for Clay to glance back, but he took up the cause as well.

"Pate, if you're still here, go help with that door! This isn't over!"

Clay didn't know whose call to action Pate heeded, but he soon heard the young man and his father in the other room. It was a one-sided conversation for the most part, with Brehmer berating and Pate occasionally trying to defend the indefensible. It was a talk better left for another time, and in private, and even though Clay had dragged the young man off his horse earlier for panicking, he hated to hear him humiliated that way.

The gunfire grew sporadic and ended in receding hoofbeats. A couple of minutes later, there was nothing but the whistle of the wind to break the stillness. Then a voice called from up-canyon, and another and another as cowhands reported in from their respective positions. Clay answered Green's shout from the *choza* with his own report, and then relayed the news to Brehmer: no casualties. But that didn't mean there couldn't still be some, and Clay in turn passed along Brehmer's order for the men to hold their positions.

Not until the night again went quiet did Clay feel a terrible weakness come over him. It was as if somebody had opened a vein and bled out all his energy and nerve. He didn't know if he could last another moment at his post, and he began to tremble as he replayed the assault in his mind.

All through the ordeal, he had acted with cool efficiency, but no coward had ever suffered the level of fear that now engulfed him.

"Mr. Andrews, I've got some water for you."

The voice was Lil's, and Clay was glad it was too dark for her to see him well. Even in the bend of the Pecos, he hadn't felt this way, but maybe everything inside him had been building toward this point from the moment he had ridden into her camp ahead of flying arrows.

Something wet touched Clay's arm, and he groped and found a water dipper. He hadn't realized the fight had dehydrated him so, and he drank quickly as he continued to scan the corral and bluff.

He passed the dipper back to Lil without thanking her. As intolerable as he considered ingratitude to be, he would rather be thought rude than to bare the coward's quiver in his voice.

"I'll get you some more," she said.

During Lil's absence, Clay tried to gather himself. Maybe it was the necessity of showing confidence for her sake, or perhaps the water began to revive him, but by the time she returned, he thought his voice might work again.

"Sure obliged, Miss Lil," he said, taking the dipper. This time he sipped rather than gulped. "What you've been through and all, I sure do admire you."

"I don't know what for."

"The way you're holdin' up."

"I got any choice?"

The quiet way she asked it, and her note of sadness, made Clay regret that he had said anything. But he couldn't let her question linger without response.

"Life sure ain't treated you fair," he said. "Once you've had time to grieve over losin' your husband —"

"Only good thing that's gone on," she interrupted.

Despite the need to maintain surveillance, he faced her in the dark. "Ma'am?"

As she replied, Clay no longer heard melancholy, only bitterness.

"Wasn't ever no husband to me. He took me for a slave when I was fourteen. He might've made out like to Papa that I was to be his wife, but a slave's what I was."

Clay couldn't have been more stunned if a bronc had kicked him in the head. "Are you sayin' . . ."

"It's just like it sounds. He and Papa made a trade, and before I knew what was happening, he was hauling me away in his wagon. He carried me to the preacher man — Mama insisted on it — but it never was no marriage."

"My Lord, Miss Lil." Now Clay's voice didn't want to work for an entirely different reason.

"He was mean and spiteful and if I didn't do like he said, he laid into me with his hand. He might as well had a leash on me, for all the living he let me do. You're the first person I even talked to for six years, and I couldn't've done *that* if the Indians hadn't done what they did."

"I . . ."

Damn it, what was there for Clay to say? For anybody to say? The way he saw it, she was grieving for a lot more than somebody who had died. She was grieving for a life she had never had.

As close as Clay had felt to her before, Lil's revelation drew him far deeper into her world. It was too much to digest right now, considering that the Comanches might launch another assault any minute. But at least he might give her a little more of what she apparently had never had: encouragement.

Clay could distinguish her form in the gloom, and he set the empty dipper in the gun port and did something that propriety didn't allow: He placed a hand on her shoulder.

"Miss Lil, all of that makes me admire you that much more."

He started to say more, but a firearm boomed and the dipper flew right between the two of them.

"Get down!" he cried, dragging her to the floor.

Clay stayed there only a moment before popping up with an Army revolver cocked to fire. Through the gun port, he saw shadows racing across the empty section of corral.

"Comin' again!" he shouted to Brehmer. "What are they still after?"

"Rest of the horses! Don't let them have them!"

Clay swung the barrel of the Colt with the flight of a silhouette and pulled the trigger. He didn't think he hit anything, but he hoped a round or two might discourage them again. But these were Comanches, who had met his father's resistance on the San Saba with even greater ferocity, and Clay wondered if he needed to save one pistol ball for Lil.

"Something's going on outside the door!" yelled Brehmer.

Clay took a bead on another moving

shadow and fired again, but it was like shooting at fleeting wisps.

"There's smoke coming around the edges!" Brehmer continued. "They must have doused it with coal oil and torched it!"

If the marauders' intent was to distract them in order to steal the rest of the horses, they were doing a good job of it, thought Clay. But an already grim situation abruptly grew worse.

"Mr. Andrews! The roof's coming down!"

Clay wheeled at Lil's cry and felt debris pepper his shoulders. From the midway point of the ceiling came metallic dings as something impacted the earthen roof. It persisted — quick, sharp reports that shook the latticework of supporting brush.

"They're diggin' through!" he exclaimed. "Get in the other room!"

But now the air was growing thick with wood smoke, and he could hear Brehmer coughing and yelling to Pate for the water bucket. Clay didn't know whether Lil left or stayed, for a fist-sized patch of night appeared in the ceiling. He took aim, and the moment something blotted out the stars, he fired.

The muzzle flash lighted the room for an instant, but as the starlight reappeared and the digging ceased, the walls stayed alive with a flickering glow. The inner doorway was even brighter, and from it funneled such a hiss and snap of burning wood that Clay knew a bucket of water wouldn't be enough.

He rushed into the room to find fire engulfing the outside door and its bracing table. Already, the flames had leaped to the latticework of brush and were spreading rapidly. The obscuring smoke stung his eyes, but the way the hot soot burned inside his chest was almost more than he could bear.

Wheezing, Clay pressed forward, drawn toward racking coughs at the far wall. Pate was down on hands and knees and Brehmer was over him, bending at the waist with a supporting hand against the mud bricks. Clay couldn't find Lil, but he heard gasps from behind and he turned to see her in the inner doorway, the smoke surging past her like dust in a big blow. The gun port and breached roof, as small as they were, had created a draft both powerful and deadly.

The station was a death trap, and its work was all but finished.

"We got to get out!" he told her. "Stay with me!"

He ran to Brehmer, who sank ever nearer his son on the floor. Clay was all but overcome by smoke himself, and communication was impossible when he could no longer find a breath. But Brehmer must have sensed what couldn't be said, for he helped Clay drag Pate to his feet.

Clay left the young man in Brehmer's care and rushed to the burning door. The heat was unbearable, and he shielded his face with his gun hand and reached down for the only upward-angling table leg that wasn't on fire. The table still had structural strength, and as he dragged it toward him, the table's bracing edge remained caught under the knob and pulled the door back.

Clay expected to see night, but it came only in glimpses through flames that outlined the doorway. The situation was almost a matter of choosing death by Comanches or death by fire, but pistol balls stood no chance at all against fire.

Clutching Lil's arm, he downed his head and pulled her with him through the flaming doorway.

Clay fell into a night boiling with smoke and alive with gunfire. He lost his grip on Lil as she went down with him, and when he squirmed around to face her, he discovered her dress on fire. He wanted to shout a warning, but his bitter cough wouldn't let him. He slapped at the flames, drawing her attention, and when their combined efforts didn't work, he threw himself across her legs.

Clay paid a price in burns, and Lil probably did as well, but he succeeded in smothering the fire.

Only now did Clay realize that Brehmer and Pate were beside them, dark shapes against streaming ribbons of yellow. Pate was sprawled, but a kneeling Brehmer was coming about with his six-shooter, the barrel swinging above Clay's shoulders. The ground was shaking, and as Clay turned to a growing tumult behind him, the revolver's report exploded in his ear.

Pounding hoofs were in Clay's face, and a few of the horses shied and broke away from the herd that stampeded toward the river. Then he was up on a knee as well, pivoting with the .44 and finding a mounted figure almost even with him. It swept past too quickly, but down the long barrel of the Colt he saw another oncoming rider and fired. Simultaneously, an arrow imbedded in the ground at his boot and the warrior surged by, the apparent beneficiary of another errant round.

Clay sprang up, but the raiders were past now, disappearing in the night with more horses. All he could do besides wheeze was run after them a few steps and shoot futilely until the hammer clicked on empty.

CHAPTER 9

During the night, the roof collapsed, and by daybreak the old mail station was in ruins, a set of smoldering adobe walls standing like a monument.

The Comanches had dropped a few horses, not enough to handle a spread the size of the Bar W's, but as river riders responded that morning to the column of smoke, the good news was that every man in the lower and middle sections was accounted for. Fortunately, the raiders hadn't made off with the store of powder and lead, and Clay wasted no time in casting .44-caliber balls for his personal revolver and replenishing his bullet bag and powder flask.

It would be a long, dangerous ride downriver to Horsehead Crossing and on to Fort Stockton, but now it was doubly important that he and Brehmer talk with the commanding officer. The raids were adding up quickly, and Brehmer observed that never had a US Army presence on the Pecos been so vital. Equally essential, the Bar W's needed horses, and any ranches that might be located adjacent to the post would be the nearest potential suppliers.

Brehmer delayed departure to allow time to assess the losses, rest, and regroup. Even in light of the uneventful days that followed, Clay wasn't keen on leaving Lil behind. But taking her along through such exposed country was out of the question, and Green agreed that she would be safer holed up in a *choza* with several armed men. Besides, once Clay struck out for Fort Stockton with Brehmer's party, there likely wouldn't be enough horses at headquarters to invite another raid.

In late afternoon a few days after the attack, Clay stepped outside his *choza* and saw Lil approaching from the gulch's mouth with a bundle of folded clothes. She had on the same simple calico dress that she had worn during their ordeal on the Pecos, but now it was cleanly laundered. For a couple of days she had helped salvage items from the torched station, and Clay had made a point of working beside her so they could talk. In the evenings, he had continued to find excuses to be around her, and he didn't think he had ever enjoyed anyone's company so much. Now that the cleanup was over, however, the soot still clung to his clothes and he was embarrassed for her to see him so disheveled. Still, she would have been a sight for sore eyes if not for one thing.

She wasn't smiling.

Clay couldn't find much to smile about either, for it dawned anew on him that she would be leaving. He had dwelled on it a lot in view of what she had told him about her marriage, and as he pondered the matter again, she stopped before him.

"Brought your clothes to you all laundered," she said. "I had them laying out by the wash pot, so they didn't get burned up." Her voice was lifeless, and her eyes were sad and had heavy bags underneath.

Belatedly, he tipped his hat. "Sure obliged, Miss Lil," he said, taking the garments.

They stood in an uncomfortable silence before Clay added, "I'll be leavin' for Fort Stockton at first light."

"I know. I wanted to get your belongings washed in time."

"Well, you sure done that, ma'am."

Another uneasy silence ensued, as though Lil didn't know what to say any more than he did. Then she reached into her dress pocket and quietly said, "I almost forgot."

When she withdrew her hand, Clay saw

the leather pouch.

"It was in your shirt pocket," she said as she gave it to him.

The water-stained leather had bulk and weight, and Clay recognized it from the dead man's boot. He positioned the bundled clothes under his arm and spread the draw-string opening.

"Funny thing about this," he said, spilling the contents into his palm.

"What is it?"

"Just little rocks, I guess. I was hopin' they was pistol balls when I found them." He dug into the pouch, came out with a wad of paper, and began unfolding it gently. "Piece of a map in here too. Peculiar thing to stick in a man's boot before buryin' him."

When Clay looked up, Lil's eyes were wide and glued on his hand. Even more striking, her face had paled to the color of a new wagon sheet.

"Somethin' the matter?" he asked.

She seemed incapable of doing anything but gaze at the brittle half page that rustled in his fingers.

"Ma'am? What's eatin' at you?"

"You *did* find it. What he was looking for. All he ever talked about. The reason he dragged me out in this country. The grave he helped dig and the one he got killed hunting for."

"Who? You mean —"

Now she looked up. "The old devil that called me his wife."

"Miss Lil, maybe I'm just tired or somethin', but you've got me plum' dumb fuddled."

She continued to seem stunned, but she began to talk, her words halting, her sentences fragmented. Clay listened, never interrupting. What she had to say was disjointed — a story jumping here and there, forward and backward — but by the time she finished, Clay thought he had it pieced together.

Back in the fifties at a place called Chadbourne, Casner had been present when a grizzled prospector named Ben Simkins wandered in with a big bear story about a portion of a treasure map he had found in a cave full of skeletons off the US Army's upper El Paso road west of the Pecos. Although Casner only glimpsed the fragment, he watched the old man pay for supplies with gold nuggets. Soon afterward, Simkins wagoned away, supposedly bound for the cave and the rest of the map that would point the way to sacred Mescalero gold in the Guadalupe Mountains.

With three other men, Casner trailed Simkins west, hoping he would lead them to the cave and the map's missing half. On the Pecos, however, the old man evidently realized he was being followed, forcing them to swoop down and try to seize his secret by force. When a search of his person and belongings failed to turn up any clue, they staked him to the ground and denied him water until he might give them answers.

For two days they kept him there, the dehydrating sun taking its toll, but the old prospector held out stubbornly. By dawn on the third day, he was dead, and all Casner and his companions could do was conceal their misdeed. Scooping out a shallow grave, they buried Simkins and threw his belongings in the river.

On the way back to Chadbourne, the men came under attack by Comanches, and only Casner and one other man survived. After a winter brutal with pneumonia, nobody but Casner had remained alive.

"The more he drank, the more he talked," said Lil. "I never knew how much of it was the God's truth and how much he dreamed up. But he told it over and over, how later on he got to thinking they didn't search the man good. The boots, he kept saying, they never looked in his boots. We finally loaded everything up and come out here, just so's he could find that spot again and look for a map. He didn't reckon on how hard it would be to find a grave that wasn't marked. Guess he didn't figure on getting scalped neither."

Now it was Clay who was stunned. "My land! I never heard the like." He examined the rocks in greater detail. When they caught the sun, they seemed to come alive. "I've never seen a gold nugget — you? Sure don't shine like —"

Like Molly's locket, he wanted to say.

"Barely seen a silver dollar. Mr. Casner sure didn't have no gold."

Clay turned his attention to the yellowed and water-stained page, which was torn almost diagonally with the greatest width at top.

"Let's see if we can make any of this out," he said, shifting about so that he and Lil stood shoulder to shoulder.

It was a fragment of a crude map, all right, labeled with landmarks. There was the Pecos, unmistakable in its sinuosity, and Pope's Crossing up by the New Mexico line. On west of the river, the map gave distances from point to point along the El Paso road until, toward the headwaters of the Delaware River, the way veered toward twin hills set between identical larger ones.

Clay studied the fragment for so long that he burned every detail into his memory, even though it wasn't his intent. The way to Skeleton Cave seemed so straightforward and logical that, if the map was accurate, a child might have ridden to the location.

But maybe it was all a big joke that had cost too many men their lives.

Lil must have poured over the map as carefully as he, for she placed a delicate finger on Skeleton Cave.

"All he talked about," she said, "and it's right there where anybody could find it."

"Like as not, they'd get scalped by Apaches tryin'. As bad as Comanches are on this side of the Pecos, they say Mescaleros are a lot worse across it. See here where it says 'gold' and 'G-U-A-D-A'? The rest of it's tore off, and the map too, but that's got to be the Guadalupe Mountains. All the way back in San Saba, I used to hear there wasn't a worse place for Mescaleros."

In silence, they stared at the fragment for another minute or so before Clay folded the page and returned it to the pouch. The rocks, he kept in his palm a while longer, noting the muted shine as he stirred them with a forefinger.

He poured the objects in on top of the map and placed the pouch in her hand.

"Miss Lil, I don't know what to make of all this, but a man wouldn't hide this in his boot if it wasn't worth somethin'. Anyhow, I figure you got a better claim than anybody."

"You're the one found it, Mr. Andrews."

"Yeah, but you're the widow of the man that was lookin' for it. I'm not sure I'd show that map to anybody — some people take a real fever when it comes to that sort of thing. But if there *is* some gold in those rocks, might help you get a start wherever you end up."

Clay hadn't intended to turn this into a conversation about Lil leaving, but he blurted the words before he realized it. Moments before, Lil had seemed anything but happy, but now her face blanched. Even worse, she began to shiver despite the oppressive heat that beaded the back of her hand.

Her reaction confused Clay, but maybe it wasn't so strange, considering all that she had told him.

"I know you're feelin' lost," he said.

"Been that way since I was fourteen."

"I know, and it ain't right. It just ain't like it ought to been."

"How . . . how long you think before wagons come through?"

"No idea, miss. Guess they'll be here

when they get here."

Now, she looked at him with those pinched eyes, and suddenly it was Clay who felt a sense of loss. He didn't want her to go — he just *didn't,* damn it — and yet he had no right to ask her to stay.

"Will something come by before you get back?" she pressed.

"Don't expect we'll be gone all that long. I'm sure you'll be seein' us come ridin' in 'fore you know it."

Lil dominated Clay's thoughts as he struck out for Fort Stockton an hour before first light. With him rode seven men — Brehmer, Green, and five more Bar W hands — a small army necessary to guard any horses they might drive back. An equal number of men remained at headquarters, but Clay wished that Green had stayed back instead of Pate. If it came to protecting Lil, Green had already proved his mettle, while Pate was nothing but a liability.

Before the morning was half over, Clay met a sight he didn't want to see.

Conestogas. A lot of them, strung out along the road. Bearing determinedly toward him through a haze stirred by laboring wheels and the hoofs of work oxen and beef cattle.

Clay could hear the screech of axles and the rattle of kettles as the Conestogas rocked to the uneven turf. He could hear the creak of swinging grease buckets and see the ruffle of dusty wagon sheets. He could hear sharp voices call out *Gee!* and *Haw!* as drivers walked beside the teams and popped whips against ox hide.

He could hear and see everything that he wished he couldn't.

In his mind's eye, Lil was already there, trudging alongside the haggard women. Her skirt was flying around her dusty shoes as she filled the possum belly under the wagon with cow chips and mesquite-root fuel. She was pressing on through life, bound for a faraway place, yet taking time to scold a young child for getting too close to the wheels that could crush.

Crush.

Those relentless wheels could destroy more than flesh and bone, and Clay knew it in a powerful and personal way. Before he returned from Fort Stockton, they would snuff out a spark that might have kindled something life-changing in him.

He wouldn't even get to tell her good-bye. She would be gone, a wisp that had passed through his life so quickly that it would seem she had never existed. And through all the dark nights to come, when he would have only vengeance and Molly's memory to give him purpose, he would regret letting her get away before he had even had a chance to know her.

Clay was third in line behind Brehmer and Green, and by the time the lead Conestoga's oxen plodded by on his left, he saw a rider nearing from ahead. Astride a mule, the stranger was a diminutive man with a tawny goatee and curly hair long enough under his black slouch hat to suggest a lot of weeks on the trail. There was a tiredness in his dark eyes as he pulled rein, but the lever-action 1866 Winchester across his saddle spoke of appropriate vigilance in Indian country.

"Might you have seen Indians?" the stranger asked in an English accent as Brehmer pulled up abreast. Dust powdered the Winchester's brass frame, but not enough to dull the glint.

"Struck my headquarters hard a few nights ago, up the road at the Narrows," said Brehmer with a nod back. "We're on our way to Fort Stockton to see what can be done about it. This your company?"

The stranger glanced at the passing Conestogas. "My name is Fremont, out of Fort Smith in Arkansas. We embarked with thirty-seven wagons and acquired fifteen more in Texarkana. We lost three people to the cholera a few weeks ago, but now it is Indians that concern me."

"Well-armed, I guess," spoke up Green, whose humor had been subdued since the night attack.

"One of the requirements in the contract. At least one firearm per family."

Brehmer took control of the conversation again. "Then I feel confident enough in your ability to provide safe passage to ask something of you. There's a recent widow stranded at headquarters who's lost all she had. This country's no place for her and she needs the company of other women. Could you take her and see that she gets a fresh start somewhere?"

No! a part of Clay silently pleaded. *Tell Brehmer no!*

"It would not be up to me," said Fremont, tugging on his goatee. "One of the families would have to take her in. How far to your headquarters?"

"Imagine you'll be making camp there this evening," said Brehmer.

"I can inquire during the march. If a family is agreeable, she can head up the river with us in the morning."

It was all too sudden, too certain, too lasting. The odds were, before Clay even reached Fort Stockton, Lil would be gone, really gone.

"Where's the end of the road for you?" A strange hoarseness hung in Clay's throat as he asked.

"California," said Fremont.

"By way of Fort Stockton might've been better protected," said Brehmer.

"I expect California is no closer one way than it is the other."

The company captain and Brehmer talked more before Clay rode on with the Bar W bunch, but as the Conestogas creaked by at Clay's side, he heard only one word again and again.

California.

The place was so far away that it might as well have been a point of light lost in a night sky.

Adrift in all the what-ifs, Clay was only vaguely aware as he and his companions worked their way downstream, alternately riding and then walking and leading their ponies. They camped in some nameless bend of the Pecos, and when they swam their mounts to the west side at Horsehead Crossing late on the second day, Clay relived the ordeal he and Lil had endured in waters so similar. More than ever, he struggled to accept that at this very moment, she might be bound for a world in which he could never have a place.

Chapter 10

Three days had passed.

For Lil, the dramatic events of the past week and a half had come so rapid-fire that she was still reeling. Once before, her entire world had turned upside down, but that experience did nothing to bolster her confidence now. On the contrary, the past and the present seemed to merge into a devastating hell bent on destroying the tiny bit of hope she still secreted away.

She thought of Clay, and her heart ached in a way that was at once similar to, and different from, the feelings she had known when Casner had whisked her away from her family. Not until she had set out with the Fremont wagon company had she realized how much Clay's mere presence had buoyed her. All through the first day's march upriver with the Conestogas, as the hanging dust — and more — had watered her eyes, she had cast wistful glances back toward the Narrows in the hope that she would see him ride up. Nevertheless, bend after river bend only expanded the wilderness behind, just as an equally uncaring wilderness swelled inside her.

But maybe Clay wasn't the man Lil thought he was. Maybe time would have proven him as heartless as Casner and her father. Maybe it was for the best that she would never find out.

Maybe. But she didn't believe it for a second.

The wagon company captain had placed Lil with a onetime storekeeper from Fort Smith, Arkansas, and his four motherless children, ages twelve, nine, seven, and two. Lil's role seemed to be making sure the older children stayed clear of the wheels and rattlesnakes while she carried the two-year-old. It was good to have a task on which to redirect her energies, though the situation only reminded her of the siblings she had lost on that black day in East Texas.

On this morning, Lil's two-year-old ward was growing heavy, not to mention the aggravation of the boy's position against the pouch of nuggets in her dress pocket. She wanted to let him walk a while, as she had done early that morning, but the baked alkali that now burned through her leather soles would have tortured a child's bare feet.

Lil had already given up looking back for Clay when a dark shadow swept across her path.

"Damn. What a pretty lady you are."

Startled, she found a rider pulling up alongside on a foamy bay. Twenty-four or so, with scraggly red whiskers and a cowboy's rigging, he immediately presented a striking contrast to the cowhand she yearned to see. For one thing, this stranger had cursed in her presence without apology, and his comment was shockingly inappropriate.

Such violations of accepted conduct were not lost on a second unfamiliar rider who came up just beyond him, the two men's profiles rising up side by side against the sky.

The second rider's eyes narrowed, and he freed up his right hand with a transfer of reins. "Fin, you want me to knock you off of that bronc?"

The cowhand he had addressed as Fin turned to him. "What you jawin' about?"

The second cowhand, thinner and burned darker, took a final draw on a cigarette and threw the butt in Fin's face.

"Watch it!" exclaimed Fin, dodging. "Thing's still got fire in it!"

"Can't you see she's spoke for? What you think she's got in her arms?"

Fin looked at Lil again, prompting her to glance at the child. "I'm just carrying him, is all," she said.

Considering what happened next, Lil was sorry she had volunteered the information. Fin immediately cut his horse in front of her, forcing her to stop. As he grinned down at her, there was something troubling about his bloodshot eyes — a suggestion of dissipation that she had seen only in Casner.

"My, my, this *is* my lucky day, seein' how you's not took. Name's Fin. What's yours, pretty lady?"

Past the V formed by the bay's angling neck and the cowhand upright in the saddle, Lil saw the Conestoga's ruffling sheet surging onward.

"I'm falling behind," she said, starting around the horse's nose. But the animal moved with her, continuing to block her way.

"What you hurryin' off for?" asked Fin. "We ain't even got acquainted yet."

"Let her be," said the second cowhand. "We got bog to ride."

Fin looked at his companion. "Well, ain't *you* the responsible one. Them stuck cows ain't goin' nowheres. I ain't neither till I get this pretty lady to give me her name."

"Yeah, well, boss would have a thing or two to say about that."

Fin's gaze wandered over Lil suggestively. "Old man Brehmer ain't around. But Pretty Lady here sure is."

His mention of Brehmer reignited Lil's hopes of seeing Clay again. "So we're still on the Bar W's?" she asked.

"Ornery ol' devil don't want a fellow to have a bit of fun," said Fin, still surveying her.

Lil's estimation of this stranger dropped even lower. Here he was, talking about fun, while her life had been about survival for days now.

"You're in my way!"

Lil turned to see the trailing Conestoga's ox team plodding past as the grumbling driver came up from behind with reins in hand. It was the rider named Fin who needed to yield ground, and he did so with a reluctant sigh. But as soon as the driver edged by with a pop of his whip against ox hide, Fin took his horse directly across her course again.

"I've got to go," Lil pleaded, forced to angle uncomfortably near the Conestoga as she started again around the bay's nose.

But the impolite stranger was determined.

As if cutting a heifer out of a herd, he reined the horse across her path so sharply that the animal's shoulder bumped her hard.

Even as Lil stumbled, she thought she could right herself against the passing sideboard. She threw out a hand, but found only the top of the revolving wheel. Her fingers rode the curved felloe for a mere instant, but its quick downward arc carried her with it. She fell against the whirling spokes, a helpless pawn with a young boy on her hip.

Something solid — the iron tire maybe — struck the side of her head, and she was down under the wagon, the dust bitter in her mouth as stars danced against the undercarriage.

Through her fog, she heard the distant cry of the child, but a corner of her mind told her that he was still in her arm and that she had to escape the crush of the charging rear wheel. She didn't even know that she rolled, but abruptly the specks of light played against an overhead sky as the wheel surged by so close that it yanked her hair.

Silhouettes blocked the brightness as her daze subsided, and she found three figures hovering over her beside the stationary Conestoga. One was the former storekeeper, his finger fierce in her face.

"Near got my boy killed!" the man yelled. "Look how you skinned him up! You damned sure ain't traveling with *my* wagon!"

Lil sat up as he gathered his children and stormed away. The second cowhand withdrew also and led his horse after him, and Lil heard enough to realize that the stranger was trying to explain that the mishap hadn't been her fault. But the Fort Smith man wouldn't listen, instead waving him off even as the cowhand persisted.

Fin's voice abruptly drowned out the conversation. "Sure lost your balance. Here, let me give you a hand, Pretty Lady."

He extended his arm, the kind of thing Casner sometimes had done after putting her on the ground. Ignoring the gesture, Lil began rising on her own, but she felt his fingers on her arm before she came to her feet. Not so casually, she stepped away and brushed the dirt from her dress.

"Lost somethin' out of your pocket."

At Fin's comment, Lil looked around to see him stooped over the leather pouch. A nugget had spilled out, a shining presence stark against the bare alkali.

"Say, what you got here?" he asked.

Fin was already scooping up rock and

pouch, and Lil remembered Clay's warning about how some men reacted to such things.

Fin rolled the little rock around in his fingers as he stood. "Sure does shine. Fool's gold or somethin'?"

Lil couldn't have told him if she had wanted to, but one thing was certain: A fool had died looking for it.

"That some kinda paper inside?" Fin pressed.

A corner of the map was exposed, and before Lil could stop him, Fin began withdrawing it with a thumb and forefinger. She was conditioned to subservience around a domineering man, but the sheer gall of this stranger awakened something in her.

"That's mine," she said, reaching.

Her hand never got there, for the stranger pulled the pouch away.

"Hold on now, Pretty Lady," said Fin. He turned his back to her, but she could tell by the rustle of paper that he was determined to inspect whatever was inside.

"Looka here. You got more of these little rocks."

Lil stepped around his shoulder and reached for the items again, but the cowhand whirled away.

"Don't be in such a hurry, Pretty Lady. Let's see what this paper here is."

Lil protested again, but Fin didn't seem to care. He continued to spin as she chased his hand. She traced a full circle in the dust, but it was like trying to catch her shadow. By the time the two of them made another revolution, he had the map unfolded, and whatever he saw at first glance so fixated him that he stopped and shoved her away.

Lil stumbled back and went down, the second time in minutes that Fin had put her in the dirt. For a moment she was aware of only the bruising hardness under her hip and shoulder, and then came a quick *pop!* like the strike of an iron-shod hoof against wood. She turned her head, seeing a wind-tossed page fluttering out of the sky as Fin fell backward. She felt the impact right through the ground as he landed violently and rocked back on his spine, his boot heels flying up.

The second cowhand stood over him, his fist clenched as he glared down. "You don't treat a girl thataway. I gave you fair warnin'."

Rubbing his knuckles, the cowhand stepped across Fin and approached. "Let's get you up, ma'am."

The map had settled on Lil's dress, and she took it as the wind lifted the edge. She was fully capable of rising on her own, but she accepted the cowhand's assistance and regained her feet. Once more, she began to dust herself off.

"Sorry what the no-account's cost you," said the cowhand. Then he turned to Fin, who lay wallowing on the ground. "You've troubled her for the last time. Pick yourself up and get on your horse."

Fin clambered up and staggered away, dripping blood from his mouth. As both cowhands mounted up and rode upriver, Lil set about gathering the scattered nuggets that could make fools out of men, and corpses out of fools.

All that day and the next, as Fin nursed his lacerated lip and quietly rode the river with the cowhand who had caused it, he dwelled on that page fragment he had held for mere seconds. He could remember nothing of the map except a crooked line labeled "Pecos River" and a place marked "gold" and "Guada" at the jagged tear. Maybe maps to lost gold went for the price of a drink in some places — a cowhand from San Antone had told him as much — but this one had been accompanied by physical evidence.

As Fin dug the shiny little rock out of his shirt pocket, the possibilities boggled his mind. Knocked senseless as he had been, he didn't know how he had managed to hold onto it. Maybe it had been the doing of the dark man inside him; regardless, not until Fin had ridden a mile or two upriver had he even discovered what was in his clenched hand. As large as a robin's egg, the rock was unusually heavy for its size, and as his palm swayed to the gait of his horse, sunlight danced in the object's wrinkled contours. Except for a yellow tinge, it resembled metal slag from a black-smith shop.

Rasping his thumb across the lump's pit-ted face and rough edge, Fin wished he knew a little about prospecting. The truth was, he was clueless about the characteris-tics of unrefined gold. Nevertheless, as he thought about that leather pouch, the rock became like a fire burning in his hand.

Fool's gold, hell! Why would Pretty Lady have had the slag side by side with a map if both weren't genuine? Wasn't she headed straight up the El Paso road for the Guada-lupes, right where Simkins's mine was sup-posed to be? He had to have that fragment — now! Hadn't his aspirations centered on the lost Simkins mine ever since he had heard all the talk at the Bar W's? He damned sure hadn't been concentrating on riding bog and stamping around knee-deep in mud.

The sun was already setting across the Pecos when the two cowhands rode into the Bar W upper headquarters below Pope's Crossing. Here on an elevated flat a mile or so off the river, smoke rose from a small cook fire at a chuck wagon set among scrub mesquites and yucca. Around the glowing coals were a half dozen men, digging into plates piled with beans and beef. Like most bog riders who had spent extended hours in the saddle, they seemed content with hot grub, black coffee, and the anticipation of a good night's sleep in the bedrolls stretched out nearby.

But a dreamer like Fin wasn't so easily satisfied. Were he to get it in his head that there was easy money in the wind, he would have set out to rope the currents. A mere wisp of promise could light a fire under him — but this time he had the kind of evidence that he could see and touch and roll around in his fingers.

And the key to it all lay back up-trail with Pretty Lady.

Fin carried that thought with him as he unsaddled his bay and turned the animal over to the jingler, who bore the responsibility of looking after the horses. Even after plopping down before the fire with a plate of chuck and a cup of steaming coffee, Fin stared at the gray ash among the coals and saw only the map that he had held all too briefly.

He was only vaguely aware of the conversation taking place around him, but he didn't have to listen to know that there were more wild horses ridden over a plate of beans than anywhere else. Staying in the saddle astride a sunfishing bronc was about all a six-bits-a-day cow herder dared dream of, but Fin supposed that he didn't fit the mold typical of his profession.

"Put in a million days out here, still won't get you a million dollars."

"What's that, Fin?"

Fin didn't realize he had spoken out loud until the cowhand at his left posed the question. A gangly man with a thick mustache and a jaw set crooked by a long-ago horse kick, Bill Tom had come out to the Pecos with Brehmer's first herd.

"Just sayin' here we are," Fin said, "wearin' out our backsides ridin' for this outfit, and what do we got to show for it 'sides tobacco money?"

"Three square meals a day, I suppose," said Bill Tom. "And knowing we can respect ourselves for a job done right."

A half chuckle came from across the campfire. The slender cowhand who had split Fin's lip stood there, a skeptical look on his dark-burned face. Ever since the incident at the Conestogas, he had spoken only when necessary. Now, though, his words came freely.

"Some hands don't have any pride in their work, Bill Tom." Despite the salutation, he stared straight at Fin.

If there was anything Fin had learned, it was not to cross someone who had already knocked the tar out of him, so he directed his response to Bill Tom.

"When I first rode in other day, I tried gettin' you boys to go lookin' for that lost gold in the Guadalupes." He pronounced *Guadalupe* "War-Loopy," as everyone in camp seemed to.

"Yeah, well," said Bill Tom, "I expect my answer's the same now as it was then. Good way to get our scalps dangling from some Apache war lance."

"If enough of us was to go in together, we could fend 'em off," said Fin. Avoiding only the man across from him, he scanned all sides of the fire and found the faces attentive.

"Some mighty big country across the Pecos," said Bill Tom. "Figure on turning over every rock till you find it?"

Fin stole a glance at his hard-knuckled nemesis through the rising smoke. "We was all talkin' about old man Simkins a few days ago," said Fin, "how he come back from that cave full of skeletons with half a treasure map."

"What of it?" asked one man.

"I think I seen that map today. A pretty lady's got it back at some wagons. I seen enough to figure it'll take us right to that cave and the other half. Put the two together and we'll be bossin' old man Brehmer 'stead of him bossin' us."

The cowhand across the fire must have realized what Fin had in mind, for he cursed indiscreetly, drawing everyone's attention to his scowling face.

"Told you to leave that girl alone," he snapped. "If you didn't get the message, let's you and me step out behind the wagon."

Fin lowered his gaze and went quiet, and no one bothered to press him for more information. He guessed that everything he had said sounded too much like a big bear story. But with every red-to-yellow-to-red pulse of the coals in the fading light, he saw only that fragment of map and Pretty Lady's face.

The stars were brilliant points of light in a black sky as Fin slipped out of his bedroll and crept past all the snoring figures. Drifting campfire smoke and the *yip-yip* of coyotes accompanied him to the wagon tongue that pointed by design to the North Star, a standard orientation practice that, on a stream as crooked as the Pecos, proved helpful even in daytime. He turned north with it and, just inside the mesquite chaparral, came upon a shifting shadow that was all he could distinguish of the night horse. Staked to a big yucca, the animal was already saddled for quick use should the need arise.

Speaking quietly to reassure the animal, Fin gripped the bridle by the cheek and gathered up the dragging reins. Freeing the horse, he mounted up with a squeak of leather, only to hear a sudden voice from beyond the yucca.

"Who's there?"

Startled by the jingler's voice, Fin spun. He realized that a muzzle flash could end his big ideas in a hurry if the man mistook him for an Indian.

"Don't be shootin' — it's me!" Fin

warned quietly.

Within moments, a rider approached out of the dark. "That you, Fin? What are you up to?"

"Think I dropped somethin' back down the river. Thought I'd have a look-see."

"In the dark? You got better eyes than *me.*"

Fin swung the horse downriver. "Be back in a little bit."

"Better watch for Indians."

"If I can't see them, I figure they can't see me neither."

Squeezing the horse with his thighs, Fin and the dark man inside him rode away into a night that abruptly held images of not only Pretty Lady, but much, much more. As if they were there, shining through the gloom in haunting reminder, he saw another horse's forelegs reaching out again and again in desperate flight from San Saba once the news had broken.

CHAPTER 11

Once more a castoff with no family to claim her, Lil trudged aimlessly alongside the Conestogas for the rest of the day. At camp that evening, a kindly woman gave her desiccated vegetables and pemmican and loaned her a blanket for the night, but only after the husband made it clear that it would be a onetime thing. Lil couldn't blame him; they had two children with another on the way, and he simply couldn't take on any more responsibility.

The next day, a spiritless Lil dropped farther and farther off the pace until she was abreast a vehicle with a wobbly rear wheel. Eventually the driver was forced to halt at a point where the road almost touched the Pecos.

As men gathered to effect repairs and other wagons rumbled past, Lil wandered lost and forlorn to the sharp riverbank. She stood there, tasting the brine in the air as it wafted up, and saw more than currents rush by, red and tossing in the sunlight. In her mind's eye she distinguished two men, bound by Pecos happenings that had caught her up and set her adrift in a sea of tomorrows frightening in all their unknowns.

One of the men was alive, to the best of her knowledge, and the other was dead, and yet it was the dead man who wouldn't leave her alone. Casner had reached out from that shallow grave to steal away her hope yet again, and whether it made sense or not, she blamed it all on the map that he had foolishly given his life in search of.

Except for a word or two, Lil had never learned to swear, even though Casner would have been the ideal teacher. Now, though, she summoned up every vile epithet that she could think of and cast them silently at that wretch of a man for what he still tried to take from her.

She wouldn't let him! He had taken enough already, and she would do whatever she must to keep him from denying her again.

Lil took the leather pouch from her pocket and withdrew the fragile page. As she had done with Clay at the Narrows, she studied the fragment, noting what it showed and what it didn't show. There were the Pecos, a crossing labeled "Pope's," and a trail leading west. But there was even more that she gleaned, particularly the place marked "Skeleton Cave." The rest of the map was missing, except for a star and the designation "Gold of Guada-" in the jagged bottom corner.

The way to Skeleton Cave seemed as simple as before, but how to get from the cave to the supposed gold was a shadowy naught reserved for fanciful dreams.

And maybe for the better, thought Lil. She knew firsthand what the promise of unearned riches did to a man's soul.

That is, if Casner had ever had a soul.

Lil shook out the shiny rocks and cupped them in her hand. Strangely, she counted only four, though she thought there had been five. No matter the number, they and the map were bridges between Casner's grave and any hope she had of truly escaping him. It was almost as if they were his way of holding her under curse. How else could she explain the incident that had led to her dismissal by the only family willing to take her in?

The wind was gusting, as it always seemed to on the Pecos, and Lil relaxed her grip on the map. The currents lifted it and carried it over the bank, where it rose and sank and rose again, before diving to the tumbling waters. The paper floated there, carried along with the surge, before a downstream ripple pulled it under.

The shiny bits of slag, whether worthless or valuable, she held a little longer as she considered Clay's kindness in conveying them to her. Was she betraying him by throwing them away? Would he have understood? Did it even matter anymore, since she would never see him again?

She didn't know the answers, which was why she dropped the rocks back inside the pouch instead of tossing them in the river.

Lil heard a saddle shake behind her, and she turned to see company captain Fremont riding up as his mule kicked up dust. Pulling rein before her, he folded his hands across the saddle horn and stared down at it. Lil watched the wind ripple his goatee for so long that she thought he would never look up, but he finally did so with a heavy sigh.

"I learned of you falling under the wagon," he said.

"It wasn't my fault."

"That child could have been killed. My company has lost two girls that way over the years. Facing their people afterward is not something I want to do again."

"I can't travel with them no more," said Lil.

"No, ma'am, you cannot."

"What's to come of me?"

Again, Fremont glanced down, and she thought she heard regret in his reply.

"There is a man I know looking for a wife, and he is not likely to find one between here and California. We've got an ordained minister in the company to do the marrying."

Wedded, just like that. A man she didn't even know, carrying her away. Consummating the marriage under a wagon and setting her on course for domination and abuse that would never end.

Before Lil would let that happen again, she would throw herself in the Pecos.

"You may think on it overnight," Fremont added.

Reining the mule about, he rode away to rejoin the screeching Conestogas as they rolled relentlessly toward tomorrow.

So that's how it would be, thought Lil — one night to come to a decision. She wondered what would happen when she told him no. Would Fremont cut her out of the company and leave her to fend for herself? In a forsaken place where if the sun didn't kill her first, Comanches were sure to do worse?

Lil turned and stared down at the boiling river, which seemed to beckon from its heartless depths.

In a dimly lighted room with plastered adobe walls at Fort Stockton, Clay could hear the Yankee flag flapping on the parade ground outside as he stood with Brehmer across from a major seated at a cluttered desk. Clay related in detail the attack on Lil's wagon and their discovery of Casner's body, but when Brehmer began to recount the raid at Bar W headquarters, Clay's mind wandered upstream of the Narrows. Lil was there somewhere, marching ever farther out of his life, and he could hardly bear the thought.

All the way from Horsehead Crossing, he had dwelled on her increasingly, for there seemed a void inside him that swelled with each passing hour. Everything in accepted conduct cried out for him to forget her — this fragile young woman whom society dictated should be in mourning, off-limits to his or any other man's attentions. It was something that every honorable person should have respected, even given Lil's unique circumstances. But Clay knew the gaping cavity that was inside him, hollowed out by an all-consuming yearning for something he didn't have.

He was letting her get away. She was gone already, and he hadn't done a damned thing to stop her.

Clay remained a disengaged bystander as the major expressed his willingness to set up a temporary encampment at Horsehead, from which the Ninth Cavalry could make regular scouts up the Pecos. With one goal accomplished, Brehmer turned his attention off-post and set about replenishing the depleted remuda with saddle stock from a ranch on nearby Comanche Creek. The succeeding days dragged by, each as long as any Clay had ever known, and he continued to be distracted even as he helped cut out Brehmer's newly acquired horses and point them for Horsehead.

The drive back to Bar W headquarters was uneventful, except for Clay's anxiousness. He realized that his hopes of finding Lil still at the *chozas* should have been tempered by realism, and yet his anticipation soared as he helped turn the herd up the little canyon toward the corral. A slender figure, hazy in the billowing dust, rushed from the fire-gutted station walls, and Lil so dominated Clay's thoughts that her name broke quietly from his lips.

But it wasn't she.

"Receive a favorable price for the horses?"

Even if Clay hadn't distinguished the voice over the hoofbeats, the emerging image of paper and pencil in the figure's hand would have been identification enough. Brehmer was too busy to respond to his son, and Clay assumed that no one else had the right to reply. But as soon as the last horse trotted into the corral and Green secured the gate, Clay reined his mount about and came up before Pate.

"Miss Lil about?" he asked.

"She embarked with the wagon company that Father evidently arranged for." Pate took a folded page out of his shirt pocket and extended it. "She left this for you."

Clay took the letter. He was crestfallen, but he didn't want Pate to see it in his face. Swinging his horse about, Clay unfolded the page and began to read as a fine dust settled over Lil's script.

Dear Mr. Andrews,

I am sorry I am unable to thank you in person for your kindness and protection over these days. I will never forget it. The wagon company is leaving now, so I must hurry and say good-bye. We never know

what tomorrow will bring — only Provi-
dence does — but if not for Him sending
you I would not even have a tomorrow.
God bless you, Mr. Andrews.

Mrs. Casner

P.S. I have watched all night for your
early return, but I know your arrival is days
away.

Clay stared at the letter until it became a blur that summoned up powerful memories. In an uncaring world, two people adrift had connected under the most trying of circumstances. As he relived those moments, the memories began to draw something confusing out of his closely guarded emotions. What it was, he wasn't sure, but he did know that inside him was a growing ache unlike anything he had ever felt before.

He dwelled most on Lil's postscript — *"I have watched all night for your early return"* — and in it was enough of a suggestion of something unvoiced that a question began to rage in his mind.

Do I go after her? Is that what I got to do?

From beside Pate, Brehmer's voice shook Clay out of his reverie. "We'll rest up tonight and start upriver tomorrow with horses for the upper headquarters. You'll both be going with me."

Just like that, the decision to follow Lil up the Pecos had already been made for Clay, and with a silent cry of elation he realized that it was the only choice with which he could have ever lived.

Far into the night, Clay lay awake in a *choza* and thought about Lil. Oddly, he pondered most her stubborn belief in something more. Whether she called it Providence or God, Lil seemed reassured by simply believing that He already saw their tomorrows and had the power to help them get there.

How could she believe such a thing? With all she had been through, how could she think like that? If there was a God, He had to be utterly heartless, the way all her yesterdays had led to Casner. Didn't she have sense enough to see that nobody in the sky gave a damn about her?

But strangely, Clay found himself longing for the very assurance that Lil had. After all, his God-fearing mother had planted just such a seed in young Clay, and for years he had never doubted it.

But that had been before he had found Molly stretched out across a blood-soaked bed.

Chapter 12

Fin didn't have any idea how to wrest the map out of Pretty Lady's hands, but he and the dark man inside him thought on it the rest of the night as he rode downriver.

He couldn't very well strong-arm it away in front of all those emigrants, but a dreamer like Fin never worried about details. After all, someone had once told him that "a man doesn't find a treasure; a treasure finds a man." And Fin figured the chosen man might as well have his name.

Right before daybreak, he came upon a large horseshoe of Conestogas rising like a fort out of the floodplain. Through the sixty-foot breach secured by ropes, he saw exaggerated shadows play against wagon sheets as figures moved before flickering campfires. He couldn't distinguish a picket, but he knew that in Indian country a nervous guard might shoot him out of the saddle without even a challenge.

"Halloo!" he shouted as he drew rein.

Abruptly, nothing but firelight danced against wagon sheets. As the troubling stillness lingered, Fin feared the worst and bent over the saddle horn so that the horse's mane brushed his hat brim.

"Identify yourself!" a voice demanded.

Fin relaxed a little, but he kept his roan's head between him and those wagons. "I ride for the Bar W's! We got this whole country!"

All that broke the silence for the next half minute were a murmur of voices and the crackling of campfires. Finally, at a shouted invitation, Fin took his bronc forward to meet several men who had gathered at the breach in the corralled Conestogas. Beyond the double ropes, camp was astir again as smoke curled against oxen ready for yoking.

A small man with a dark slouch hat and a pronounced goatee stepped forward through the ropes as firelight caught the lever-action 1866 Winchester at his side.

"Dangerous country for a lone man about," he said with a distinct English accent.

"Ol' river's bad for boggin' and we's spread pretty thin," said Fin.

Fin shifted his horse's position a little in order to scan the enclosure past the man's shoulder. He hoped to see Pretty Lady among the milling people, but the shadowy faces darted in and out of the firelight. He needed a better look, and he wouldn't get it from here.

"Sure could use a cup of coffee," said Fin.

"Coffee, we have. You may tie your horse to the wagon."

"Much obliged," said Fin, dismounting.

"My name is Fremont. You can give me a report of what lies ahead. Two of your riders passed through my company yesterday, I was told. I did not have an opportunity to speak with them."

Concerned that the blame for Pretty Lady's mishap may have fallen on his shoulders, Fin decided against acknowledging that he had been one of the Bar W hands. After securing the roan, he followed Fremont through the ropes and on to a popping fire near a Conestoga at the nine-o'clock position in the enclosure. Every step of the way, Fin glimpsed faces all about but couldn't make out the young woman from the day before.

He took a cup of coffee from Fremont, and the two men hunkered at the fire as smoke teased with a changing wind. The Englishman plied him with questions about the road, and Fin told him what he knew while stealing glances past the swaying flames. Pretty Lady was there somewhere, and so was that map, but Fin was still clueless about his next step.

Once Fremont seemed satisfied with the report, the Englishman changed the subject. "I assured a man by the name of Brehmer — he seemed to be in charge — that I would try to take a widow with us. I fear it will not work out. I may need you to escort her back to your headquarters."

The last thing Fin wanted was a widow woman to nursemaid in a long, dangerous ride to the Narrows with nothing to gain by it. That called for somebody fool enough to be satisfied with having done the responsible thing, and Fin didn't view life that way. Hell, he was chasing lost gold!

When Fin hesitated, the Englishman added, "The company will loan a horse. I have not the men to spare or I would see to it myself."

"Well, I got a lot of river to ride, and that ain't my section." Through no fault of his own, Fin had spoken the truth. Lifting his cup to his lips, he looked through the rising steam in continued search.

"I feel your employer would be in favor if he understood," encouraged Fremont.

Fin heard, but his focus was now across the enclosure. That dainty figure, sitting by the rear wheel of the Conestoga with the ripped wagon sheet . . .

"Your reluctance to assume more responsibility is understandable," persisted the Englishman. "Until I speak with her again, I am unsure there is even a need. But should there be, I will pay you a week's wages."

If there was anything that could seize Fin's attention, it was money, and the quick look he gave Fremont must have spoken volumes.

Fremont rose. "Come with me."

The fire hissed as Fin threw the rest of his coffee in the coals and followed. He still had no intention of going to the Narrows, but at least he could pass among the obscured faces discreetly and maybe get a better look below that torn wagon sheet.

Working their way clockwise along the wall of Conestogas, they weaved through haggard women who loaded cast-iron cookware as children yawned and stretched underfoot. Meanwhile, the men of the caravan began to drift across the enclosure to yoke the oxen, which pulled best in the cooler morning hours. Shadows continued to hide the features of all but the nearest individuals, but if Fremont would hold course for a little longer, Fin could at least satisfy his curiosity about the figure in spotted calico below the torn wagon sheet.

Soon Fin was there, stopped at the Englishman's shoulder before a kneeling girl who folded a blanket on the ground. Her head was down, but she looked up as Fin's spurs ceased jingling and he saw firelight reflecting in the unmistakable pinched eyes of Pretty Lady.

"My, my, what a . . ."

Fin started to say more, but he was so surprised to learn the widow's identity that the words wouldn't come. She seemed just as startled to see him, but Fremont either didn't notice or dismissed it.

"Mrs. Casner," the Englishman said in greeting. As she rose trembling, she cast eyes back and forth between the men, and something akin to compassion entered Fremont's voice. "I believe it is *Lil,* am I right?"

"I guess."

Her voice was that of someone with a crushed spirit — and for a moment, Fin heard another girl, weeping in the strewn hay as he had fled the barn on a day that seemed strangely near again.

Fremont went on. "When I made my suggestion yesterday, you lost all color. I fear you have not changed your mind."

She gathered the blanket to her breast as if seeking comfort in it. "I . . . I need to give this back."

"I explained my predicament already, and I confess I am at a loss. Fortunately, this gentleman from the Bar W" — he faced Fin briefly — "what is your name, sir?"

"Go by Fin."

"This gentleman offers a solution. Are you willing to let him escort you back to headquarters?"

"They don't want me there," said the girl, who was even prettier than Fin remembered.

"Surely Mr. Brehmer will understand once you explain," assured Fremont. "Perhaps he can place you with the next company through."

Pretty Lady fell silent, but Fin felt her eyes probing him even as he looked down and scratched the caked alkali under his hat brim. While the Englishman pressed her for a reply, Fin concentrated on stirring the soil under his boot. But when he heard Pretty Lady agree in a reluctant whisper, he looked up and flashed her a grin as big as a mountain range that hid mysterious gold.

Maybe, just maybe, there was truth after all in that crazy claim that a treasure found a man instead of the other way around.

By sunup, Lil was riding downriver, rocking

to the gait of a spotted appaloosa. Immediately ahead, a roan nodded along under the rein of the Bar W hand who had identified himself as Fin.

As wary as Lil was of this boorish stranger and the dangers ahead, she was so alive again. She was going to the Narrows, a place she had thought she would never return to, and Clay would be there. Once more, she would see him, this man who had done so much for her.

For a while, Lil reveled in the kind of buoyant hope that had been missing throughout all the cruel years. But as the saddle chafed her thighs and the sun flared in silent fury, doubts began to gnaw at her.

She would see Clay again, all right, but what of it? Even if she longed for their friendship to grow, circumstances would never allow it. Wasn't she riding back merely to tell him good-bye as soon as the next willing emigrant company passed through?

As disheartening as that thought was, Lil was troubled even more by the prospect of meeting an accommodating caravan before she ever reached the Narrows.

Lil was just out of sight of the Fremont Conestogas when Fin wheeled his horse about, forcing her appaloosa to halt.

"We need to talk, Pretty Lady."

He brought his roan back and stopped abreast so that the horses faced opposite directions. Fin's animal crowded so close that Lil's leg was almost pinned.

"Let me see that pouch you got," he said.

Lil had hoped their game of *ring-a-ring-a-rosie* was over.

"What for?" she asked.

"Come on, let me see that thing." Fin's hand darted out and groped her dress in the vicinity of her pocket. "Where you keepin' it?"

"Don't," she pleaded. "Please quit."

Lil had tried kindness with Casner too, but it hadn't worked then and it didn't work now. She was ready to produce the pouch herself, but when she attempted to do so, Fin's searching fingers were in the way.

"Stop fightin' me," he said, evidently misinterpreting. "I ain't hurtin' you."

Lil's horse slung its head and seemed ready to spin away, forcing Fin to reach for its bridle instead of her pocket. The development gave Lil an opportunity to end this, and by the time he calmed the appaloosa and turned back to her, she had the pouch out and extended.

"That's real smart of you, Pretty Lady," said Fin, taking it eagerly.

He parted the drawstring top as he sat

back, a sunlit figure stark against the distant horizon. Lil already knew this for a big, lonely country, and life in it was already fragile enough without another fool like Casner in the mix.

Fin's hand showed a sheen of sunlight as he emptied the bag. The four rocks, he dropped into his shirt pocket, a brief diversion before he dug for a map that Lil had already committed to this half acre of hell. When his fingers came up empty, he gave a quick look inside before muttering an oath and throwing the bag away.

Under his roan's angling neck, Lil saw the cracked leather catch on a shin-high mesquite beside the road.

Fin tightened his lips and looked at her. "You best hand it over, Pretty Lady."

"I don't have it no more."

"Oh, you got it, I bet. Let's see what else is in there."

He leaned across to search again, but Lil was a step ahead. Before he could touch her, she pulled the pocket out and exposed its calico lining, bright against her faded dress.

"Wha'd you do with it?" Fin demanded. He reached across her saddle and tugged elsewhere on her dress. "You got more pockets?"

"Just the one."

"So where is it, then?"

"I threw it away."

Fin went red all the way from his sloping jaw to his bottom-notched ears.

"You want me to take ever' stitch of clothes off of you lookin' for it? You better fork it over, Pretty Lady."

Long conditioned by the same wild look in Casner's eyes, Lil shrank and wished she still had the map to give Fin. But all she could do was tell him the truth.

"I threw it in the river."

"Hell, Pretty Lady. You expect me to believe that?"

"Caused trouble, was all it did."

It was *still* causing trouble, Lil thought, just as Clay had warned. She glanced at Fin's hand, wondering when the back of it would strike.

"Be a lot more trouble if you don't give me the damned thing," he said.

"Mr. Casner died 'cause of it. Anybody goes looking for those two little hills between the big ones probably will too."

"Hills?"

"That cave there with the skeletons in it. By the other river, west a ways."

Leaning back squarely in his saddle, Fin folded his hands across the saddle horn and stared at her. "Seems you learned that map awful good, Pretty Lady. Think you and me's gonna be spendin' some time together."

CHAPTER 13

For Clay, riding drag through an alkali haze, the scene ahead played out over the dusty rumps and wind-tossed manes of two dozen horses.

Pate was the first to point out the "Indian sign" beside the road, and Green was the rider who snatched the leather pouch from a shin-high mesquite and held it up for Brehmer to see. But it was Clay who responded with purpose, gigging his bay into a lope that quickly carried him past one trotting animal after another.

Before Clay could join the men, Brehmer evidently dismissed the find as inconsequential and the riders dispersed, leaving Green on the verge of dropping the bag below his stirrup.

"Green, you look in that?" Clay asked, pulling up before him.

Green glanced up at Clay and then inspected the pouch again. "Cracked like a saddle that ain't never seen soap. Somethin' from them wagons we come across, I guess."

Yeah, thought Clay, *but maybe it started out in a dead man's boot.*

Green offered him the bag, and Clay took it and felt the cracked leather for himself. He could tell by the way it collapsed in his hand that it was empty, but he checked inside anyway. For a moment he relived it all: the Pecos River grave, the wagon camp siege, the face-to-face talk that had ended with the bag in a dainty palm. And now it had been discarded, its contents removed beforehand.

Clay didn't know what to make of it. Certainly, Lil had come this way, trudging alongside scores of emigrants bound for California. If she had lost it, why was it empty? If she had thrown it away, why had she bothered to remove the rocks and map?

Green chuckled. "Lookin' that thing over like you lost it yourself."

Clay lifted his gaze. "Guess I did, sort of."

"Well, that's a heck of a trick. Thought you come out from San Saba."

"Did. Found this above Horsehead in a dead man's boot."

"A what?"

"Grave, but I didn't know it. Bag had

some shiny rocks in it and some kind of map."

Green slid his fingers under his hat. "I ain't got the lice, but you've got me scratchin' anyhow. If you come by here gettin' to the Narrows, you sure come a roundabout way."

"Said I *sort* of lost it. I give it to Miss Lil back at headquarters. Don't know how come it empty and layin' here."

"If I was walkin' all the way to California, I'd look to lighten my load too."

Pate must have grown curious about the conversation, for Clay turned to see him riding up. Clay didn't think that he had ever seen anyone quite as ill-fitted to a saddle; all the way from the Narrows, the young man had fought against his roan's gait instead of conforming to it.

"Did I hear discussion about a map, Green?"

"I swan, Pate," the older man said. "Them squinty little eyes can't see for nothin', but your ears is a different matter."

"A map to where?" pressed Pate.

"Just part of one, really," said Clay. "Showed to end up at some imagined gold in the Guadalupes."

Pate's eyes went wide. "Old Ben Simkins's mine? I've been taking down accounts from everyone I could."

"Always lookin' for a story, ain't you," said Green. "Meanwhile, your pa's about to have a conniption fit. Guess we did quit on him, all right."

Sure enough, when Clay looked around he saw Brehmer with his jaw set firm as he stared back at them, a single drover with two dozen horses that had come to a standstill.

"Uh-oh," added Green. "Here he comes, and he don't look happy."

Clay's mind was still on Lil as he watched Brehmer approach, but the stern look on the owner's face as he drew rein before them was enough to jolt any six-bits-a-day cowhand back to the here and now.

"I'm not paying you men to sit here and quilt like women," said Brehmer. "Right now I'm paying you to drive these horses."

"Father," spoke up Pate, "Clay informed us that the leather bag is Miss Lil's and that it contained a treasure map and nuggets."

"Heard more than I thought," said Green.

"I didn't say they was nuggets," interjected Clay. "Not if you mean gold, anyway. I wouldn't know gold if I saw it, but they might've been."

"So what's that got to do with getting these horses to upper headquarters?" challenged Brehmer.

"Father, there could be a good story in this," said Pate. "You know how the men all talk about Simkins's lost gold."

"Hell, son," growled Brehmer, "that's all you ever think about is scribbling some damn fool story. You ever going to learn to do a man's job?"

Pate looked down, clearly unable to endure his father's glare. Clay, despite his differences with Pate, once more felt embarrassed for the young man at having to endure his father's criticism in front of the hired help.

"Oh, he'll come around," said Green. "If he keeps ridin' with me, 'fore long he'll be able to outsmart a ol' bronc good as any of us."

Clay wasn't so sure about that, but it was good to see that Pate had a mentor as patient as Green.

"Young'n," Green said to Pate, "we can start with fallin' back in place with them horses."

Green, Pate, and Brehmer reined their mounts about and would have ridden away if Clay hadn't spoken up. "Hold on a minute. Mr. Brehmer, your son might be kind of a dreamer — a little like somebody else I know — but there's somethin' about this worth talkin' about."

"I'm listening," said the owner.

Clay showed the pouch. "That map Miss Lil had — and four or five little rocks, whatever they were — they was all in this. I found it in a dead man's boot back down the river. Pretty sure it was this Ben Simkins they talk about, like Pate was sayin'."

"Simkins himself?" Pate asked in amazement.

Clay was focused on Brehmer's scowl.

"You grave robbing?" the owner accused.

"Not on purpose," said Clay. "Boot was stickin' out of the ground. Didn't know there was a foot in it till it was too late."

"Simkins himself?" Pate repeated.

"So what right you have to take everything?" pressed Brehmer, talking over his son.

"Comanches showed up," said Clay. "I was short on pistol balls, so I stuffed the bag in my pocket and lit out for Jericho. Come to find out, wasn't a bullet bag at all."

Between Brehmer's rigid frame and the neck of his bay, Clay could see Pate's eyes awash in boyish enthusiasm that not even the threat of a father's tongue-lashing could deter.

"Would you permit me to interview you?"

Pate asked tentatively. "At upper headquarters? Would you permit me?"

Green must have seen the icy stare that Brehmer gave his son. "Whoa, there, young'n," said Green. "Think we better get them broncs up the river 'fore you think about any paper scratchin'."

But now it was Brehmer who prolonged the discussion. "You still haven't told me," he said, facing Clay, "what all this has to do with Mrs. Casner."

Clay explained that he had given her the pouch and its contents at the Narrows.

"So?" pressed an increasingly impatient Brehmer.

"I warned her how some people take a fever when they hear 'gold,' and that she should keep it to herself. Findin' the bag empty this way makes me uneasy about her. Somebody might've strong-armed her."

Green looked at Brehmer. "Told him while ago she more than likely just throwed it all away."

Wondering, Clay scanned the mesquite bush, with its lacy green leaves shimmering, the bare alkali underneath, shining in the sunlight, and the floodplain, so empty and yet seemingly so eager to hide its secrets as it stretched into the distance.

"Listen to Green," said Brehmer. "I'd say

she discarded it."

"Maybe," Clay admitted. But he couldn't convince himself.

"Regardless, there's nothing we can do about it here," said Brehmer. "Likely as not, we'll catch up with those emigrants before they cross the river at Pope's. You can ask Mrs. Casner herself."

Clay mulled Brehmer's words as they all fell back into position around the herd. It was true that a drove of horses could manage dozens of miles a day, a pace so much faster than Conestogas that they might indeed overtake the emigrants before reaching upper headquarters. The owner was right: The best thing to do right now was get these horses on the move again.

But as the broncs strung out, the stronger forging to point and the weaker falling back to drag, Clay realized the complicating factor that could lie ahead. Ever since he had ridden for Fort Stockton, Lil had so filled his thoughts that he had almost forgotten what had brought him to the Pecos. He was looking for someone — for *Lucius,* who had ruled his every act for weeks after finding Molly's words.

Maybe the rumors placing Lucius on the Bar W's were true, and maybe they weren't. But with every lower division hand accounted for, the only place left to look was right where these broncs were headed.

Strangely, Clay almost hoped Lucius wouldn't be there. Clay's anticipation had built for weeks, but now that the moment might be imminent, it seemed too soon, too abrupt, too final. If the answers he had come for corroborated everything he suspected, there could never be any turning back, not when Molly's memory demanded so much.

But where would that leave Lil and him? Or did he even have a right to think in those terms?

All Clay knew for certain was that if he determined she was in trouble, he might have to make a decision that he never could have anticipated.

Maybe a night together clinging to a dangling wagon wheel had connected Clay to Lil in a way beyond understanding, for his premonition that something was wrong grew stronger as day faded and he sighted the caravan's plume of dust ahead.

Impatient, he nevertheless held his position with the herd as the horses closed the gap. But as soon as he distinguished individual Conestogas, he urged his mount up abreast of the Bar W owner.

"I'm sorry, Mr. Brehmer, but I'm goin' on ahead to check on things."

It was a statement, not a request for permission, but the displeasure Clay expected to find in Brehmer's face wasn't there.

"You do what you have to," said Brehmer. "Upper headquarters is just a mile or so more. We're taking the horses on in."

Clay gigged his bay into an easy lope that quickly made up ground on the Conestogas. They were strung out along a slight curve in the road, fifty-two vehicles with screeching wheels and flapping wagon sheets. He had encountered the caravan only days before, but now there seemed something strangely troubling about it, as if this lonely company bore terrible news.

Lil! Where was she? Good God, was she here?

As Clay overtook the caravan, he slowed his horse to a trot for the safety of the unaware emigrants plodding along. Passing them one by one, he frantically searched the faces. With each pace of his bay his fear rose, the same kind of growing terror that had gone with him across Molly's room.

There must have been fifty figures with calico hems flying around ankles, and three or four times Clay was almost certain he had found Lil. But disappointment built upon disappointment, increasing his anxiety to the point that he was beside himself by the time he came abreast of the lead Conestoga.

Forty yards ahead of the ox team, a diminutive rider with black slouch hat and tawny goatee reined his mule about to face the oncoming wagons. Clay recognized company captain Fremont immediately, and even though the Englishman began to signal the drivers with his arm — evidently to form the vehicles into a camp configuration — Clay didn't hesitate to interrupt. Spurring his pony ahead, he expressed concern even before he pulled rein before the captain.

"She's not here — Mrs. Casner's not here."

Clay apparently had stopped in Fremont's line of sight, for the Englishman flashed him an impatient look before edging his mule to the side and continuing to signal. A little guilty, Clay glanced over his shoulder at the Conestogas breaking out of march formation.

"I know you're busy," said Clay, "but I've got to find where she is."

Fremont maintained his focus on the task at hand, but he talked as he did. "I arranged for her transport back to the Bar W headquarters. Her presence had become a problem. She departed as we broke camp this morning."

Clay felt his face go hot. "By herself? You sent her off by herself?"

Now the Englishman made eye contact. "Certainly not, sir. She went in the company of a Bar W employee."

"Just the two of them? With Comanches on the prowl?"

"I had not the men to spare for an escort."

Clay spun back to the wagons. The two lead vehicles had stopped abreast, and the succeeding Conestogas were pulling up alongside in twos so that their front wheels were even with the rear wheels of the preceding two. The staggered effect quickly formed an arc that soon would be a circular corral. Off to the side, emigrants assembled out of the vehicles' path, but it was the hanging dust of the horse herd beyond that momentarily fixated Clay.

"We come from that way with horses," he said, turning back to Fremont. "If they'd been on the road, we'd've seen them."

Lines furrowed the captain's forehead as he gave Clay his undivided attention. "I assure you, sir, they embarked in that direction. I provided an appaloosa and provisions to see them to the Narrows."

The time for respect was over. "So where is she? If you run her off, where the hell is she?"

"That, sir, I cannot say. I can tell you only that she was in the charge of a Bar W employee who identified himself as Fin."

Fin.

There was something disturbingly familiar to Clay about that name, but he couldn't put his loop around it.

"Soon as you took her in, you was responsible for her," Clay charged. "Chasin' her off don't change that a bit. We got to look for her, and you're gettin' us the men to do it with."

Fremont's cheek began to twitch, and when he spoke, his words were hoarse, wavering, clearly the signs of a flustered man on the defensive.

"Sir, I indeed accepted responsibility when I allowed the Bar W Ranch to pass her into my care. That responsibility ended when I relinquished her back to the Bar W."

"The hell it did!" Clay was ready to knock him off the mule. "You took her out of a camp where there was guns and walls and throwed her out in the open with just one man!"

"He sported a revolver."

Clay knew from experience what it was

like facing an entire war party with a lone six-shooter. "You sendin' men with me or not?"

The Englishman motioned over Clay's shoulder, inducing Clay to glance back at the gathering wagons.

"I have one hundred ninety-seven men, women, and children," said Fremont. "Only six are on the payroll, and I cannot spare a single one. You may, if you wish, inquire of the families, but they have no mounts and cannot afford to abandon their wagons and prosecute a search by foot. I suggest you seek the services of the drovers that accompanied you."

Clay realized that he had no other option. But he was scared and angry and there was no one to blame except the man before him. He reined his horse about, only to spin the animal back to Fremont.

"If I find her dead, you son of a . . ."

The rest of Clay's words died in the rattle of his saddle as he wheeled his bay and rode away.

He looked left and right and back to the left again, not knowing what to do. Lil was missing, the floodplain to the west was about to swallow the sun, and it would be folly to work downstream and search by starlight.

What could have become of her? Good God, what could have happened?

He knew all too well, and it sickened him even to think about it. By sheer dint of will, he reached inside himself and drew upon wisdom, not emotion.

In soil as grasping as this, Conestogas would be hard-pressed to make eight or nine miles a day, which meant her departure point was only a few hours back by horse. But judging the miles by night would be challenging, and even if he started out now in order to be within striking distance at daybreak, he would be a lone rider facing a pitiless country that would sooner kill than give up answers.

Damn it, no matter how much the trail downriver tugged at him, he had to be smart about this. Turning his bay upstream for upper headquarters, he opened the animal up as much as prudence allowed.

He could already make out a distant chuck wagon in mesquites and yucca, along with two dozen horses descending on it. His bay's reaching forelegs chewed up the distance in a hurry, and the alkali fog raised by the herd was still settling over camp when he eased his mount into a walk on final approach. Chuck wagon etiquette required a rider to hold down his dust, and

Clay was too conditioned by the unwritten rule to violate it even now.

Suddenly he drew rein hard, frozen in stark realization. *Lucius might be here.*

Clay reached for the .44 that dangled by a leather loop from his saddle horn. Its three pounds had never felt so heavy, or the walnut grip so abruptly sweaty. Over the eight-inch barrel, he scanned camp in terrifying expectation — the weather-beaten wagon with its water barrel and cluttered chuck box, the rumpled bedrolls under a crooked yucca, the rising smoke lapping soot-blackened cookery on three sets of glowing coals. He saw everything a cow camp should have, except for men, but through the scrub mesquites ahead, riders and horses stirred among big yucca.

Trembling, Clay clutched that Colt Army revolver and remembered the oath he had sworn over Molly's grave. He couldn't disrespect her by disavowing it. He just *couldn't.* But in the time it would take him to pick his way through the brush to the remuda and cowhands, he might have to decide whether Molly or Lil was the more important.

It was a hell of a choice to make for a grieving and worried man on this godforsaken river, and as he urged his bay forward, the weeks rolled back to that blackest of moments when he had waited outside while three kindly women had prepared Molly's body for burial. To the unnerving buzz of cicadas and despondent cooing of doves, he had tossed butt after butt off the sagging porch, and when the door had creaked open, he had turned to find something worse than tears in the women's eyes.

Violated.

That's what they had told him.

Violated.

They had stood there on the warped decking, the brushwood roof hanging over them all like a shroud, and whispered a word more disturbing than any he had ever heard. And it had set Clay on a course from which there could be no retreat.

He had lived the succeeding days in a fog, except for a time when morning sunlight had glinted from a shovel blade beside a dark excavation. Momentarily aware, he had found himself repeatedly scooping and broadcasting, the dirt raining down to patter against wood. And without warning, Lucius's features had seemed to cast an ominous shadow across that three-by-six hole to which no man should have committed an eighteen-year-old sister.

Lucius, the friend.

Lucius, the suitor.

Lucius, the bastard.

At times, he had been each of these, but even a bastard wouldn't have violated a virtual kid sister who had blossomed into innocent womanhood. Or at least Clay had refused to consider it until Molly had been dead a month and his head had begun to clear. Only then had Clay learned something deeply concerning: Without once stepping foot on the homestead to share in their common loss, Lucius had left San Saba.

Then the weeks rolled forward to another day, another lonesome moment in which grief had hung in Clay's throat and heightened a now-chronic ache in his skull. Returning home on a stocking-footed bay after riding for an outfit across the San Saba River, he had reined up just shy of the house and paused in the shade of the big, twisted live oak that he had come to hate. For minutes or hours he stared down at the freshest of the graves, a sting in his eyes blinding him to everything but memories too heinous to remember and too important to forget.

With a fierce shake of his head, Clay turned from Molly's grave, only to notice something white on the ground halfway to the house. Fluttering at the wind's mercy, it was caught in a patch of wilted bluebonnets. Curious for a reason he couldn't have explained, he took his horse closer and snatched it up.

A letter-sized sheet, rain-crinkled and faded by sunlight, it was oddly stained as though something had soaked through from the other side. Flipping it, he found Molly's handwriting exploding out of a blood-smeared page.

Lucius, Lucius, why did you do it?

Nothing more, nothing less.

Lucius, Lucius, why did you do it?

Stunned, Clay whirled to the window to Molly's room that had stood with shutters swung out that dreadful day. He remembered the draft, and how it had drawn strands of her golden hair toward the opening as she had lain in death's repose across the bed, a bloody pencil beside her.

A pencil without a note, until now.

Lucius, Lucius, why did you do it?

The words had been enough to imply, not to condemn. And that was why today, far away on the Pecos River, Clay gripped his .44 and broke through the scrub mesquites at Bar W upper headquarters in search of answers.

Then he was there, caught in the suffocating haze rising from a hundred hoofs. He saw mounted figures in flashes — three on the right, one in back, three more on the left — like images through the spinning cylinder of an empty revolver. But Clay's Colt was rammed full, six loads sealed with axle grease, the hammer under his thumb ready to snap back and set the trigger against his index finger.

"Glory sakes, you expectin' Indians?"

Details still came rapid-fire, delineating men who hadn't spoken: a rider rail-thin and dark-burned, a companion with crooked jaw and thick mustache, an additional two cowhands equally unfamiliar. But Clay recognized Green's voice and found him at nine o'clock beside Brehmer and his son.

Clay relaxed his grip on his revolver, but he was still as tightly wound as a dallied catch rope around a saddle horn. He had been spared an impossible decision, but right now he couldn't find comfort in it.

"Lil's missin'," he blurted. "Mrs. Casner, she rode off for the Narrows this mornin' and we never did meet her. We got to go look."

"They tell you that?" asked Brehmer.

Clay nodded downriver. "Company captain back there. Fremont, I think's his name. Some Bar W hand's supposed to be ridin' with her."

"We got one missing, all right," spoke up the crooked-jawed man.

Brehmer turned to him. "Who's that, Bill Tom?"

"That no-account Fin you sent me. If you measured a man in dollars and cents, he'd be worth a cactus in the butt."

"That's him — Fin," said Clay. "That's the name I was give. You think he'd hurt her? He reliable enough to see her back to the Narrows like Fremont sent her?"

Pate looked at Brehmer. "Father, the captain gave me the impression you arranged for her passage."

"He said there was a problem," interjected Clay. "Important thing now's to go out lookin' for her. We got to hurry!"

Brehmer twisted around in the saddle to study the low-hanging sun. Its rays bathed his glistening face as he seemed to fall into deep thought. As his distant stare lingered, Clay traced the owner's long shadow across the remuda. Beside a forked yucca, its daggers shining in the rays, the crooked-jawed man Brehmer had addressed as Bill Tom straddled a roan and joined his fixation on the sunset. Clay knew what both men had to be thinking.

If a girl was in trouble — it didn't matter

whether she was saint or whore — she deserved everything a respectful cowboy had in the way of gumption and grit to help her. But they couldn't do it in the dark.

At the squeak of leather, Clay found Brehmer turning to speak to him.

"Let's get some chuck in our bellies and decide how to do this."

CHAPTER 14

Out of one nightmare of domination into another.

The taut rope binding Lil's wrists to the saddle horn chafed her skin as she bounced to her horse's gait at sunset. Fin rode ahead, leading her appaloosa by a towrope through broken country as thick with alkali dust as the Pecos floodplain. He had taken her far away from the river as he had circled back upstream, always keeping the Conestogas out of sight. He had mentioned, too, the need to avoid the Bar W upper headquarters on the way to Pope's Crossing.

In this moment of weakness, Lil figured that God must hate her. He must have judged her for all her failings and passed terrible sentence. During all the years with Casner, Lil had somehow endured, secure in God's love if not in man's, but now her world seemed darker than ever before.

If there was anything worse than perdition, it had to be the way she had been teased with escape from it. For a few brief days, despite Comanches and rattlers and uncertainty, she had known what it was like to revel in hope again. Judgment had been meted out on Casner, and a friend had come along to remind her that the world was not all filled with Casners.

And then circumstances had sent Clay one direction and her another, two courses that could never meet.

"You wouldn't be doing this if he was here."

Fin looked back over his shoulder. "Guess you ain't forgot how to talk after all."

"He wouldn't've let you touch me," Lil added.

"The yay-hoo that rattled my jaw? Ain't goin' near him."

"He stood up to a whole war party. He'd stand up to you too."

Fin drew rein and turned his horse to her. "Who you talkin' about?"

Lil hung her head. Would it do any good to dwell on what couldn't possibly be?

All through the purgatory that had been her life with Casner, the answer had been no. But that had been before a stranger had shown her a level of kindness that she had forgotten existed. Already, Clay was fading into the past, a memory destined to join those of siblings in dreams she could barely summon up now. Was there anything wrong with clinging one last moment to the hope that he had brought her?

She stared at the knot about her wrists. "If he knew, he'd be coming after you."

Fin gave a slight laugh — a nervous one, Lil thought. "Pretty Lady, I don't expect they's anybody in these parts that cares. That's why I come here in the first place. Nobody to get riled up about things like they is in San Saba."

Lil lifted her gaze in surprise. Hadn't Clay said he was from San Saba? Hadn't he asked Green and Pate about somebody who might have hired on?

"You got friends in San Saba?" she asked.

Fin's cheek twitched. "Not no more, don't expect. Not after —"

He seemed to catch himself, and a pallor came over his face. "Funny question you're askin'. What's it to you?"

This wasn't the kind of friend that Clay would have had, Lil thought. But maybe they *weren't* friends. If Fin was the one he had asked about, maybe there had been some other reason for his interest.

"Any more of you from there?" she pressed. "That's working up here?"

"We don't talk about where we's from. You don't need to neither. What the hell you care, anyway? She was the same way, always makin' my business hers. Least, *that's* over with."

It was the first time Fin had mentioned someone else, and there was something about the way he said it that made Lil wonder if she could exploit it.

"This how you treated her too?" she asked. "You go and tie —"

"You don't know a thing about it," Fin interrupted. His eyes seemed to go blank. "I don't care what they say — I was good to her. How was I to know she'd take it that-away? Things just got out of hand and there wasn't no stoppin' Dark Man. How was I to know she'd go and —"

For a moment, Fin seemed to have forgotten that he was talking to Lil. Something troubling seemed to have breached an inner protective wall long enough for him to start to blurt secrets. At least that's how it seemed to Lil, judging by the way his jaw dropped as if in sudden realization, followed by a strange stare with eyes that repeatedly shifted in their sockets as if loose. Casner may have been mean, but Lil had never doubted his sanity the way she abruptly did with Fin. *This wasn't somebody to provoke.*

Lil fell silent, keeping all her questions to herself as she pondered his mysterious remarks and whether he had a connection with Clay. But it was Fin who wouldn't let the matter go.

"You're about her age," he said. "What are you? Nineteen? Twenty? What different it make if, you know, somebody takes you 'fore you're ready? It ain't like you really been hurt or nothin'. Not enough to do what she done and mess my whole life up."

He pressed her to answer, but Lil sensed that it was safer right now to avoid eye contact, much less perpetuate the discussion. Meanwhile, piece by piece, she began to put together the story of the other girl — whoever she had been — and realized the girl's story had been hers as well.

They gathered around the cook fire with its ever-shifting smoke — Clay, the Bar W owner and his son, and five other men who rode for the brand. Two additional riders were absent, checking for straggling beeves away from the river.

As Clay paced back and forth nervously, the last thing he wanted to do was grip a tin plate of grub. Common sense, however, told him to force down what he didn't want. Yet with every bite of beans, every taste of airtight tomatoes and sip of coffee black enough to float a horseshoe, he wondered where Lil was that very moment.

Or even *if* she was anymore.

"We'll throw together provisions tonight," said Brehmer.

He hunkered across the fire from Clay, a ribbon of smoke curling around his sweat-darkened hat brim. At his left, Pate sat scribbling furiously.

"We'll rest up," continued the owner, "and start downriver early enough to read sign at daybreak."

Brehmer seemed ready to say more, but the rail-thin cowhand, drinking coffee from where he stood over Pate, lifted his hand as if eager to contribute. Brehmer obliged, allowing the cowhand time to swallow and lower his cup.

"I ain't got a clue which lady Fin was supposed to haul back to the Narrows," said the cowhand, "but I got some suspicions about things."

Clay couldn't imagine what he was leading up to, but his words were enough for Clay to stop pacing. Staring, he waited anxiously as the man took another sip and made eye contact with him.

"She a wisp of a girl, nineteen, twenty,

with a dainty little chin?" the cowhand asked.

As Clay considered the description that could have fit several women in the wagon company, he took in every detail in the speaker's face: the mole showing through the stubble beside his mustache, the square jaw, the firelight flickering in the dark eyes.

"Her eyes is all sleepy-looking too," the speaker added. "At least out in the sun."

"That's her — that's Mrs. Casner. How —"

"Fin and I rode through the wagons yesterday. He was awful smitten by this one young lady. He got out of hand and I had to set him straight."

He flexed his fingers, and Clay noticed his swollen knuckles.

From the opposite side of the fire, Bill Tom cleared his throat. "She who he was talking about? The one that had the map that was going to lead him to gold across the river?"

If Clay's jaw hadn't already dropped, he was sure it did now. "That's the map I give her, back at the Narrows. How is it you know all this?"

The rail-thin cowhand shook his head. "Should've guessed Fin was still up to no good about that girl. He was trying to get us all to go in with him. Back at the wagons, he knocked that little miss down with his horse. Accident, I guess. But then he picks something up that fell out of her pocket — must've been a map — and didn't want to return it. I put him on his back and he didn't have a choice in the matter. He come back up here with me and started in again. Soon as he brought up little miss, I cut him off quick and he dropped it."

Bill Tom passed his hand across his deformed jaw. "Yeah, but then he makes off with a horse in the middle of the night, and nobody's seen him since."

"I guarantee you," said the swollen-knuckled man, "if Fin headed off with that girl, it wasn't to no Narrows. He's got her across the river looking for old man Simkins's mine. And I'm pretty damned sure it ain't by her own choosing."

In one way, Clay was relieved: There might be an explanation other than Comanches for not meeting Lil on the road. But this Fin character, and the prospect of abduction with the aim of entering an Apache stronghold . . . Any way Clay added it up, the uncertainty consumed him as only Molly's death had ever done.

"She . . . she deserves all we got — all *I* got, anyway." Clay's voice was hoarse with

224

emotion. "Come daybreak, we'll already be a day behind, and we can't afford to fall any farther back lookin' the wrong direction. Either the Comanches took her off before we could meet up with her, or this Fin's makin' her take him to that cave of skeletons."

Pate looked up from his notes. "Skeletons?"

Lil's features blazed too vividly in the lapping flames for unimportant details to throw Clay off-track. "Either way," he went on, "we got a trail to find. I . . . I just don't know what to do, which trail to look for."

A troubling silence fell across camp, except for the crackling of the fire and the incessant rush of Pate's pencil across paper. Green's voice broke the quiet.

"Way this wind blows out here — got so much room to start up in, you know — tracks won't last long. How could we ever hope to track anybody over across the river?"

"Don't have to," said Clay, looking up. "I looked that map over good — piece of one, really. If they're over there, I think I can find where that cave's supposed to be."

"Skeletons? A cave of skeletons?" repeated Pate.

For several minutes, Brehmer had stayed

quiet, as if processing the details dispassionately, something Clay was unable to do. Now, however, the owner spoke with the kind of authority Clay longed to hear.

"Then it's settled," said Brehmer. "I want one man here with the remuda. We've got two others due in tomorrow. Bill Tom, you take a few men and scout downriver. If you don't find anything, I want you to keep riding and bring back those Yankee soldiers. They're setting up at Horsehead Crossing."

Then Brehmer faced Clay, and there was something reassuring in the older man's scored features. "The rest of us will go across the river with you. It's my fault she went with that wagon company, and I'm sorry things worked out like they did. I promise you we'll do our damndest, Apaches or no Apaches."

It was the best Clay could hope for, and he closed his eyes against the consuming flames and hoped that the God in Whom Lil had placed so much faith hadn't abandoned her the way He had Molly.

Stretched out on his bedroll, Clay lay awake, wondering if the stars that stared back at him were watching over Lil as well. Too, he pondered whether Molly was up there somewhere, looking down on both of them through those faraway windows into Heaven.

It would have been a comforting thought, and his mother had implied a similar thing to young Clay about his father's place in a great cloud of witnesses. But as real as Heaven had seemed to Clay then, hell had been much more of a certainty the last three months.

Green, sleeping beside him, snorted loudly enough to wake himself and roll over. As Clay heard him fall back into a rhythmic snore, he knew that he needed to get sleep as well. But how could he, when Molly was dead and Lil was gone?

Clay stared into the sky for so long that the stars blurred and seemed to merge into a single thing that danced against a black pool. Drifting toward unconsciousness, he momentarily yielded to his heavy eyelids three times, always able to follow the object's bounce whether his eyes were open or closed. The image went with him into sleep, a finger-sized bobbing stick that sent ripples through a shady pool of water.

"You got a bite, Molly!" he heard his ten-year-old self say. "Pull him up! Pull him up!"

On the San Saba River's grassy bank sat the three of them — Clay, four-year-old Molly, and ten-year-old Lucius, whose dark eyes had begin to shift strangely in their sockets. Clay had seen it in Lucius before, this warning of a tantrum to come. At least Clay had always thought of it as a tantrum, but all he knew for sure was that he should keep his distance for a while.

But with a fish bobbing at Molly's line, Clay was distracted enough to ignore the sign. Molly, gripping a short cane pole, squealed with delight and jumped up. This would be her first catch, but even though the bobber at the end of her line had disappeared underwater, she was doing nothing to set the hook.

Clay's own bobber began to run, but he dropped his pole and reached for Molly's. He could feel the weight of the hidden fish as he yanked, and with the two of them pulling, a sun perch as broad as a man's hand swung back at line's end.

Clay had never seen Molly so excited, the way she bounced around saying, "A fish! A fish!" But just as Clay grabbed the line to keep the perch from hitting her in the face, a hand darted in front of him.

It belonged to Lucius, who seized the fish and held on, despite the fins and Clay's angry, "What are you doin'!"

Clay burst up just as Lucius scrapped the perch free of the hook. It fell at Molly's feet, and before Clay could act, the fish flopped off the bank, slapped water, and was gone.

Clay looked at Molly. The corners of her mouth dropped. But it wasn't until Lucius broke into cruel laughter and Molly's eyes welled that Clay whirled on him.

Above Lucius's puffed cheeks and crooked sneer, Clay saw the bulging eyes with their crazy, darting pupils. But most striking was the blood all over his hand, a telling sign of the puncturing fins. Long ago, Clay had gotten into a scrape with Lucius during one of his fits, and had gotten the worst of it. He hadn't thought anybody could be that strong. But with Molly bawling loudly, the memory of a bloody nose didn't keep Clay from lowering his head and rushing him.

Clay caught Lucius in the stomach with a bony shoulder and drove him hard to the ground. The sky that showed through a leafy pecan tree kept changing positions as the two of them rolled in the grass. Then Lucius went off the bank and splashed water just as the fish had, and Clay picked himself up and took Molly's hand. With a glance back at the flailing arms and bobbing head, he led her away, not caring that Lucius couldn't swim.

Lucius survived, and the three of them never spoke of the incident. But by way of a taunting nickname, Clay reminded Lucius for weeks that he would pay a price if he ever did something like that again to Molly. And for a while, Lucius strangely had embraced the name.

Fin.

Clay sat bolt-upright in the Pecos night, his heart racing as never before.

CHAPTER 15

Just after sunup, Fin and Pretty Lady rode upon a grisly sight that could have served no purpose except as a warning.

It stared at Fin from the base of a big yucca to the left of the road, an arrow-riddled corpse with shoulders propped against the trunk. The head hung to one side, but the angle still showed a face frozen in a terrible grimace for every passerby to see.

The body was so badly decomposed that Fin couldn't tell if it had been a man or a woman. But he could distinguish the ants clearly enough, crawling across discolored flesh. Even at a distance, the stench was unbearable, and so were the flies.

Several yards away, at the end of the yucca's shadow trace, jumbled rocks told of a desecrated grave. Fin guessed that Apaches had done it, considering that he and Pretty Lady had crossed into their country. But warning or no warning, he wouldn't be deterred. They had swum their horses across Pope's Crossing at dusk the day before, and now as the long shadows of sunrise pointed him west, he was focused in a way he had never been before.

Ahead was his ticket to easy street where there would be no cantankerous bosses, saddle sores, or twenty-hour workdays. They would all be just memories, buried deep with other reminders of a life better forgotten, things like San Saba and Clay and Molly.

Molly.

Why was he thinking about her all of a sudden? Why the flashing images of her beneath him and the dark man, her face turning away from his would-be kisses as he pinned her against the barn's scented hay? Why the creak of the lantern as it swung from the overhead rafter, or the feel of the wind rushing through the door that screeched to and fro? Why her muffled *"No, Lucius, no, no, no!"* in his ears again?

Fin didn't know, but it all went with him with every pace of the roan that carried him past the hideous sentinel.

"Mr. Casner didn't have a lick of sense, neither."

With eight hoofs beating a cadence, Fin

barely heard Pretty Lady's subdued voice. He looked back, finding her profile against the bright sunrise as she faced the gruesome scene. It was the first thing she had said since the day before. Hell, she hadn't even looked at him.

"Got a funny way about you, don't you," he said.

Almost as if by reflex, she turned to him — at first in a tentative glance as though assessing, and then squaring her face for what would have been eye-to-eye contact had she been more than a silhouette.

"Act like you's scared of me," Fin added.

"He would've rode on past it too."

Fin took a quick look under the yucca's daggers.

"Didn't matter the fix ahead," she continued, "he'd've drug me right in the middle with him."

"Well, Pretty Lady, it's goin' to get me somethin' I ain't never had."

"It did him too. It got him a scalping."

In spite of himself, Fin cringed, and he took another hard look at the arrow-riddled corpse.

"How come you and him's like that?" the girl asked. She was suddenly talkative. "How come a person to stomp over somebody, just to get something that don't belong to him?"

"Maybe that's how some of us been treated our whole life," said Fin. "Maybe we had a old drunk for a daddy. Maybe we was hardscrabble poor 'cause he never lifted a hand except to beat us. Maybe seein' your mama kill him with a double-barreled does somethin' to you. Maybe I learned quick to stomp over people to get what I want."

They had ridden past the exhumed grave now, but Pretty Lady motioned back with her head.

"You can *want,* just like Mr. Casner did, but that's all he ever got and all some people got coming."

A shudder gripped Fin, and he couldn't keep from studying the corpse one last time. "Why don't you shut back up a while. Think I liked things better the way they was."

Nevertheless, as Fin twisted back straight in the saddle and rode on with her appaloosa's towrope in hand, the image went with him. But strangely, the mutilated body against the yucca had taken on the features of Molly, blooded wrists and all.

Forty or fifty miles straight ahead, the Guadalupe Mountains covered the west horizon like a rising blue norther. All through the first couple of days on the Bar W's, Fin had mistaken it for just that:

gathering clouds ready to swoop in. Even now, it didn't seem possible that anything could loom up so dramatically out of the Pecos barrens.

The range was like an unassailable fort, a wall that formed in the northwest and angled ever higher in working its way from right to left. Across what must have been forty miles of ridgeline, parapets stood out against the sky, while in other places, dark-gashed canyons reminded Fin of gun ports. On the range's extreme left, its highest and southernmost point, the battlement ended abruptly with a shining cliff. To Fin, it seemed as if an Apache god had taken a battle-ax to the Guadalupes and said "No more."

As the sun rose behind Fin and the rutted road gradually ascended through gray salt-bush and sand sage, spiny walking-stick cholla and prickly pear, he pondered the secrets behind that wall, or in its shadow. So far, he had never cajoled anything more in the way of directions out of the girl than a reluctant nod to the road ahead. Nevertheless, their course seemed hell-bent for the Guadalupes, and Fin wasn't sure if that was a good thing or not. She had planted seeds of doubt in his mind, and he couldn't keep from wondering if a battle-ax smaller than a god's, but just as lethal in a warrior's hand, waited for him in that Apache stronghold.

In mid-morning, Fin's horse squeezed between a pair of creosote-covered hills, eighty-foot prominences that overlooked a brief, yucca-strewn valley. At bottom, brush hugged a winding ditch that he figured for the Delaware River, if a stream so narrow could be called a river. As he looked down and across the drainage, he had his most commanding view yet of the still-distant Guadalupes. As impressive as the range had seemed before, it was awing now — awing and mysterious and maybe deadlier than any place he could imagine.

If that's where Pretty Lady was leading him, it was damned sure time to find out. He reined his horse about, inducing her appaloosa to halt where a twisted tree, bare of leaves but interwoven with green thorns, stood alone just off the road. Holding his animal crossways in the gap, he looked back and forth between the Guadalupes and the girl.

"Been nice to you up to now," he told her. "Ain't done a thing to pry directions out of you. That's all changin' right here."

She gave him a cautious first glance before facing him. "I wanted to draw that map over again," she said. "You could've had it and let me go."

He looked at her skeptically. "Now, how would I have ever knowed if you was on the square with me? This way, you ain't got no choice."

She glanced at her knotted wrists. "I'll still draw it, and you can ride on by yourself."

"I don't need you to scribble," said Fin. "All I need's for you to tell it to me."

"That mean you're letting me loose? That I can go back?"

"First things first." Fin slung a hand to the Guadalupes' ghostly haze. "There where you're takin' me? Where Apaches is thicker than heel flies?"

Pretty Lady's gaze followed Fin's arm, and as she continued to look, her brow knitted as if his words had suggested something.

"I saw what Indians done to Mr. Casner," she said, looking back at him. "I saw how they'd peeled his scalp off, and how his eyes was eat out. Buzzards was all over, pecking at him."

"I ain't talkin' about him, whoever the hell he was," said Fin. "I don't want to hear it from you neither. I'm wantin' to know where that map in your head's takin' us."

"Mr. Brehmer said the whole country over here's like a snake den, only it's Apaches. Don't matter where we go. Cross the river and they're watching the whole time."

Fin shuddered, and he turned in the saddle to check the small hill at his back. Was that something dropping out of sight behind the wind-tossed creosote bush on top?

He wasn't sure, and he didn't feel any more at ease when he reached for the .36-caliber Navy revolver in his waistband.

"Captain Fremont said they're worse than Comanches some ways," she continued, "that they'll slice you all up."

His fear building, Fin spun to her. "Quit it! I don't want to hear no more!"

"If they get a chance, they'll douse you good with coal oil and take a match and —"

The Navy six glinted in the sun as it swept up involuntarily, and Fin found himself looking at the girl's paling face over the violently quaking barrel. From boyhood, there had been terrible times when a dark corner of his mind seized him. He would become a distant onlooker, watching what he couldn't control. Usually, he would witness nothing more than innocuous misconduct — maybe inappropriate laughter or profanity. But there had been gloomy moments when his fists had flashed or he had pinned Molly on the ground and —

Afterwards, he would sometimes replay what that other part of him had done, and wonder with crushing remorse if he was even human anymore. Why did the rabid animal inside do such things? Good God, would he ever be able to keep it from acting against his self-interests?

The girl was his only hope of finding the gold, and yet all that the lucid part of him could do was watch her avert her eyes from what seemed sure to be a killing muzzle flash.

"Look at me!"

Spittle flew against Pretty Lady's cheek as the animal inside him yelled in her face. Fin could hear the thing's snorting breaths and sense the bulging eyes, feel the tension of a hand against revolver grip and the tightening of a thumb against hammer.

The girl said something — a plea or a prayer — but Fin was too busy grappling with a dark angel over control of the cocked revolver to tell the difference.

Words seemed to rise up out of a deep well, or maybe from hell itself — words that should have registered but didn't. The fight inside him was too intense, too savage, his two halves waging a war that threatened to kill them both.

Through his fog, Fin began to piece

together the words, one by one. *Dust! Riders! There!* With a powerful wrenching of his mind he tore free from his shadow self and realized that they came from his own lips.

There was an image with the words, a scene back up-trail of heat waves broken by tiny figures against a feather of dust.

"You see them?" he asked Pretty Lady, who had twisted away from him as much as her bound hands allowed. "They Indians? Would they be followin' the road thataway?"

Fin realized she was not only cowering, but trembling. Now the regret kicked in, crippling guilt at what the dark man had done.

He returned the hammer to the safe position and slipped the weapon back in his waistband. Reaching across Pretty Lady's shoulder, he brushed her cheek with the back of his hand. He did so as gently as possible, but she cringed and shrank even more.

Fin wanted to draw her to him. He wanted to free her wrists and fall into tender arms that would shelter him. He wanted to lay his head on a warm breast and close his eyes, hide from all that had happened and hear a soft voice whisper, "It's all right, it's all right." He yearned for it, *needed* it. But his search for comfort had been empty ever since he had put spurs to his horse and fled from the news about Molly.

Fin's eyes began to sting at the thought of the affliction he had borne all these years. He suspected that his father had passed it to him, for he could remember the rapid shifting of his father's eyes just before he would change into a growling animal. Clay had been the first tell Fin that his pupils sometimes showed the same frightening darting. Fin hadn't wanted to believe it, and when he had tried once tried to peer into a looking glass during a spell, the dark angel had broken it and ground his hands into the shards until the blood had run.

Fin looked at the back of his fingers. The brush of Pretty Lady's cheek still seemed to linger there, but now she leaned so far away that she would have fallen out of the saddle if her wrists weren't secured to the horn.

"Just tryin' to be gentle, is all," he said. "I ain't some kind of hydrophoby dog."

But the way she continued to cower and avoid eye contact, Fin knew that she was as unsure as he was.

He lifted his gaze, and the sight of the horsemen down in the creosote flats dragged him from his self-pity. They couldn't have been more than a half hour behind, and he could almost see them gaining ground with each passing moment.

"Better look yonder, Pretty Lady," he said, pointing. "Apaches will do worse to you than they will to me. If that cave's anywhere these parts, you got to get us to it so's we can make a stand."

Clay's stomach churned like the boiling river back at Pope's Crossing, and he didn't know which stench was to blame.

From the withers of a bronc, he looked down on human remains under the daggers of a yucca standing monument-like in a scorched wasteland. He wondered what kind of animals would commit such a sacrilege. Good God, this was someone who deserved to lie undisturbed, at rest in death if not in life.

Just like Molly.

Clay threw his sleeve across his nose to keep from breathing not only the rot in the air, but the odor of gastric juices. Still, he could hear Pate vomit, and Clay turned to find the young man leaning over the side of his roan at the party's rear.

Pate had already disgorged all that his insides had to give, and much of it still ran down the cracked housing of his saddle. Now he had the dry heaves, and he seemed determined to persist until Clay, too, would lose his chuck.

Brehmer had reined his horse about, and so had Green, and the two of them pulled up before Pate so that he was framed between.

"Straighten your butt up and get your horse past all this," lectured Brehmer. "Don't just sit there breathing this in."

Clay couldn't fault Pate for effort. The young man sat up, but another heaving spell doubled him over almost immediately. Clay didn't think he had ever heard anyone vomit with such violent groans.

"I swear, Pate," said Green, drawing rein. "You're boogerin' my horse."

Brehmer's dapple gray shied as well and almost spun away, adding to his impatience with Pate. "We're not waiting on you," Brehmer told him. "You either get that horse on down the road or we're going off and leaving you."

The owner apparently meant it, for he wheeled his gray and started toward Clay.

Clay had reason to be in a bigger hurry than any of them, but he was glad to see Green hang back and do what Pate couldn't. Taking the reins of Pate's roan, Green led the animal after Brehmer. Even more impressive, Green offered the young rider the encouragement he needed.

Brehmer came abreast of Clay, and as they rode on together down a road cut by the dark shadows of circling buzzards, the older man muttered to himself. Most of it Clay couldn't make out, but when he looked at Brehmer's squint-eyed profile against the exhumed grave beyond, he saw enough of his lips to read what he couldn't hear.

"That's why I didn't want to bring him. Doesn't have the stomach for it."

"Who *does*?" Clay asked rhetorically.

Brehmer directed a frown at him. "What?"

Clay motioned to the desecrated grave. "Nobody's got the stomach for that."

Brehmer gave the grim scene a glance. "Out like this, you better. Apaches usually keep away from the dead, but not always if it's an enemy. Killed our guide in Guadalupe Pass in forty-nine. We buried him but they dug him up, shot him with arrows again. A man goes to falling to pieces like Pate, he'll end up the same way."

"That's just it, Mr. Brehmer. He's more boy than he is man."

"Not by age, he's not. He'll be twenty-one inside of a year. I never should've let him talk me into letting him ride with us."

"With Indians about, might be glad to have that Navy revolver of his," said Clay.

"Huh! What's he going to do with it? He

might as well write those Apaches a story."

Brehmer had a point. Pate certainly hadn't shown any mettle in the time that Clay had been around him. Nevertheless, Clay pondered matters as he faced the faraway Guadalupes that rose and fell with his horse's gait. Strangely, he dwelled most on the father he couldn't really remember, and he found himself grieving for a relationship that he had never had.

"Sure hard on your own son sometimes," Clay said.

The two of them faced one another, and one look at Brehmer was enough to make Clay regret what he had said.

"That any business of yours?" Brehmer demanded.

Even with all that Clay had endured without blinking, Brehmer's tone was intimidating. Clay didn't know how to respond, so he focused again on the Guadalupes' wall, a fort no more unyielding than the owner's firmly set jaw.

The last thing Clay wanted to do was alienate Brehmer. After all, the man not only had answered his call for help, but he had organized searches in two directions and had provided the men, horses, and supplies. Indeed, just after the four of them had left the silent ripples of the Pecos behind at dawn, Green had picked up a trail swept faint by the wind. Clay hadn't been so sure about it, but the fresh manure that began to dot the road made it certain.

Still, Green hadn't been able to tell how many horses had preceded them, but now that the gusts had relented, Clay could read for himself the two sets of upside-down U's bearing straight for Skeleton Cave. Despite the dire warning that Apaches had left under the yucca, someone had been fool-hardy enough to press on.

Clay lifted his gaze to the road that disappeared in distant heat waves. Good God, Lil was out there, in the hands of a onetime friend who may have already committed unspeakable evil against Molly. And his best hope of rescuing this second girl he loved hinged on Brehmer's help.

Love.

Had Clay's feelings for Lil risen to that level? Was it possible this quickly? Could he have so swept aside the conventions of society as to admit such a thing?

He didn't have time to process it, for Brehmer cleared his throat and drew his attention.

"I don't know why I'm telling you this," said Brehmer, so quietly that only Clay could hear. "But we're out here in a dangerous country depending on each other, so I guess you've got a right to know. Pate's not like everybody else. He didn't walk 'til he was two, and he never said a word 'til he was four, and when he did, he spoke in complete sentences.

"Smart as a whip, but simple things that we take for granted — living skills, I guess you'd call it — came hard for him. But Mrs. Brehmer's a schoolteacher, and she read to him from the time he was a baby, and a month or two after she started teaching him to read, we found out he could do it as good as either of us. Never forgets what he reads either.

"By the time he was fourteen and older than some of my hands, I put him to wrangling the horses. Instead of watching the remuda, I'd catch him with his leg folded across his horse's neck and a pad and pencil in his hand. Anytime there was work to do, all he wanted to do was scribble.

"He's just not willing to take care of the essentials to get him through life, and his mother and I won't be here always. Hell, I always had the notion he'd take over my cattle business someday, but I can't see that ever happening. She insisted we send him off to boarding school, thinking the structure would do him good. He came back with the fool notion to go East and study as an apprentice with a newspaper. If I'm hard on Pate . . ."

Brehmer began to blink a lot and Clay didn't know what to make of it. But as it persisted, Clay realized with surprise and looked away, giving the man as much privacy as he could. For long seconds, there was only the *clomp-clomp* of hoofs.

"Damn." Brehmer may have chastised himself, but his emotion wouldn't go away. "If I'm hard on Pate, I do it for his own good. At some point, he's got to stop dreaming and take care of himself, because sooner or later he won't have a choice."

Clay suddenly felt guilty about the way he had treated Pate. Maybe a typical person would have deserved it, but not someone as different as his father made him out to be. When Clay had first met Pate beside a steer bogged in a Pecos mud hole, the young man had admitted being out of his element. Maybe everyone — himself included — was trying to fit a square peg in a round hole.

Clay looked down at the saddle horn. "Shouldn't've ever drug him off his horse like I done," he said quietly.

"You're lucky I didn't shoot you dead," Brehmer growled.

Stunned, Clay whirled. Everything about

the man — the stiff posture and tight jaw, the fiery flush and narrow eyes — told Clay that he meant it. For an awkward moment that stretched on and on, the two men stared at one another, Brehmer glaring and Clay accepting it.

"Yes, sir," Clay acknowledged.

"It's one thing for *me* to be hard on Pate," Brehmer added. "It's another thing for somebody else to do it when they don't have any stake in his welfare. Now that you know, don't expect me to be so forgiving next time."

CHAPTER 16

With the rise of a strong wind, Clay's worry increased tenfold.

Under an unforgiving midday sun, he trudged beside Green as the four of them led their tiring horses down a road swept bare. Clay would have stayed in the saddle and forced the pace, but Brehmer — now compassionately on drag with Pate — had insisted that they rest their animals.

Even now, Clay was aware that it was the prudent thing to do. But as the dust crawled around his boots and he snugged his hat down for the dozenth time, he was tempted to dig his toe into the stirrup and gig his bay into an all-or-nothing run.

Clay knew that if he didn't overtake Lucius by Skeleton Cave, he might never be able to. He wouldn't know where to look, and Lucius could fade into an Apache-infested wilderness of bony hills and rocky washes where the howling wind would wipe tracks clean faster than a horse could make them. He would disappear with Lil, or do worse to her, and she would be gone, as surely as Molly was gone. And there wouldn't be a damned thing anybody could ever do about it.

The bastard! He would tear Lucius apart with his bare hands!

Clay couldn't believe how all of this had worked out, the fusing of past and present that had set Lucius again at the center of a situation involving someone Clay cared about. It was almost as if this constituted a second chance that Clay didn't deserve. The first time, he had stood idly by as Lucius had openly courted his sister — his *sister,* for God's sake. The spells of madness . . . the abusive tongue . . . the quick fists . . . Clay had seen it all, and still he had failed to protect, and Molly may have paid for it with her life.

Now, though, Molly and Lil seemed strangely melded into the same vulnerable person, one girl in desperate need. If he could just get to her in time, maybe it would be like reentering that San Saba room soon enough to stifle the bloody flow.

"Green, we got to go. We just got to."

Green turned his weathered face to him. "I know the hurry you're in," he said, rubbing his chiseled jaw. "I got a pretty good notion what you think of that girl. But like I said, you got a lot more gall than you do smarts."

"But he's *got* her. Don't you understand? Once he gets to the cave and leaves it, that map in my head won't do us no good."

An abrupt gust almost lifted Clay's hat, and he saw the older cowhand seize his own brim.

"Wind ain't helpin' none, all right," conceded Green, studying the distance. "See where the road climbs up 'tween them little hills, couple of hundred yards? Let's rest these horses till we get to that tree in the gap. Crucifixion thorn, looks like."

"A what?"

"*Corona de Jesus,* Mex'cans call it. Crown of Jesus."

"Never heard of one."

"The crown of thorns?" asked Green.

"No, the tree. My mother used to read me about the other one when I was little."

"Well, we get up there, you'll see why they call it that. Not a leaf on it, just thorns all twisted together. Sure must've made the blood run."

"Blood?" asked Clay.

"The Good Lord's," said Green. "Guess you didn't listen when she was a-readin'.

Figure it all ties in with the ram caught up in the thicket by the horns. You know, the one Abraham used for a offerin' instead of his boy."

Clay was surprised. Green had never spoken much of anything except cowboying. "How you know so much about it, Green?"

"I was a preacher back where I'm from."

Now Clay was outright stunned. "I'll be damned."

Green flashed him a toothy grin. "Sure hope you ain't," he joked. "Yeah, little town of Cora there on the South Leon, Comanche County. Had me a Baptist church by the sawmill. Wife and little girl's still there."

"Green, you surprise the hell out of me."

"Now *that,* I hope I can take like it sounds," said Green, with a customary laugh.

Clay saw the cowhand in an entirely new light. Thinking back, it occurred to him that he had never heard Green curse. His demeanor, his patience with Pate, his willingness to give Clay the benefit of the doubt when he had pulled the young man from the saddle — it all added up now.

"What in the world you doin' out on the Pecos?" asked Clay. "It's like the back porch to hell out here."

"Yeah, well, doin' the same as the Good Lord. Holy Ghost led Him to the wilderness to work through some things. Got me a wagonload to sort out."

Clay considered the San Saba events that had set him on his own course for the Pecos, and he knew that if there had been anybody behind it, it sure hadn't been a God who cared.

A dubious half laugh broke from his lips. "What kind of troubles can a preacher have? Even before Miss Lil, things was gnawin' at *me* to where I couldn't hardly take it."

"Soundin' like you needin' to talk about it."

Clay let out a weary breath and checked the distance. "We catch up with them, won't need to no more. It'll be over."

"What'll be over? Sure you don't want to talk it out?" asked Green.

"Don't hear *you* sayin' much," said Clay, focusing on the twin hills covered with creosote.

"Fair enough. Let's just say I rode out of town the middle of the night, it a-pourin' down rain and me a-dodgin' the grand jury."

Clay turned to him. "Grand jury? What could a preacher ever done to have that happen?"

Green didn't answer, and Clay didn't

press the issue. There were some things a man had to figure out or do for himself. And avenging a sister was one of them.

When they reached the twisted tree, which stood as tall as a man on horseback, Clay saw for himself the thousands of long, green thorns springing like leaves from the gray branches. It certainly wasn't difficult to imagine weaving a crown of spines from a cutting or two, all right. For a moment, Clay remembered the security of his mother's arms as she had read to him about it, and he wondered if he would ever have that kind of peace again.

"Looka there! See the dust?"

Green had swung up into the saddle and was pointing west-southwest. Clay looked for himself, but he couldn't see a thing until he stepped up into the stirrup. Sure enough, on a ridge a little to the left across an eroded valley marked by yucca and a crooked drainage, a dirty-white smudge stood out against the deep blue of the faraway Guadalupes.

"That two riders I can make out?"

Brehmer posed the question from behind, but Clay was already spurring his horse down into the badlands.

I'm comin' after you, Lucius! He cried

silently. *All the way to hell before I let you do it again!*

Lil longed for death.

Swaying in the saddle, her wrists rubbed raw by her bonds, she closed her eyes against the approaching hill with rimrock aflame in the fading sunlight. Her entire world was on fire, and death was the only sure escape. Even if she freed herself from the saddle horn and eluded the man who led her appaloosa, so what? She would still be just as much a prisoner, trapped in a life that had shown so little mercy.

Back at the ditch-like Delaware, Fin had untied Lil long enough to let her drink from the small stream — "got to take care of my map in that pretty head," he had told her. But sustaining her dignity had been the last thing on his mind; he hadn't even allowed her to take care of bodily functions in private.

"Ain't runnin' away on *me*," he had grumbled.

Now she was far upstream to the west-southwest, deep in despondency as the sun began to vanish behind the Guadalupes' distant wall. Intellectually, she was aware that the map was proving surprisingly accurate in its depiction of topographic features; even the rimrock ahead resembled a specified landmark. But a person courting death wouldn't have cared a Rebel dollar about getting to Skeleton Cave, except that there was something about Fin's crazed eyes that made her think that there were better ways to die.

She looked at his sweat-darkened back, a sharp contrast to the white foam on his roan's hindquarters. "Can't keep riding, come dark," she said. "Won't see land-marks."

Fin turned in the saddle and seemed to check over Lil's shoulder. "They's still back of us, whoever they are. We'll stop when there ain't none of us can see no more."

Lil rode in silence as the yelp of coyotes ushered in a night so dark that the horse and rider before her were mere suggestions under a hazy band of starlight. She wondered who might be following, and whether the death they might mete out would be more merciful. For a moment, the idea that they might offer her succor crossed her mind, and then reality denied her even a chance to consider it.

Still, she could remember the hope she had known so briefly that he now seemed like a passing vapor. Kind, reassuring, protective — Clay had been all of these, and more. Even now she thanked God that He had let her experience a fleeting measure of how life always should have been.

Fin waited to stop until the gloom was so thick that Lil thought he wouldn't be able to untie her from the horse. Long minutes later, however, she lay trussed with hands at back in scorching soil with a clump of brittle sand dropseed under her head. She could taste the grit as she squirmed, unable to find a position in which she might bear the night.

Fin lay beside her, a shadow so close that she could smell his sweat.

"Can't you undo me?" she asked. "Can't rest like this, not another night like before."

For a long while, there was only a loafer wolf's faraway howl, like a lost soul's forlorn cry among all the callous stars that looked down. With Fin's silence, Lil's fear grew, for she couldn't see what was in his eyes.

"I'll untie you, Pretty Lady," he finally said. "I'll let you loose if you . . . if you'll just hold me for a little bit."

In his voice was a strange note of insecurity, and she didn't know what to think. But that didn't keep her from scooting away in the sand a little more.

"I don't mean to scare you none," he went on, his words increasingly emotional. "I — I

258

just need holdin'. That's all, just holdin'."

She heard the crackle of brittle grass, and then a silhouette blotted out the jeweled sky.

"Please," she begged.

"Dark Man ain't here. He's the one hurts people. I don't ever hurt people. He's the one does it. I don't like when he shows up, doin' bad things, always doin' bad things. I didn't want him hurtin' Molly thataway. She looked at me so funny, like it was me doin' it. It was him, wasn't me. You know I'd . . . *Molly!* I — I'd never . . . *Molly!*"

He began to sob, his words no longer distinguishable except for one last plea for Lil to hold him. When she never responded, the silhouette withdrew, and she remembered the long-ago night when her father had been forced to shoot the family dog that had changed so quickly into a frothing beast.

CHAPTER 17

Against a daybreak sky glowing red, four close-set hills rose from gloomy badlands across the Delaware gulch.

From her appaloosa on a bluff overlooking the river's dark channel, Lil was struck by the hills' precision. The two outermost were identical squat cones of impressive size. Between them, equally spaced, were replicas one-third as large. The map had shown these landmarks to be only two miles across the Delaware, but the haze of dawn gave the impression of great distance.

And greater mystery.

But Lil didn't care. A cave of skeletons, a matching half of a map, the promise of riches — none of those meant anything to someone who had no reason for being except to find a merciful death. The only good thing about this was that everybody who went looking for the Simkins mine had a way of ending up dead.

"You seein' what you need to?" asked Fin from the roan on her right. "Them four teat hills?"

If the map hadn't lied, Skeleton Cave would be there, all right, although Lil couldn't fathom why any cave in this forbidding country would be filled with human remains. Maybe it had been the price they had paid for undertaking their own cursed search.

"Well, Pretty Lady?" pressed Fin. "You —"

Both horses unaccountably shied, as if they had caught a disturbing scent. When the animals pointed their ears into the south wind in alert, Lil and Fin checked as well. At first she could see nothing but yucca silhouettes in a murky flat of creosote, sand sage, and javelina bush. A wolf maybe, or —

A firearm boomed, and there was bedlam.

A ricocheting bullet whizzed by and her appaloosa bolted, jerking the towline out of Fin's hand. Fin's horse must have stepped on the dragging rope, for it went taut violently, dropping Lil's animal to its knees and throwing her across its neck.

"Apaches!" shouted Fin.

Lil's mount was up in an instant, but with her hands tied to the saddle horn, she was at the mercy of the appaloosa's instincts. A horse was a herd animal, however, and when Fin's roan started down the bluff into the shadows, the appaloosa went with it.

Forty feet below, they struck bottomland and broke through thick sage and salt bush. Then came catclaw that shredded Lil's dress, and the thorny limbs of scrub mesquites that scourged her legs. Her appaloosa labored in grasping sand deposited by flood, but the horse nevertheless kept pace with Fin's roan.

Another shot from behind echoed through the hollow, and moments later Lil's pony squealed to a third shot that staggered it. She thought she would go down under the crush of a wounded animal, but the appaloosa regained its stride from what must have been a grazing ball.

Thrown off-balance, Lil looked up over her horse's ears and saw Fin's Navy six in her face. The revolver roared at virtually point-blank range, and the fact that Lil heard it and saw the muzzle flash told her she was still alive. She had just enough time to duck before Fin squeezed off a second shot over her shoulder.

"Gotta let 'em know we's fightin' back!" he cried, twisting back straight in the saddle.

At least that was what Lil thought he had said. For a few seconds, a piercing ring in her ears didn't allow for much more than guessing.

A hundred yards across the bottomland, they burst upon a sudden ditch only yards wide. Fin's horse didn't slow, and neither did Lil's. Her appaloosa sat back on its haunches as it plowed down a twelve-foot bank of sheer sand to a flowing stream six feet wide. Lunging across, the animal dug its hoofs in an equally steep far bank and started up after the struggling roan.

Such a climb required the best in a horse, and the tight quarters demanded even more. When Fin's roan slid back, there was no place for Lil's appaloosa to go but squarely into the roan's hindquarters. For a moment, there were not two horses but one, ready to take Lil down with it in the Delaware's ditch. Then the animals somehow separated, and Lil felt the power of her appaloosa as it lunged upward again.

All the way up was a fight, but Lil and the appaloosa broke out on top behind Fin. Something sharp poked Lil in the back, and when she turned she found a feathered arrow marked with red and white bands in the cantle of her saddle. Beyond, she saw a pursuing Apache all too close in the mesquites and catclaw, while more Indians poured off the bluff where the chase had begun.

In the light of dawn, Lil saw the nearest warrior in greater detail than she wanted. Below a war cap with waving eagle feathers, dark straight hair flew across a face painted white with a streak of black across the nose. A calico garment trimmed in red draped from his shoulders, while his breechclout left his legs bare against a gray horse that looked even more jaded than Lil's appaloosa.

But as chilling as the Apache's appearance was, it was nothing compared to the sight of him bending a single-arc bow nocked with another deadly arrow.

"He's on us!" she cried.

She turned to hunch over the saddle horn but met another muzzle flash from Fin's revolver. Shaken, she glanced back, not knowing which Fin had fired, the dark man or the one who had sobbed. Whoever he had been, he had felled the gray horse and thrown the Apache over its head.

"Gotta make a stand!" shouted Fin. "That cave hereabouts?"

It was, at least according to the map. But to a girl bound to a horse, a hundred-yard lead over an Apache war party gave her about as much chance as a snowball under a Pecos sun. Casner had once told her that Apaches never violated a captive woman for fear of incurring bad luck, but Lil wondered if anybody had ever informed the Apaches.

"Where's that cave!" Fin demanded again.

"Let me ride!" answered Lil. "Cut me loose!"

Fin rode a few more strides, and then wheeled his horse with an oath and seized the appaloosa by the bridle. Taking time they didn't have, he pulled out a pocketknife and slashed her bonds. In rapid succession, he freed her horse from the towrope, passed her the reins, and fired another round over her shoulder.

Together, they fled up a thirty-foot bluff, rifle balls peppering the ground about them. Even after Fin yielded the lead out of necessity, creating a buffer between Lil and the Apaches, she expected to catch a ball in the back any second. All she could do was hug the horse's neck and coax the animal to greater speed.

For half a mile, she ran the appaloosa across a sandy divide thick with bear grass and prickly pear. All the way, Lil searched the nearing hills for a cave, but through the appaloosa's flying mane she could see only unremarkable slope. Then the animal's hoofs pounded across a slab of chalky rock and they dropped into lowlands where twisted yucca stood like hoodoos.

For more than a mile, Lil pressed the appaloosa past red-berried tasajillo and century plants, through prickly pear and barbed cholla, across exposed gypsum in arroyos lined with catclaw. As badlands gave way to a steep incline, even the higher hills vanished.

But the Apaches hadn't. Puffs of dust that raced alongside to another burst of gunfire told Lil they were there, and a glance back showed that the warriors had narrowed the gap on Fin to sixty or seventy yards.

The slope was rocky and crowded with knife-like bear grass, and the tiring appaloosa struggled as it carried her up an angling ridge between sharply cut drainages. She topped out before the southernmost hill, dominating the skyline a quarter mile ahead. Close range had given all four hills a different look; now she could see features that set each apart.

The outside cones, which rose two hundred feet, still shared a lot of similarities, although the one before her was rockier and had more folds. A greater difference distinguished the eighty-foot inner hills. The nearer of the two had gullies with walking-stick cholla, but the farther was bare all the way up to a jagged ridge of solid rock that capped the summit. Thirty feet thick, the stony mass looked like the backbone of a monster squatting across the crest, ready to swoop down.

The monster had an eye.

Lil saw it, and for the first time Casner's years-old story of a cave of skeletons took on real meaning. It hadn't been enough for Lil to hold the map for which he had wasted away his life, or even for her to meet up with someone else just as convinced that the lost Simkins mine was real. Only now, staring up at a small keyhole of sky showing through the cliff, did the wonderment seize her. Bored entirely through the midway point of the great rock, the eye almost seemed to beckon.

Another ricochet screamed past, breaking Lil's trance long enough for her to find Fin topping out behind her.

"There!" she yelled, pointing to the cave.

Then she urged her horse into a run and considered how ironic it was that she had to depend on her abductor for survival. Maybe she wanted to live, after all.

Across a sterile plateau marked only by cholla, the appaloosa's forelegs reached out again and again for the cave, the powdery gypsum flying. For fifty yards, Lil and Fin seemed alone, but then another rifle ball kicked up dust and she knew that the Apaches had gained the plateau as well.

Escape seemed hopeless and death sure, but no more sure than on that night when she had clung to a wagon wheel with Comanches above and a raging river below. Clay had seen her through it — *she,* a total stranger — and even though he was out of her life, she owed it to him not to give up now.

Soon she reached the rock-capped hill and gigged her horse up the slope. The loose gypsum offered poor footing and the incline grew increasingly steep, two factors that tested the exhausted animal. Twenty feet shy of the cliff's base, the angle became too much, and for a moment Lil fought to stay astride a rearing horse with forelegs pawing air. As the squealing animal twisted with her, she was helpless to do anything but let the inevitable take its course.

The cliff flew up and she was down, rolling in the gypsum beside eight hundred pounds of bone and sinew. Bitter dust billowed, but as she came to her hands and knees she saw the reins dragging the ground and seized them. An arrow thudded down, pinning the hem of her dress to the slope. She tore free and rose with the horse, and then dragged the unencumbered animal up to a stunted yucca at the base of the cliff.

From here, the opening was no longer visible, but Lil knew it was there, a dozen feet above. Rifle balls pinged against rock as she quickly hitched the appaloosa to the yucca and clawed the cliff face. There didn't seem to be a hold, not a crack or a bulge in arm's reach, but she used opposition force — her shoes against yucca stalk, her hands against wall — and worked her way higher. She was aware that Fin had brought his horse up after her and was attempting to secure the animal, but she could also hear him fire again.

As Lil planted her shoe between the yucca's crowning daggers, an arrow pierced the trunk. Missing her by inches, it gave her a foothold that allowed her to stand upright and reach a deep crack angling down. Growing up, she had been a tomboy, out-climbing her brothers in the hickory tree behind the house, and desperation brought back her skills. She kicked at the wall as she pulled herself up, and frantic moments later she hooked a forearm over the cave's opening.

She got a boost from below, Fin's firm hand trying either to assist or shove her out of the way. Regardless, a glance down showed that he was at her heels, the arrows and rifle balls bouncing off the rock around him.

Lil squirmed inside to face a current blowing through from the other end, sixty feet distant. There was something eerie about the way the wind moaned, as if it carried the far-off cries of the damned. Too, a musty smell spoke of death instead of life in this crudely eroded hole five feet across and strewn with skull-sized rocks.

Fin fell inside beside her, his Navy six and a bullet bag with powder flask in his hands. His legs were still below, and he abruptly seemed to be losing ground, sliding closer to the precipice.

"He's got me!" he screamed.

Seizing a rock, Lil pivoted on her hip and peered over the edge into the painted features of an Apache with a grip on Fin's ankle. She used both hands to drive the rock down, and when it hit flush with crushing force, the Apache fell away.

Fin clambered on up and twisted about, flattening himself at the brink to defend the cave, his revolver a silhouette against first sunlight.

"They's after the horses!" he yelled, shooting over the edge.

A ricochet wailed past Lil's ear, and she

realized that even though the sharp angle protected against direct gunfire, they were far from safe. She whirled, recognizing also that the second opening doubled the chances of Apaches breaching their stronghold. She found only a glare at the far end, but in the ambient light she noticed another passageway branching off to the right. Located midway down the corridor, it seemed to have depth, judging by how dark its jagged outline was. If the Apaches stormed the tunnel, the passage might be one last place to fall back.

Leaving Fin to reload his Navy six, Lil crawled for it, feeling a chill as she considered the secrets this cave might hold.

CHAPTER 18

The scene through the cave's side passage took Lil's breath away.

Human skeletons. A lot of them. Resting in ghostly twilight on a rock shelf against the left wall of a room whose reaches were in dense dark.

Something told Lil not to go inside. Maybe it was the sight of all the grimacing skulls, or perhaps the whisper of the musty current in her face. Possibly, everything about this place reminded her too much of the Pecos country grotto with its devil-eyed rattlers. Nevertheless, the hum of another ricochet spoke even louder, and she squeezed through the cleft to twist back around and assess the defensive possibilities.

On a day that had seemed so hopeless, she found encouragement. From here, a man with a revolver might hold off an entire horde — or at least until his ammunition ran out. And with a maximum load of six rounds, that might not be long. For the first time, Lil wished for the double-barreled shotgun back at the Narrows. But what good would two more rounds do when God only knew how many Apaches were out there?

Aided by a crack of daylight above, Lil counted thirteen skulls among the bare bones. But on the floor below was a four-teenth set of remains, with distinctive characteristics. This skull alone had a long, narrow face and relatively flat crown, sug-gesting that he hadn't been of the same people. But most striking were the intact section of tawny hair and a feathered arrow that pinned shredded trousers to a thigh bone. Looking around, Lil saw shrunken leather boots and remnants of a hat.

This man had been different. And he had died a long time after the others, who must have been ancient Indians. For all Lil knew, fifteen or twenty years might not have passed since the clothed man had drawn his last breath here.

Lil stood, finding ample headroom, and the change in angle revealed something on the wall on the shelf side of the entrance. Stepping over the boots, she went closer. At first she took the etching for Indian art, but as her eyes adjusted to the shadows, she made out a rough map. But that wasn't all. Strung together below it were crude letters, as if hurriedly carved by knifepoint.

CAPTURED — APACHES — 1849
TO SACRED GOLD — GUADALUPES — 1850?
ESCAPE — CHASE
APACHES OUTSIDE — SCARED TO ENTER

At first, Lil thought that was all, and then a foot or so above the floor she found one last entry, hardly more than scratching, as if it had been the work of a man too weak to rise.

HURT BAD

Lil looked back at the remains on the floor. He had bled out right here, whoever he had been. He had crawled into this cave to escape Apaches, and he had carved his own epitaph in the rock and had bled to death.

She wondered if she should add her own words before it was too late.

But even as survival remained central to Lil's thoughts, something else was at play. Casner's big talk of lost gold had never interested her, but all the mystery now swept her up. Turning, she quickly studied the landmarks engraved in the wall: Skeleton Cave, the Delaware, the mountains to the west, a canyon, and a place marked *Gold of Guadalupes.*

The map seemed oddly familiar, and she searched her memory as she ran her fingers along the rock, tracing the crook of river, the squiggly ridgeline, the sharp notch denoting a canyon. Where had she seen this before? How *could* she have?

Then Lil realized. From Skeleton Cave on west, the fragment of map that Clay had given her at the Narrows — the map Casner had died looking for — had been a replica of segments of what she now saw. It was as if someone had stood here and copied it.

Right now, Lil would have traded all the gold in the West to be away from Fin and those Apaches. She wished they would kill each other, but there were so many Indians that she realized it wouldn't happen.

Strangely, what she couldn't see in the room's black recesses seemed even more frightening than what she knew to be outside, and Lil kept glancing back in fear that something would pounce on her. She didn't think she could be any more unnerved, but then a war cry rang out and she spun in terrified search. The cry was still echoing when she heard the thunder of a revolver, followed by a second report, a third.

"They's comin' both ways!" shouted Fin.

Lil bolted for the cleft, intent on doing what she could. Maybe she could fend the Apaches off with rocks long enough for Fin to fall back here — *Fin,* the unbalanced man who already had put a cocked Navy six to her face. What kind of choice was that, having to decide between evils?

Sliding her shoulders through, Lil found two silhouettes in fierce struggle at the first entrance, a fight that Fin ended with a gunshot that drove the Apache backward off the precipice. Whatever else one could say about Fin and his dark counterpart, they knew how to kill.

Bitter smoke rose up even thicker, but something else dimmed the light. Whirling to the opposite opening, Lil saw a shadow drop down from outside and crouch against the sky.

"Behind you!" she yelled.

Fin must have pivoted at the same time, for he fired two quick shots that repelled the Apache before the hammer of his revolver clicked futilely against an empty cylinder.

"Gotta reload!" he cried in panic, reaching for his powder flask.

Lil knew it could take him four or five minutes to ram in six fresh loads, time they didn't have with assaults on two fronts. At first, she had hoped the Apaches just wanted their horses, but now it was clear they wouldn't be satisfied with anything less than blood.

Maybe she should have carved her epitaph into the rock after all.

Just as that image raced through her mind, she thought of what was already inscribed there — *Apaches scared to enter* — and she remembered something Casner had told her. For all their bravery, Apaches had a mortal fear of the dead, so much so that they wouldn't even refer to deceased relatives by name.

Lil rushed back to the rock shelf, knowing it was her only chance. She seized a skull in either hand, and scooped up a third and a fourth against her breast as bones clattered down at her feet. She sprang toward the sound of more war cries and dropped to her knees at the notch that opened to the main passage. She didn't waste time peering out; extending a skull through, she rolled it toward the tunnel's far end and hoped that a rock didn't stop it too soon. It was still rumbling when she set another skull on course for Fin.

"They's backin' out!" shouted Fin.

Now, Lil looked for herself. The first skull had lodged against a rock, but she glimpsed a dark shape retreating through the opening beyond.

Lil squeezed through, a jag ripping her dress and scraping her shoulder as she gained the main passage. She gave Fin a quick look, guessing that he was probably bewildered by the skull in arm's reach.

"Put them on the edge!" she yelled, tossing a second one in his direction.

Then she scrambled away to mark the other entrance in the hope that the dead would keep them alive.

They lost the riders in the night, and not even the map in Clay's head made much difference now.

The four of them sat their horses under a late afternoon sun and stared at a pair of gaunt mustangs, pawing at the mud in a water hole with tracks leading to it from all directions like wagon wheel spokes. Clay and the others had struck out at first light into a stiff south wind that carried the topsoil away in swirls. Under waning stars, as they approached a rock palisade that he recognized from the map, Green picked up a trail in firmer footing just off the road. The problem was, it bore a little south of due west, a course that would take it away from the Delaware and Skeleton Cave.

In the muted light, Clay, Brehmer, and Green talked it over, weighing a certain trail against hunch. Green was for tracking the two horses. Pate, who so far had kept quiet, wanted to continue for the cave, but Clay wondered if he was driven more by a search for a story than any thought of rescue. Brehmer, while acknowledging that he tended to agree with Green, said he would leave the final decision to Clay. Torn, Clay heard himself justify a choice he would come to regret.

"Maybe he had his reasons for leavin' the river."

Throughout a brutally hot day in which Clay had downed two airtights of tomatoes, they had proceeded to track the two horses straight toward the Guadalupes' highest point. Now, watching the two mustangs continue to paw the mud, Clay realized the consequences of his mistake.

"Sure sorry," said Green.

"Not your fault," said Clay. "We had no way of knowin'."

"I told you we should continue for Skeleton Cave," spoke up Pate. "I told you, but no one would pay me any mind. You wouldn't listen when I said we —"

Brehmer wheeled his dapple gray to Pate and drew back his quirt. "I threatened to kill a man if he ever laid a hand on you! But by God, that doesn't mean *I* can't!"

Clay had never seen such abrupt rage seize anyone but Lucius, and he was as shocked as Brehmer's son.

"What did *I* do?" asked a cowering Pate.

For anxious moments, Brehmer's quirt hand hovered in indecision. Then he lowered it with a sharp breath and turned his horse away.

Clay hung his head. "It's all right, Mr. Brehmer," he said quietly. He reined his horse about and started back for the Delaware. "Pate told me, all right, and I wouldn't listen."

CHAPTER 19

Even a few minutes before sunset, the dark man still whispered to Fin at the cave's mouth.

Guard the horses! You're dead without them!

Only twice, in the assaults of morning, had an Apache made it as far as the mounts, but each time the warrior had chosen the greater feat of counting coup in battle with Fin rather than steal the animals. Throughout the siege the dark man had been there, whispering and sometimes seizing control. Fin wished he would go away, but the soulless thing was a presence that couldn't be swayed.

And so Fin still held his position as the lengthening shadows accentuated every fold in the double hills across the sudden drop. Beside his boot at cliff's edge perched a skull, watching over the desert sea like a figurehead on a ship's prow. Throughout a long, tense day, as Fin had nervously smoked one cigarette after another, the skull had done its job, and so had the specimen he had dropped over the precipice. For confirmation, Fin had periodically wormed his way to the rim, brushed cheekbones with a man long dead, and peered down. He did so again now, finding the horses still secured and the skull caught against the stunted yucca.

Farther out, past the hill's base and beyond rifle range, he had glimpsed Apaches once or twice. Fin hadn't seen them for hours now, but he figured they were still there, biding their time until he and Pretty Lady grew foolish enough to descend from this house of the dead.

When night comes, ride out of here, whispered the voice.

He would, but not before looking this hole over good. He had watched Pretty Lady come and go through a cleft midway down the passage, and the skulls she had produced verified this place for what it was. All the stories of lost Guadalupe gold had always included a reference to a cave of skeletons, and whatever it was that made this landmark special had to lie in its recesses.

Now, if that dark corner of his mind would only let him find out.

Soon the sun sank behind the hidden

Guadalupes, casting a coppery pall across the badlands below. The gloom was greater in the passage behind Fin, and as he retreated from the precipice, he expected the dark man to stop him with another admonition to guard the horses. But no such order came, and Fin crept on to the cleft, before which Pretty Lady lay curled in sleep.

Even though that other part of him had stood his ground against Apaches, Fin felt a strange reluctance to go inside. Heavy dark hung over the notch like fog in a midnight graveyard. Too, there was something crypt-like about the cool air that whistled from it, a musty draft with just enough suggestion of decay to remind him of the arrow-riddled corpse at the big yucca.

Fin nudged Pretty Lady with his boot, startling her. "Show me what's in there."

The girl glanced at the cleft as she sat up. "It's too dark now."

"Said show me."

She looked at him a moment, as if she had learned to check his eyes to see who was in control. He doubted that she could determine much in the fading light, but regardless she went ahead and squeezed through the notch. Following after her, Fin found himself in inky night that seemed without boundaries except for the rough floor below and the ceiling at arm's length above. As his eyes dilated, however, skeletons began to take shape on what seemed to be a shelf of rock.

Going closer, Fin stumbled against something that poked his shin. He couldn't make out more than a dim outline until he reached down and found the feathered end of an angling arrow. What in the hell . . .

Digging out a match, Fin struck it on the rock overhead. The match head flared with a hiss, illuminating a chamber of skeletons. The bones on the rock shelf were bare, but shredded garments draped the arrow-pierced remains at his feet.

His heart hammering in anticipation, Fin turned and scanned the room as the flame flickered in the draft. He couldn't make out much in the black recesses, but when he pivoted again to the skeletons, he glimpsed what appeared to be writing on the wall beside the cleft.

He lurched toward it in a frenzy, three words exploding out of the rock. TO SACRED GOLD! In seconds he was there, passing the flame across what seemed to be a map. Skeleton Cave, the Delaware, the —

The match unexpectedly burned his fingers, and he reflexively swore and threw it down. He dug for another as it continued to burn at his feet, a faint flame growing fainter. Just as he realized the match was his last, the flame went out, plunging everything into dark.

Fin drew upon every curse word in his vocabulary before he remembered the matches in the war bag behind the cantle of his saddle. Wheeling, he rushed for the glowing notch, only to collide with Pretty Lady.

"Out of my way!"

Fin shoved her aside and squeezed through, but he managed only a couple of steps through the tunnel's twilight before the dark man seized him.

Stop! the voice told him. *When night comes, ride out of here.*

Fin argued with him, and when that didn't work, he tried a different tack. *Let me ask Pretty Lady! Let me ask her to get a match!*

But rather than listen, the dark man continued to whisper. *When night comes, ride out of here. When night comes . . .*

Sinking to the unfeeling rock of Skeleton Cave, Fin buried his face in his hands and grieved for all the things the dark man had always denied him. And for a moment, he hoped the Apaches were still out there, summoning up courage for one last assault that would bring him rest, if only through death.

■ ■ ■ ■

From a bluff overlooking the Delaware gulch, Clay recognized the four conical hills showing in ghostly wisps through thick dust hanging against the rising sun. But that wasn't all that he brooded over from the back of his bay. Even after the rise of a brisk wind, the bluff's churned ground told of scores of passing hoofs a day before.

"They was in a all-out run," said Green, who alone had dismounted. He bent over with a hand braced on his knee and traced the tracks with a bony finger. "They come out of the yucca and headed straight for the river like they was chasin' somethin'."

Clay swallowed hard. "I — I don't like the looks of this."

"Just 'cause they was chasin' it don't mean they caught it," encouraged Green. He lifted his gaze to the four cones in the distance. "You sure them hills is what we's lookin' for?"

"I'm sure enough. If they look like it to me, they would've to Miss Lil too. If those Apaches . . . all 'cause I chose wrong yesterday . . . if she's . . ."

"No use dwelling on what we don't know," spoke up Brehmer, urging his gray off the bluff. "I expect we'll find out soon enough."

Clay couldn't even imagine the effect on himself if he found Lil stretched out pale and cold, a San Saba nightmare repeated. If he had to stare again into eyes like Molly's — eyes that looked back but couldn't see — he figured his very sanity, or worse, would be at stake.

He rode after Brehmer in a daze, the emotion and dust both choking him. His temples pounded to a silent *No! No! No!* at the signs of a running fight: a horse carcass festering in bottom land, an arrow marking the Delaware's far bank, more arrows in the crushed sage and bleeding cacti of a low divide. The beaten trace continued across badlands rent by arroyos, past guarding yucca, up a plateau where the four hills dominated the skyline.

Still, the trail continued unbroken, leading the four riders to the bottom of an inner hill capped by sheer rock set apart by what appeared to be a cave.

"I'd say most of them horses stopped right here," said Green, motioning to the disturbed soil all about. "But look yonder how the slope's kind of sloughed, like maybe a couple of horses been up it."

Clay saw, all right, and he didn't wait for any more explanation. He spurred his horse up the hill and persisted in the climb past the point of safety. When the grade grew extreme, he dismounted and, reins in hand, scrambled the last twenty feet up to a stunted yucca at cliff's base.

There was a human skull beside the yucca, and more cigarette butts than he could count.

"They was up here!" Clay shouted with a glance back at the others.

He hitched the horse and turned to scale the rock without forethought. He wanted this over. Whatever he would find up there, he wanted this *over.* The not-knowing would kill him, almost as surely as another pair of lifeless eyes staring at him. Twice in his blind haste he managed a couple of feet before sliding back, and then on his third try he braced his boot against the yucca and found a slanting crack that carried him on up.

Clay broke out on top beside another skull in the five-foot mouth of an empty cave passage littered with more cigarette butts.

"Lil!"

There was no answer except the hollow return of his own voice, but down the wall he spotted a tatter of cloth flying like a little flag from a jag of rock bordering a shadowy cleft. He rushed awkwardly for it and snatched it up, a shred of calico that matched Lil's dress.

A slight wind moaned through the notch, and Clay looked at the gloom inside and was back at the door to Molly's room. He couldn't do this. Damn it all to hell, he *couldn't.* He would find her cold and stiff and drenched in blood, and it would be more than he could take. Strangely, he wanted to pray, just as his mother had taught him, but he knew that if there was anybody in the sky who really cared, none of this would have happened in the first place.

Clay seemed oddly detached, as if it were somebody else who edged through the cleft and stood. At first, the shadows were dense, despite a splinter of light above, but that distant part of him struck a match and the images exploded out of the dark.

Bones, scattered among skulls on a shelf. More bones at his feet, along with decomposed remains with an imbedded arrow. Black recesses that demanded a second match, and a third as he frantically searched and identified the boundaries of a chamber without any sign of Lil.

But beside the cleft, Clay found something etched in the rock. He had just stepped closer when he heard stirring, and he turned to find Brehmer squeezing through the cleft, with Green and Pate following close behind.

Clay held up the tatter and noticed that his hand shook. "She . . ." He had a hard time finding breath enough to talk. "She was here. But there's no sign of either one of them now."

"Well," said Green, "least we know we's not chasin' ghosts, that the two of them's really over this way."

"Do you think the Indians took her?" asked Pate.

Clay had already asked himself that, but there was something about hearing someone else voice the possibility that made him flinch. Good God, Apaches! What would they do to her? What had they *already* done?

Brehmer breathed sharply and whirled on Pate. "Hell, son, you ever going to learn when to keep something to yourself?"

Pate lowered his head, and even with all the things that tormented Clay right then, he felt sorry for him. He was glad to see Green encourage Pate with a pat on the shoulder.

"Better get your paper out," Green told him. "Looks like plenty to scribble about. See them skeletons? Looka here at this one with the arrow in him."

Pate still seemed chastised as he looked

up with a quiet question. "What do you suppose happened here, Green?" Then his voice gained energy. "Look — is that a map in the rock?"

They all went closer, and even though Clay's match had burned out, there was plenty to see in the twilight. Clay wasn't sure what to make of the brief words, but there was something disturbingly familiar about the map.

"This man with the arrow in him must have done it," said Brehmer, looking over the remains. He reached for something among the bones and came up with an open-bladed pocketknife. "Funny how a man's mind works in his last moments."

Green seemed to examine the wall intently. "Take a whole lot of imaginin' to figure this one out. Pate, you's the storyteller. Why don't you put it all together for us."

As Pate took his time studying the scene, Clay was sure that Green's suggestion would only expose more of the young man's deficiencies. But Clay was wrong.

"What a story this is!" Pate could barely contain his excitement. "It's all right there, Green. Apaches captured this man in eighteen forty-nine, and a year or so later they took him to a sacred site in the Guadalupes where there's gold. He escaped and they chased after him and shot him in the leg with an arrow. He got to this cave and climbed in here where they wouldn't follow."

"Awful scared of the dead, them Apaches are," interjected Green.

Clay gained new respect for Pate. Maybe he came up short in a lot of ways, but in others he was smarter than any of them. But Clay was doing more than listening; on a hunch, he scoured the cave floor with a lighted match. He was looking for something in particular, and as he picked up a dusty wad of paper, he figured he had found it.

Pate, still breathless, went on. "I've got to write this down! So he was lying here about to die, but he had already come down with the fever you told me about, Green — how gold does things to people — and it drove him to carve all this in the rock."

"As though his scratchin' would make any difference," opined Green.

"It made a difference to *somebody,*" spoke up Clay, who had peeled open the wadded paper. "It made a difference to Ben Simkins."

Clay knew that everyone was looking at him, but he was back on the Pecos, tugging on a boot buried in the alkali.

"I've been standing here listenin'," Clay continued, "and I think I know how the rest of the story went. Maybe there never was any Simkins mine. Maybe he just stumbled on this cave in his prospectin' and went back to the settlements spillin' a big bear story."

"You've got our attention," said Brehmer. "What's your reasoning?"

"The piece of map I found in Simkins's grave on the Pecos is a dead ringer for part of what's in the rock here."

"I'm still not following you," said Brehmer.

Clay handed the Bar W owner the rumpled page that formed a rough triangle. "Listen, I just found this. See how it matches the wall if you was to cut the rock catty-cornered? If you put this page alongside what was in that boot — same map as I give Miss Lil — the two parts would join up perfect. Simkins stood right here and copied the wall, and then tore the page in two and throwed the rest away. It was like he wanted just enough to flash to people to get them worked up."

"You mean he was using false pretenses to get financed?" asked Pate.

"Grubstaked and liquored up both, I

imagine," said Green. "I heard the story a hundred times, how a tore map and some colored rocks got him a steady stream of dollars from fools itchin' to believe. Looks like he finally had to answer to his Maker for it on the Pecos."

Clay supposed that only he and Lil knew how that had come about, but Casner's misdeed didn't matter much anymore. *Lil was missing!*

"But none of that proves the map in the rock here's not real," insisted Pate. "Or that Simkins didn't trail it out and find it. Green, don't you think he at least *believed* there was something out here? Why else would he have been back out on the Pecos?"

Clay had to admit that Pate had raised a good point; the Pecos certainly wasn't a place a man went without a reason. Too, there had been those nuggets. They had come from somewhere — maybe right from the pockets of the dead man here, especially in light of what he had apparently written in the rock.

But Green had his own ideas. "Maybe Simkins was like the ol' prospector who got to the pearly gates. Decided it was too crowded inside, so's he starts a rumor about a big strike in hell. When ever'body starts downhill with their picks and shovels, he takes right in after them. 'Might be some-thin' to that rumor after all,' he says."

Clay wagged his head and swore under his breath. Here he was, swapping ideas about imaginary gold, while Lil — where was she? Good God, he had to do something — now!

But it was Brehmer who laid out a course of action. "All this storytelling can wait. Pate, copy that map down item for item. We don't want to forget any of it." Then he turned to Clay. "You inclined to think like I am? That Fin saw all this and maybe's still dragging Mrs. Casner along chasing after gold?"

Maybe, thought Clay. Maybe Lil was still alive, safe from Apaches if not from Lucius, and on the way right now to sacred gold high in the Guadalupes. *Maybe* wasn't much to hang a man's hopes on, but Clay was fresh out of anything else.

CHAPTER 20

The evening before, clouds had moved in, rendering the night almost as black as the depths of the cave. An owl began to hoot, and Fin took it as a good sign. He had heard that Apaches believed the spirits of the dead spoke through an owl, reason enough for even the bravest warrior to flee its curse. Pretty Lady descended from the cave mouth first, but a morose Fin was right behind her, feeling his way down the slanting crack in the cliff and searching for the stunted yucca with his boot. He found it, and soon they were leading their horses down the slough-ing slope at a northerly angle that would take them away from the last place he had seen Apaches.

They must have reached the hill's base at a point opposite the northernmost cone, although Fin couldn't see well enough to be sure. The key now was to get out of the im-mediate vicinity of Skeleton Cave while the hard dark still gave them a chance.

Mounting up, they dropped off the plateau, a blind descent for a person but not for a horse. Even so, footing was treacherous and cacti thick, and the roan didn't reach the lowlands any too soon for Fin, who had sunk into deep despondency. For more than an hour they rode through an arroyo-slashed flat where hoodoo yuccas loomed up like restless spirits of the ancient dead. For a while back in the cave, Fin had come close to joining them, and maybe that would have been better.

The wailing wind, interrupted at times by another hooting owl, seemed to speak to him as he slumped in the saddle. It told him that his quest for Guadalupe gold wasn't over yet, that even though he hadn't been allowed to return to the chamber of skeletons, the way forward was clear. Braced by the prospect, he straightened and looked across at Pretty Lady.

"You seen that map in the cave, didn't you," he said quietly. "You sure 'nough seen it."

The only response was the patter of hoofs in sand.

"I don't expect you to clam up no more," Fin went on. "You're either gonna talk to me or to him about it, and he ain't near as nice."

For just a moment, a word seemed to catch in her throat. "Who you mean?"

"*Him*. Dark Man. The one that almost put a thirty-six ball 'tween your eyes."

"You know then, like you were saying. The way you change all of a sudden."

"Not me changin' any," Fin said defensively. "It's him. He's there all time, whisperin' and tellin' me this and that. He gets ready to take over, no stoppin' him, 'less I put a ball in my own head."

Abruptly, the part of Fin that had been gentle with Molly — the part that could still remember a time before the dark man — yearned for someone to understand, to show compassion, to forgive.

"You ever seen a doctor?" she asked, surprising him.

"Won't let me. Never would let me."

"Maybe . . . maybe if you was to go to one, he could do something."

"Doctor can't drive a evil spirit out. Man by the name of Green back at the Narrows, he was tellin' me about them. How they get inside a person to where he ain't hisself no more. That's me. Been me for a long time. Least, I finally know who to blame it on."

Pretty Lady went silent, and Fin supposed

she had a right. It was an awfully lot for even him to absorb, much less accept. Strangely, though, he felt better for having told someone.

"You're not a praying man, are you," she said finally.

"Whoever done enough for me to start jabberin' to him?" Fin challenged.

"Praying's not something you do just when things go good. It's what you do when you need help."

"Well, Pretty Lady, your help's all *I'm* needin'. I know you seen that cave scratchin' good. Maybe gold will tickle the dark man same as it will me. Way I see it, the three of us is just gettin' started."

For the better part of an hour, Clay helped comb the base of Skeleton Cave hill for a trail. There was plenty of agitated soil, along with a few deeply cut tracks that had survived the wind, but no clear trace showing two sets of hoofs leading away. Eventually Clay lifted his gaze to the Guadalupes' massive ridge twenty-five miles northwest, and when he took his bay toward it, the other riders fell in behind.

They were in the heart of the Chihuahuan Desert now, and even on its fringes it had lived up to its name. Much of what stretched before Clay was sterile, a depressing off-white freckled with the dull green of cacti or shrubs. The mountains' blue escarpment rose up in sharp contrast, suggesting everything that these badlands were not. But those heights lay under the same swollen sun, and Clay wondered if life there was any less fragile than here.

It looked as if he would find out, all because he had faced a decision the day before — one choice out of two — and he had let Lil down.

His fault. All of it, from that moment on. Hell, even Pate had known better. And now there was no way to make amends, except ride for those mountains and keep riding until he either found her or died in the attempt.

As the day wore on, the four of them walked and led their horses as much as they rode. At one point, Green fell back to trudge a stretch of lechuguilla with Pate. Clay, just ahead, could hear Green warn about these "shin-daggers" that could knife a man through his boot uppers. It wasn't long, however, before Green worked the conversation around to the finer points of throwing a loop.

In the cave, the cowhand had rallied the young man's spirits by appealing to his interests, but it was clear that Green hadn't given up on making a cowhand out of Pate. Clay wondered if Pate would have had any better luck turning Green into a writer.

Later, as they rode through tasajillo and wind-whipped sotol, Green joined Clay on point, well ahead of Brehmer and his son.

"Sure good about lookin' after Pate," said Clay.

"Yeah, well, he just needs a little learnin', is all. I expect I was the same way once upon a time."

"Nothin' like learnin' a job from the ground up. But you've took him under your wing like nobody I ever saw."

"Guess I need it 'bout as much as he does," said Green. He glanced over his shoulder. "A young'n like that, you just got a little while to make a difference. 'Fore you know it, they's all growed up and decidin' for theirselves."

Clay looked at Green. He was an uncomplicated man, or so it had seemed, and a person could usually read an uncomplicated man's thoughts right in his face. But Green had hinted at something deeper.

"Pate might not ever say it," said Clay, knowing it wasn't his place to pry, "but I bet he appreciates you treatin' him like your own."

A dark sadness seemed to come over Green. He bent his shoulders, and only after a troubled sigh and a slight shake of his head did he look up again.

"I expect that boy's as close to bein' mine as I'll ever get from here on out. Don't expect I'll ever see my little girl no more. Always be a ten-year-old in my mind long as I live — a ten-year-old I'm through bein' a daddy to."

"My land, Green, how come?" The moment Clay asked, he wished he hadn't.

Green momentarily lifted his gaze skyward, and Clay saw his eyes glisten a little.

"Good Lord's got His plan," said Green, his voice wavering. "My girl might not have me, but that boy back there does."

Clay may not have understood the *why,* but he understood the man. "You're doin' good by him, Green. You sure are."

Green closed his eyes and a tear squeezed out, prompting him to turn away.

"I wish . . ." Clay had a hard time getting words out. "You know, Green, wish I'd had a preacher man like you to get me through some happenin's a few months back. You and my mama was a lot alike, the way you think somebody watches over things."

"Preacher needs to set an example, not do like I done," Green said with odd bitterness. Then he seemed to gather himself. "You's *still* workin' through some things, ain't you."

Turning, he faced Clay, two troubled men staring into each other's souls.

Clay wanted to tell him. He wanted to open up about all the hurt inside and share the grief and worry and the crushing burden of losing his faith in something better. But talking things out wasn't the way of a cowboy, not even one as tormented as Clay.

"It's in your eyes," said Green, holding his stare. "It's there so bad it's like I'm lookin' at my own."

Uncomfortable, Clay turned back to the Guadalupe's ridge, which now extended almost entirely across the horizon. He had told Green two days before that as soon as he caught up with Lucius, the things that gnawed at him would go away. He wondered now if that was just another foolish hope.

"Green . . ." Clay rasped his hand across his bristly face. "Green, is revenge so bad a thing? I mean, is it somethin' a man will get over once it's done? Does it even make him feel any better?"

When Green didn't answer immediately, Clay looked across and found his face with the pallor of a dead man.

" 'Avenge not yourselves,' " Green whispered, his shoulders slumping. "Right there in the Book, plain as day. 'Avenge not your __,' "

His head dropping, Green turned away and hunched over the saddle horn, a portrait of a man distraught. But he continued to mutter.

" 'Vengeance is mine; I will repay, saith the Lord.' " The cowhand shook his head. "It's the *Lord's* right, just like it says. Ain't mine or nobody else's, just *His.* "

"You talk like you been there, Green."

"It's a dark place you don't want none of, guarantee you. You can get forgive for it, but what you done don't ever go away."

Clay wondered if all of this had something to do with the daughter Green couldn't see anymore — and maybe that grand jury — but he wasn't going to ask.

Green faced him. "You was talkin' like catchin' up with Fin, maybe killin' him, would ease things with you. Probably needs killin', all right, and one of us sure might have to do it before this is over. Just make sure you's doin' it for the right reason."

"That's just it. How much cause makes a killin' right? What if they was to hurt somebody you care about?"

Green flinched. Clay had been on the verge of telling him about Molly and Lucius

304

and all the reasons he had lost faith in a God who cared, but there was something about the twitch in Green's cheek that told Clay there would be a better time.

They pushed on, careful not to overtax the horses or unnecessarily deplete their provisions, especially the airtights of watery tomatoes. Survival, not just their hopes of rescue, demanded wisdom in a wasteland so unforgiving. The map, discouragingly vague about landmarks immediately west of the Delaware, didn't show a single water hole ahead. There would be no logical reason for Lucius, with a day's head start if he was even out here at all, to tarry anywhere long enough for Clay and his companions to overtake him soon. Ahead, though, loomed the Guadalupes, with a promise of gold that would lure Lucius like a magnet. Somewhere in that palisade yawned a canyon marked at its mouth by possibly a waterfall or dry pour-off, or so the map showed. Lucius would be looking for it, and Clay would be looking for Lucius.

By the time the sun fell behind the Guadalupes, the Bar W riders were close enough for the range to command the western sky. From below, it was difficult to gauge the escarpment's size, but the almost indistinguishable trees high on the rim gave Clay some idea. The abrupt slopes, hardly less barren than the desert lowlands, must have sprung up almost a vertical half mile.

These were *mountains,* not the hills back home that sometimes were known by that term. Majestic, imposing, intimidating — they were all of these, and the deep canyons hewn out of their rocky face were no less so.

"Never seen nothin' like it, Green," said Clay. After walking for almost an hour, the two of them rode abreast again, well ahead of Brehmer and Pate. "How'd somethin' ever get that big?"

"Good Lord done it," said Green. " 'He that formeth the mountains, The Lord, The God of hosts, is his name.' "

After Green had been all but silent for hours now, Clay was glad he had found his preacher's voice again.

"You really believe all that, don't you," said Clay.

"Just like I do about the stars declarin' the Good Lord's glory. It's all right up there for ever'body to take in."

"I just thought, you know, after your" — Clay started to say *daughter* — "after whatever it is eatin' at you, you might have second thoughts about it all."

"Can't deny what I'm seein' now," said

Green, his face turned toward the ridge, "and I expect I won't be tonight neither when I'm lookin' up at them stars."

Clay studied the mountains — a fortress rising up so dramatically out of the desert. He couldn't even imagine the power it must have taken to mold that battlement and fling it north and south as far as he could see.

"Say He *did* make all this, and the stars too," Clay said. "What makes you think somebody with all of that to take care of would give a damn about me and you?" Clay hadn't meant to say *damn;* ever since he had learned that Green was a preacher, he had tried to curb his swearing around him.

Green reined up and turned to him, leading Clay to stop as well.

"That's 'cause I know Him *here,*" said Green, bringing a hand to his breast. "He don't live in no mountains or stars neither one. Good Lord lives right *here.*"

Had anyone else said something like that, Clay would have shrugged it off as nonsense, but he had come to have deep respect for this cowhand.

"Should've knowed my mama, Green. She raised me up tellin' me just that sort of thing. Sometimes I . . . Sometimes I wish I could still think like that."

"If you believed it once upon a time, Good Lord's still got you in His hand. Time you least expect it, He's liable to knock you on your butt and ask how come you's kickin' at Him so hard."

Strangely, it was a comforting thought, the most comforting Clay had known since the last time he had gone to camp meeting with Molly. But at the same time, the memory of her reminded him of all the reasons he couldn't accept what Green had said.

CHAPTER 21

In this mad search for a canyon that might not even exist, Lil didn't know how much more she could endure.

They had spent an entire day reaching the escarpment, and another day and a half paralleling its base and crossing gulch after gulch. Cut deeply into the bedrock, these ravines that emptied out of the heights were all but impassable. Again and again, she and Fin would trace the rim of a gorge for half a mile just to reach the bone-white rocks below, only to face a far bank just as steep. And always another ravine waited beyond, past lechuguilla so thick that it was impossible to avoid. Her appaloosa's legs bled from a dozen wounds, and so did hers from all the times she had dismounted and led the animal.

At least Fin no longer kept her bound, except at night. Their desperate flight to Skeleton Cave seemed to have convinced him that a sudden attack could demand the best of her limited riding skills to stay alive. After all, the only map he had was inside her head, even if its points of reference thus far had been so vague that Lil doubted that the man who had drawn it on the cave wall could have followed it.

Ever since the Delaware, she had looked for an opportunity to escape. But Fin was a crazy man, and a crazy man was just as likely to act against his self-interests as for them. He might kill her for even trying. Indeed, all through this day, he had grown increasingly agitated, and considering the daunting nature of the terrain, it seemed only a matter of time before everything came to a head.

It finally happened as they scrambled out of another dispiriting gorge with horses in tow. The ascent almost drained Lil's strength, but she used the appaloosa's stirrup leather to drag herself to her feet. Her lungs heaving, she leaned against the foamy animal and found the escarpment swimming against the sky. It was just as dominating as ever, just as stubborn in its refusal to suggest any connection with the map. On down its base another hundred yards, a boulder-strewn rise restricted her line of sight, but she could guess what was beyond.

Standing like a brace for a great wall, the angling ridge was sure to precede yet another gulch at a canyon mouth.

Something seized Lil's arm, spinning her about.

"You take me for a fool, Pretty Lady? Waterfall, hell! In a place this dry? At the mouth of a canyon?"

Fin's face was flushed, a redness muted by dirt and stubble that glistened with sweat. But it was the eyes that she keyed on, eyes dark and wild but not yet deranged.

"Never said no waterfall." She almost didn't recognize her own voice, a hoarse whisper that crawled up tiredly from her throat. "I said it was drawed like a egg pointed down, with wavy lines running down through it."

Fin sank his fingers into her arm. "What's that supposed to mean?" He took a vise-like grip on her head and twisted it around to the escarpment. "You see anything like that there?" He twisted more. "Down there, up there?"

"Please quit it," she rasped, trying to pry his fingers loose.

"You rather Dark Man do it? Huh? That what you want? Him wringin' your neck? Been wantin' to, damned straight. Been wantin' somethin' else first, though. Ever' since we laid eyes on you, him and me's been fightin' this out, just like we done over Molly. Let her alone, I told him, but Dark Man wouldn't listen. He got his way and I had to get out of San Saba fast before they figured out why she killed herself."

It was the raving of a demented mind, but Fin wasn't through.

"Dark Man don't ever worry. Won't even give things a second thought. But I'd lay awake at the Bar W's, thinkin' I was bein' sneaked up on, afraid her brother was out there in the dark. Even stopped callin' myself Lucius, but that wouldn't mean nothin' if Clay ever got a look at me."

His hand still on her head, Fin shoved her back against the appaloosa. But Lil was stunned for an entirely different reason as he turned to his horse.

Clay!

In an instant, so many things made sense — all the way back to the moment when a stranger fresh from San Saba had shown up at her wagon, and the next day when he had asked about a certain "Lucius Cox" whom he wouldn't acknowledge as a friend. Until this moment she had forgotten that name, but now it seemed to echo from the mountains. The motivations of two men — no, three, for one of them plunged in and out

312

of insanity — all showed clearly now, so much so that she was buoyed by the hope that Clay might follow Fin even here.

At Fin's gruff order, Lil struggled back into the saddle, and they rode on for the obscuring ridge that angled down from the escarpment. As the appaloosa picked its way through lechuguilla, there were too many thoughts for her to process, but she managed to focus on what it would take to escape. Even with talk of Apache atrocities, she hadn't been able to distract Fin, but now she might have something far more powerful. Still, with the dark man lurking behind those eyes, she knew she was taking a chance.

"He's coming after you," she said. "Clay was at the Narrows with me. He's coming."

Fin rode framed against the mountains, a man dwarfed but more dangerous than ever. "Tired of you jabberin' about what somebody coulda done or woulda done. Ain't happenin'. Never was, so just shut up about it."

"I didn't know it before — just wishing — but I do now. You'll be laying there sleeping, maybe it'll be tonight, and he's going to slip up on you and —"

"Don't press your luck, Pretty Lady. Just 'cause I blurt out a name, it don't mean I can't see right through you. Oh, yeah, you know him. Like hell! You think I —"

"Clay Andrews."

Fin went silent, a quizzical expression on his face. He reined up and looked down at the saddle horn, and Lil pulled rein too and watched as the seconds tolled by.

"So I give out his last name too," he said, looking up. "Dark Man whisperin' like he is, don't know half of what I said. You think you can just —"

"Lucius Cox."

"What?"

Lil had talked over Fin, but his reaction was that of someone who had understood. His jaw dropped, and as flushed as his face had been before, it went just as pale.

"I can tell you all how Mr. Andrews looks, too," she added. "Blue eyes. Hair kind of sandy. Leaner than you are, and he never would swear around me."

Fin seemed too stunned to speak, but he was alert enough to cast a concerned glance behind him. Lil realized that she had pricked something unnerving in him, but she still didn't know if it was to her benefit or detriment.

"Nobody at the Narrows knowed me," Fin eventually muttered. "They knowed Fin, but they sure as hell don't know any Lucius.

SOB would never figure out who was who. You're lyin' like a ten-cent whore."

"He don't need a name to tell people how you look. I know now he come out to the Bar W's just to hunt you. He took a job there, I expect just so he could look better. By now, he's asked up and down the river and figured out who you are."

Fin looked over his shoulder again. "Still don't mean a damn thing. I ain't on the Pecos no more."

Now, Lil fell back into wishing out loud. "Those wagons was on Mr. Brehmer's range. I bet word got out you took me off. I bet Mr. Andrews has got even more reason to hunt you now. I bet the horses we saw a few days ago was him coming to kill you."

Lil didn't think it was possible for Fin to blanch more, but he did. He drew his Navy six, and it shook in his hand as he twisted in the saddle to scan the lowlands on his right and the lechuguilla behind, the mountains on his left and the slanting ridge ahead. Finally he waved Lil forward with the revolver.

"Clay be damned — Apaches too, the filthy animals. You're takin' me to that waterfall or egg or whatever it is or, by God, Dark Man will do what he wants to with you."

Lil thought fast. "You can stop the dark man, just like you told me. Your revolver."

Fin slung an arm to the mountains. "When they's gold there somewhere? When I'm fixin' to get the only break I ever got?"

"You couldn't ever enjoy it. He's got you just like you got me."

"What do you know about it? I'm the one lived with him all this time."

"So chase him off. Make him know he don't have a choice." She nodded to the revolver. "Put it to your head and show him. Cock it and start to squeeze it and show him."

And while you're squeezing, I'll yell out about Apaches and maybe your finger will twitch!

Fin looked at his Navy six and seemed to consider what she had said. But the moment passed quickly.

"Threats don't scare him none," he said. "Ain't scared of me or nothin' else much except the time Clay liked to drowned him."

What Lil's suggestion couldn't do, Fin's own reference to Clay apparently did. He spun again, looking for things that couldn't be seen.

They rode on, a desperate girl and her rattled captor, both at the mercy of a dark thing lying in wait.

Clay had the uneasy feeling that eyes watched him, and with Lil still in Fin's hands, he didn't need to be any more troubled.

The desert had followed them inside this slashing maze in the Guadalupes, and even after brutal miles, it showed no signs of letting go. To call this a sun-seared canyon land wouldn't have done it justice. Maybe the trenches of hell would have been a better fit.

After searching the escarpment's base for a full day, they had reined up before a canyon mouth gaping like the jaws of something that might have come from damnation. From a bed of white rocks gleaming in the dying sun, barren mountains angled up fifteen hundred feet on either side, a pair of scarred slopes rising to meet sheer cliffs. Most striking was a natural face etched across hundreds of feet of towering precipice at Clay's right. The array of cracks, surface irregularities, and runoff chutes — all brought to life by shadows — roughly matched the simple sketch in the cave.

Even after Brehmer studied the formation for himself, he continued to refer to it as a waterfall; maybe he had seen one sometime. But in the cliff's fine details, Clay found something entirely different, and he figured Green was to blame.

Clay saw the face of a man crowned with thorns and streaming with blood.

From a catclaw bush just inside the canyon, Green had plucked a tatter of calico just like the one in Skeleton Cave, and they had ridden deeper. Now, they were off their horses and preparing for nightfall at this intersection of rock-strewn drainages where a small pool had collected below a large boulder, just as the map indicated. The horses needed water, and so did they, and from the appearance of things, these mountains might not have any more to offer.

Even at dusk, heat radiated from the bleached rubble underfoot. It was like a fever burning through Clay, and when he looked up to scout the surrounding bluffs and high cliffs, the sweat dripping from his brow half blinded him. But no matter how many times he searched and found nothing, the nagging feeling that he was being watched wouldn't go away.

As the four of them sat beside their saddles and downed supper in a growing dark, he mentioned it.

"You too," responded Brehmer. "I was

hoping it was just me letting something I heard once get the best of me."

Pate reached for a sheet of paper he had weighted down with a rock. "Just a moment, Father."

Brehmer gave him an impatient look. "Is there ever a damned thing more important than grabbing a pencil?"

Clay was tired, and growing even wearier of Brehmer's unrelenting criticism of Pate. Even with some understanding of the dynamics between the two, he hoped the young man would achieve his dream someday, if only to prove his father wrong.

Brehmer now seemed reluctant to continue, but Green spoke up.

"You fixin' to tell us, ain't you? I kinda had the same feelin' about eyes bein' on me."

Clay didn't think Brehmer saw his son and Green look at one another, but Green nodded to Pate as if to say, *He'll tell us yet, young'n.*

Brehmer did.

"Forty-nine. Big party of soldiers was laying out the El Paso road and I had the beef contract all the way from the settlements. We got to Guadalupe Pass, south end of the mountains, and the army had an Apache scout, Tats-ah-das-ay-go. Supposed to mean

Quick Killer. I got to talking to him one night and he had my hair standing on end before it was over.

"Said Apaches think these mountains are sacred. Spirits are up in here, and the only way Apaches ever connect with Ussen — he's like God to them — is through these spirits. Quick Killer went on to say there's gold here too. That's why I never thought any of this talk about a mother lode was all that far-fetched.

"Trouble is, Apaches think gold is sacred, some kind of symbol for the sun and I guess Ussen himself; I don't know. But you'll see Apaches wearing silver, but never any gold, and Quick Killer said it's because nobody can touch it without riling up all these mountain spirits.

"Quick Killer was some kind of medicine man, and he looked at me at one point and said something that shakes me up a little when I think about it, considering where we are. He said there'd come a time when I'd go looking for the yellow metal and make all the spirits mad, that they'd be watching me every step."

Clay wished there was still good light; the hair had risen on the back of his neck, and he wanted to scan the rimrock one more time.

Green laughed a little, more out of ner-vousness than mirth. "Well, long as them things just watch, guess we's all right."

"That's not all Quick Killer said," Breh-mer went on. "He told me there'd be seven of us, and the closer we got to the gold, the angrier the spirits would get."

"Whew!" said Green, with another little laugh. "Yeah, I can rest easy now, seein' how bad he is at prophesyin'. Just the four of us."

"And two more ahead," said Pate. Despite Brehmer's earlier reprimand, Clay could hear the young man's pencil sing against paper. He hoped it would be readable come daylight.

"Six in all," acknowledged Brehmer.

Maybe, pondered Clay. Or perhaps Quick Killer had been right. Perhaps the Apache medicine man had looked inside Fin and found not one person, but two.

Seven.

That thought didn't do much to calm Clay's nerves. He didn't want to ask Breh-mer more, but he forced himself.

"So what did this Quick Killer say was goin' to happen to these seven people?"

Brehmer's voice seemed to echo through the night. "Said three of us would die when we got there. I'd heard all I wanted, so I didn't ask him anything else."

CHAPTER 22

Three.

The word stayed in Clay's mind as he lay on his bedroll and listened to a powerful wind moan from the lofty rimrock. When he had ridden out to the Pecos, only his search for Lucius had given him reason to live, but Lil had changed that. Now, he couldn't sleep for worrying about what the Apache holy man had said. Which three of them would die? And when? Would there be any warning, or would they just be here one second and dead the next?

But that wasn't all that preyed on his mind. As black as this night was, Clay didn't think it was possible to hide any better, but the sensation of being watched hadn't gone away. On the contrary, it seemed stronger, and he rolled over and found the grip of his revolver, as if .44 balls would do any good against Apache hants.

Clay sat up and scanned the night. He

could hear Green snoring beside him, while from the boulder overlooking the water hole came quiet voices that he recognized as Brehmer's and Pate's. Brehmer had volunteered for first guard, but he had ignored Pate's offer to take his own turn during the night. Clay, to be sure, wouldn't have been comfortable with Pate in such a position, but he wished Brehmer had handled the matter better. Maybe the two of them standing watch together was Brehmer's way of letting Pate feel good about himself.

But as Clay listened to their rising voices, it was clear that father and son weren't seeing eye to eye. Clay knew it wasn't any of his business, but something about the conversation led Clay to put on his boots and get up.

"You treat me as if I were helpless," Pate was saying. "You do it in front of the men just as if we were alone."

"Start showing me something and I'll stop doing it," Brehmer said sharply.

"That's not fair, Father. Have you ever read anything I've written? Just because I'm not proficient with guns or horses or ranch work doesn't mean I'm unable to accomplish anything. I'm sure Alexandre Dumas wouldn't have done so well either trying to extricate a mired steer."

"Who?"

Clay had never heard Pate defend himself to his father before, so he was glad to hear the young man do so. But as Clay started through the night for the boulder, he realized that he was just as clueless as Brehmer about Alexandre Dumas.

"That's exactly the problem," Pate continued. "You don't have any appreciation for literature, or the artistry and hard work it requires. Whenever I try to speak with you about it, you give me a look that could shrivel a cactus. Doesn't it matter what I want for myself? Everything's always what *you* want for me."

"What I want is for you to be able to take care of yourself," said Brehmer. "I'm talking about the essentials, the getting by, day to day. Not some foolishness that has to do with paper and pencil. Might as well be an old hen scratching in the dirt for all the good it does."

"You're always criticizing me that way. You don't ever hear me speak harshly about your cattle business."

"Damn it, son, what I do's something you can reach out and grab. It puts food in your belly, and money in the bank for lean times. One of these days, I won't be around anymore, and neither will your mother.

You've got to learn to do things for yourself."

"Before we ride out tomorrow, will you read what I wrote at camp yesterday evening? It's only three pages, but I want to show you something I *did* learn for myself."

Unexpectedly, Clay heard his own voice respond as he neared. "Why don't you read it, Mr. Brehmer?"

From the boulder came quick stirring, punctuated by a revolver hammer clicking back.

"Hell!" exclaimed Brehmer. "Good way to get yourself killed, sneaking up that way."

"Sorry," said Clay. He went closer, finding their shadows on the rock.

"What was that you were saying?" Pate asked him.

Now that Clay had time to think, he decided not to repeat it. Besides, he figured the young man had heard clearly the first time.

"You think Father should read what I've written?" pressed Pate.

"What I think is that it's none of his damned business," said Brehmer.

Clay maintained his silence, but the young man wouldn't let the matter go.

"He thinks you should read it, Father. It won't require but a minute or two."

Brehmer swore quietly. "See what you started up?" he demanded of Clay.

Clay knew he should turn and walk away, but he was tired and on edge and, he supposed, looking for a fight, even if it was with the wrong person.

"I didn't exactly start it," he said. "I think you two been goin' at it a while."

One shadow rose and came closer. "What goes on between me and my boy's between us, not anybody else," Brehmer snapped.

Clay held his ground, his face burning hotter. "Back at headquarters, maybe. But you told me yourself we's all in this together. All Pate's askin' is you read somethin'. Don't sound like too much to ask."

The shadow came within arm's length. "Damned lot of nerve you've got."

"I just like to see ever'body be give a chance, is all. I —"

Something struck Clay solidly in the chest. He was already stumbling back before he realized Brehmer had shoved him with both hands. Clay's boots twisted in the rubble, but he managed to stay on his feet.

"Hey, what's goin' on over there?" came a voice from across camp.

"You've got to stop them, Green!" exclaimed Pate. "They're fighting!"

They weren't fighting. There was no way

Clay was going to hit someone more than twice his age. He realized he must have lost his mind to argue with the man he counted on to help find Lil. If Brehmer rode out of these mountains at daybreak and took his son and Green with him, where would that leave her?

Abruptly a silhouette was between Clay and the Bar W owner.

"Rocks a-hurtin' my bare feet ever' step over," said Green. "Better been for a good reason."

"Forget it, Green," said Clay. "Nobody throwin' punches. Just talkin' some."

"A right smart amount, from what I could hear over there." Then Green's silhouette turned away. "You all right, Mr. Brehmer?"

"Butting in where it's none of his business." From the tone of Brehmer's voice, he was still ready to deliver a fist.

"Still say I'm right," said Clay, trying to keep his own anger under rein. "If you don't think so, ask Green about it when you cool off. Need to appreciate Pate for what he is instead of what he never will be."

"Didn't see *you* so satisfied with him, dragging him off his horse that time. Damned hypocrite's what you are."

This time, Clay listened to his inner voice. He retreated to his bedroll before he did something that would only make matters worse.

Worried that the Bar W owner would abandon the search, Clay spent more hours awake than asleep that night. By the time Green roused him for last watch, he had sorted things out, and it wasn't a favorable appraisal of himself. Damn it, Brehmer wasn't his enemy; Lucius was. Clay had just let exhaustion and nerves get the best of him, and he couldn't blame Brehmer for responding the way he had. If the torturous ride from upper headquarters had worn so heavily on a twenty-four-year-old, Clay couldn't imagine what it had done to a man Brehmer's age.

At first light, Clay left his post on the boulder and approached Brehmer as the older man threw a saddle across the dapple gray.

"Mrs. Casner don't have a thing to do with what's between us," said Clay. "I hope you don't hold last night against her and stop helpin' me look."

Brehmer stretched the cinch strap down behind the horse's forelegs and set about buckling it. "Not doing this for you," he said curtly, without even a glance in Clay's direction. "I'm doing it because it's my fault she left headquarters in the first place. I'm the one that's to blame, and I'll do whatever's in my power to make it right."

Clay was still standing there, debating whether he should thank him or not, when Green approached. Clay was afraid Green would say something about the row and stir things up again, but he didn't.

"Wind sure blowed up high last night," said Green. "Could hear it just a-screamin' from the rimrock."

"These mountains are bad for wind," said Brehmer, adjusting the strap in the cinch ring. "Had to strip off all the wagon sheets that time in forty-nine. Couldn't have stood it, a wind that hard. I grabbed hold of a wheel, and still thought the wagon would turn over with me, way it was bouncing. Never was so glad to put these mountains behind me."

And yet here he was back again, thought Clay, giving his all despite age and unwelcome advice and more threats than a man could count. Brehmer may have had his faults, but he had qualities that Clay couldn't help but admire.

From the water hole, they took the drainage's left fork and traced its winding course past ledges guarded by agave and hedgehog cacti. Clay thought of this place as bone canyon, for the chalky rocks in the wash looked the part, especially in the early morning sunlight. Already, he could feel the baking heat of the bluffs that stairstepped up on either side, and he could just imagine what this place would be like in the afternoon.

By mid-morning, however, a dark overhang specified by the map turned them up a sharply rising side canyon. For a mile or so, it was manageable for horse and rider, but finally they had no choice but to dismount. As Clay struggled with his bay up through grasping ocotillo and walking-stick cholla, he took heart in something Green noted.

"See there front of us, how the rocks is stirred up? Somebody sure been up this way, all right."

"How long ago?" Clay asked. "Can you tell?"

"Pretty recent. Looka here at this bare spot, where that thousand-legs is crawlin'."

"The centipede, Green?" asked Pate.

Green knelt before the centipede and traced the ground with his finger. "See the horse track he's in, young'n? Way the wind blowed in the night, must've been made this mornin'."

This morning!

Clay lifted his gaze to a rock shelf high up

at the canyon's head, where an upright form stood against the sky. For a moment, he made himself believe it was a person.

"She's up there, Green!" he exclaimed, brushing past. "We got to go!"

In his haste, Clay slipped in the rubble, but he was up quickly and dragging the horse after him, all senses fixed on the ledge.

"Hold on there," said Green. "Just a Spanish dagger you're seein'."

But Clay kept on, pushing himself relentlessly up the steep rise.

"Oughtn't to wear yourself out," Green added.

Clay fell a second time, a third, and by then his chest heaved so violently that all he could do was lie there gasping at his horse's hoofs.

"Air's rarified at this elevation," said Pate.

From behind, Brehmer complained sullenly. Most of it, Clay couldn't make out, but he thought he could hear something like "any damned fool should know better." Clearly, Brehmer hadn't dismissed their clash.

Green, for his part, was more subtle, but the message was the same. "Ain't a stretch to make up ground in. We better take it easy till we top out."

But as the morning wore on, Clay wondered just when that would be. They skirted the ledge at the canyon head and reached the Spanish dagger, only to find a rocky shoulder angling up sharply to the left. His boots slipping, Clay led the way up it, his lungs laboring as he dodged lechuguilla and pincushion cacti that grew where it didn't seem possible. His bay was reluctant, fighting him through the reins. But Clay wouldn't be denied as he and the animal gained shelf after rocky shelf, only to find something always higher bending out of sight above.

Just as he reached a band of lichen-stained rock too abrupt for a horse, he heard Pate call out from below.

"Something's wrong with Father!"

Clay turned, looking past his animal's tail and fetlock to the figures strung out down the slope: Green and his dun ten yards behind, Pate and his roan another twenty yards back and retreating more, and the dapple gray standing over a man on hands and knees at rear.

Clay wrapped his reins around a barbed ocotillo stalk and rushed down, losing his footing almost immediately and sliding several feet on his buttocks. He got up, only to slip again. When it happened a third time, he didn't know if he had a seat left in his britches, but he managed to reach Brehmer almost as soon as Green did.

Pate stood helplessly over the downed man. "Father, you all right? You all right? Can I do something? What can —"

"Go write me a story," Brehmer mumbled without looking up. "How this old man wasn't tough enough."

It was inappropriate and ill-timed, considering Pate's obvious concern, but Clay took it as a good sign. At least Brehmer was well enough to mock his son's passion.

"Let me in here, young'n," said Green. He brushed past Pate and dropped to a knee at the man's shoulder. "What is it that's ailin' you? Can't catch your breath?"

Brehmer was breathing hard, all right, but he was also shaking his head like a dazed goat. "Every time I look up I get dizzy, things start going dark a little. Long as I keep my head down, it doesn't bother me."

"Been drinkin' enough?" asked Clay. He turned to Brehmer's son, who was closest to the dapple gray. "Pate, get a airtight of tomatoes opened up."

As the young man rushed to do so, Clay checked the sky. "Sun will bake your brains out here."

He took the dapple gray by the bridle and shifted the animal's position so that Brehmer had at least a semblance of shade. Still, with the underlying rock burning right through the soles of Clay's boots, he knew that Brehmer was like a man with his head in a stove.

When Pate came back with an open air-tight, Green sat Brehmer up and gave it to him. "Small sips at first, just like you was drinkin' molasses," Green told him.

As Brehmer did as instructed, Clay considered their options, but he waited until the owner emptied the can before suggesting anything.

"Up there where my horse is at, we've got to turn along a line of rock. Don't know for how far, but you'll be able to ride a while. You make it up there if we was to help you?"

Brehmer lifted his head, only to lower it immediately. "Still the same way. I look up and I get lightheaded, things start fading."

Nevertheless, Brehmer climbed to his feet, aided by Green's hand on his arm until he shrugged it off. "Long as I keep my head down," said Brehmer, "nothing to keep me from going anywhere I want to. Just can't see where I'm headed, is all. Where's my reins?"

Green passed them into Brehmer's grip, and the owner started uphill with chin down. He was struggling, but so were all of them, and Clay knew better than to offer help.

Soon after they mounted up, they caught a break. The band of rock turned them left along an almost-level course that allowed them to stay in the stirrups longer than Clay had expected. As they followed the curve of the mountain, Clay found something that he hadn't seen since the desert flats: sky that didn't begin at a point almost overhead. A quarter mile ahead was a shallow saddle of land that separated the mountain from a flat-topped crest at its left. The sister peak couldn't have risen more than another eighty feet, and its grade appeared gentle.

In minutes, they were on the sister peak's rocky but grassy summit, only to face an even greater maze than down in hell's trenches. In every direction stretched an endless chain of haphazard hogbacks and gaping canyons. Clay had never imagined that any place could be so wild; it was as if somebody had hacked these mountains with a knife as big as Texas.

Up until now, they had managed to follow the map without problem, but Clay wasn't so confident anymore. He had no idea how a person could navigate such broken country, which extended all the way to a haze that danced on the horizon.

"Hold up here a minute," he said, pulling rein beside a gnarled juniper. "Pate, let's see that map you sketched."

The young man obliged, and as Clay studied the rustling page in a tugging wind, Green cried out.

"Across yonder!"

Clay looked up to find the cowhand pointing west across a plunging gorge. Against a line of junipers no more than two hundred yards away, a figure on a paint pony surveilled them from the rim of a cliff. The Indian was there only a moment, and then he wheeled the horse and disappeared into the brush.

"He seen us!" exclaimed Clay.

"Who did?" Brehmer asked. "I looked up and things faded — what was it?"

"It was an Indian, Father," said a breathless Pate. "Sitting there looking at us. An Indian."

"Apache," said Green. "Sure 'nough Apache."

"I don't like this, Green," said Clay, still watching the far rim. "They know we're here now."

"Expect they knowed it since we rode in. Surprised they ain't showed themselves till now."

"What are we going to do?" Pate asked in

337

alarm. "Father, there's Apaches you can't even see. What are we —"

"You're the one wanted to come along," said Brehmer. "Tried telling you it was dangerous, but you kept at me till I finally said yes to shut you up."

Clay checked the map again. If he wasn't mistaken, that very cliff was one of the landmarks, but the prospect of reaching it in this puzzling high country was daunting.

Slipping the map into his pocket, he led the riders north along the gorge's edge and found a neck of land extending west at its apparent head. Perhaps a hundred feet lower than where he was now, the ridge was only fifty yards wide and dropped sharply hundreds of feet on either side, but it promised a link to the far rim.

"I don't have a choice," he said, reining his bay about to face the others. "I'm cross-in' over to where we saw that Indian. That's what the map says do, and I expect Lucius — Fin, you call him — already done just that. It's different with y'all, though. Mr. Brehmer, you're not feelin' good, and Pate, I know you're not any more anxious to tangle with Apaches than me. Green, y'all do whatever it is you have to, and I won't hold it against you."

Clay turned his bay down the gentle slope

to the neck of land and didn't look back, but he could tell by the sound of hoofs that three horses trailed along behind.

The sun burned with a deadly anger as midday became afternoon, and afternoon early evening. In a zigzag ride bearing generally south, they had seen no more of the Apache. But Brehmer, in his head-down position, had pointed out a cigarette butt under one of the piñon pines that began to intermix with the thickening junipers. Without doubt, Lucius had been this way, chasing a greedy dream at the expense of a girl who already had faced so much in life.

Just five minutes. That's all Clay wanted with the bastard.

In a stretch of twisted piñons so thick that the thin air was suffocating, Green ducked under a limb and came up on Clay's right.

"Been wantin' to call you on this all day," said the cowhand. "Think you called Fin 'Lucius' or somethin', if I was hearin' right. You know him from somewheres? Or did your tongue just get all tangled up?"

Green had offered him an excuse in case he didn't want to talk about it, and Clay appreciated it. But he didn't suppose there was any reason to keep matters to himself when Green had stuck with him all this way.

"Lucius Cox," said Clay. "Him and me

sort of growed up together, back in San Saba. I'm the one started callin' him Fin for a while."

"And here I was, figurin' you was after him just 'cause of the girl. Expect they's more to it, ain't there."

Clay glanced back and found Pate and Brehmer lagging out of earshot. "Lot more. But Miss Lil's sure part of it now."

"Still figurin' on killin' him?"

Clay looked at the cowhand, framed against the passing piñon limbs. "Don't think I ever said I was, exactly."

"Yeah, but a man don't talk about revenge in the middle of a chase without it meanin' somethin'."

Clay turned his hand over in a half shrug and faced his horse's ears again. "Gettin' some answers, maybe killin' him, all right, is just about all I've thought about ever since . . ." He shook his head. "I know you talk against it."

Green started to respond, but Clay continued before he had a chance.

"Green, he killed my sister." He turned and stared at the cowhand. "Might as well done it, anyway. I think he violated her, and she done the rest."

Green went ashen, but at the same time a terrible anger seemed to sweep over him.

His eyes narrowed and every muscle in his face tightened except for a twitch at his cheek. His lips began to move silently, and if Clay hadn't known better, he would have thought the cowhand was swearing under his breath.

"Makes me want to go gunnin'," Green said through gritted teeth. "Lord help me, makes me want to go gunnin'."

Clay was surprised that such a statement could come from Green.

"Whole reason I come out to the Pecos was to find Lucius," said Clay. "Then I met up with Miss Lil, and things got a little blurry. Then he goes and takes her off — Miss Lil, the only other girl I ever cared anything about. *Both of them, Green. He's tryin' to take both of them away from me.*"

Green looked down and seemed to grapple with himself as he rode in silence for a long while. Again, those lips moved in silent anger as his twitch grew worse.

"What would you do, Green?" Clay asked. "If you was in my place, what would you do?"

Clay didn't think a man's features could show greater anger than Green's already had, but he was wrong. The rage in his eyes became more than words could describe.

"I been in your place," growled the cowhand. "My girl ain't but ten, and a man outraged her, just like you was sayin'. Member of my own church, and he outraged her, and the law let him go."

For a moment, Clay couldn't catch his breath. "God A'mighty, Green. What did you do?"

"I killed the son of a bitch. God forgive me, I killed the son of a bitch."

"Green! Need help with Father!"

For a moment, Clay was too stunned to react to Pate's summons. But as Green wheeled his mount, Clay looked back and saw Brehmer slumping in the saddle as Pate reached across for him.

Clay reined his bay about and trotted the animal after Green, who seemed to have an awareness that Clay didn't. Green reached the dapple gray in moments and stepped off his horse, but he still had to lunge to catch Brehmer as the man slid off the gray's far side. Even with Green's supporting arms, it was more of a controlled fall than a dismount.

Under an adjacent piñon, Green laid Brehmer back on shaded pine needles. Pate was obviously distraught as he jumped off his horse and rushed across to hover over them. "Father! Father! Father!" he kept saying.

"Not so close, Pate — let him get some air," warned Green. "Here, stir some up with his hat."

Clay secured the horses, and by the time he came up on foot, Green had Brehmer's head up and was pouring tomato juice down him. Clay was glad that Green had set Pate to fanning with a hat, for aiding his father in such a way seemed to help both of them. Soon, Brehmer showed signs of being alert again.

"Guess I've made those mountain spirits plenty mad," he rasped. "Taking their pound of flesh and then some."

After rallying briefly, Brehmer lapsed into semiconsciousness again. Plainly, he was in no condition to ride. With sunset approaching, Clay and Green left Pate to watch him while they tended the horses in advance of nightfall.

The best forage was near the rim of a deep canyon on the east, or maybe it was southeast; all the meandering on ridges had confused Clay. Regardless, after he had helped unsaddle and stake the animals, he retreated to a jutting point. Sinking to the scorching rock at cliff's edge, he considered matters as he watched the shadows creep up the far canyon wall. He didn't realize that Green had followed until the cowhand eased down beside him.

"Don't like how this is shapin' up, Green," Clay said tiredly. "Don't like it at all."

"We's run into some bad luck, all right," agreed the cowhand.

"No way Brehmer's goin' to be able to go on. You and Pate got to start back with him in the mornin'. Can't just send Pate by himself; you got to go with him, or neither one of them'll make it. Brehmer gets down off of these mountains, breathes better, he'll probably be all right."

"Lord willin'," said Green. "But goin' off and leavin' you . . . A place like this . . . Apaches prowlin' like they is. And that sorry bastard with that girl still."

Clay looked at him. "Never heard you cuss before, Green."

"Yeah, well, Book says they's a season for ever'thing. Cussin' too, I imagine. If anybody deserves it, it's those two SOBs that hurt our families."

"I feel awful what happened to your daughter. I know what it done to you, and I feel awful."

Green took a deep breath and his jaw began to tremor. He started to say something, but choked up and turned away. As he brought a hand to his eyes, his shoulders commenced to shake.

Clay, too, abruptly saw things through a mist, and he thought how strange that their stories were the same — or would be once he overtook Lucius. He placed a caring hand on Green's shoulder, and the two of them sat there lost in emotions that men rarely displayed. Clay finally found words.

"When . . . when I catch up with Lucius, find out he's to blame, you and me will be just alike, Green. We'll have both killed the bastards that took our families away."

Green whirled, his eyes wide and wild as he clutched Clay by the collar. "You ain't doin' it! You hear me? You tell me you ain't doin' it! Won't bring nobody back, just take a lot more away!"

Green released him and stood, but Clay just sat there shaken and looked up as the cowhand railed on, even as his voice calmed a little.

"I can't never see my daughter no more or wife neither, and even though the Good Lord might've forgive me, I'm gettin' what I deserve. Right now you got a shot at somethin' with Mrs. Casner, but you go to murderin' and you'll lose ever'thing you got. Just like me."

Green stormed away, spooking the grazing horses as he disappeared between them.

CHAPTER 23

Clay needed time to think, and to do it, he had to be alone. He dug out a couple of airtights from his dwindling supply and returned to sit on the rocky point, where he forced down supper as crickets chirped and a troubling dark fell across the canyon.

Green had spoken from experience. He had paid a terrible price for avenging his daughter, and it had taken away his very life. In some ways, the man who had outraged her had been the lucky one. His suffering had ended in a moment, but Green's would follow him all through a tortured existence in which there could never be rest.

Was that where Clay was headed? Would he rescue a girl he had come to love, only to throw away any chance that they could ever be together?

He wished there were an answer. He wished for even more. He wished he had Green's faith that bestowed forgiveness even while demanding an accounting.

He heard footsteps behind him, and he spun with .44 in hand to a shadow inside of shadows. "Who is it?" he challenged.

The shadow froze. "Me. Pate."

Clay relaxed. "Come on over, Pate. How's Mr. Brehmer?"

The silhouette came up before him. "Green says he's sleeping. I couldn't tell in the dark. Earlier he was sweating profusely and tossing. Green thinks he has a fever."

"Been rough on him, I know."

Pate sat down nearby. Clay still had more solitary thinking to do, but he wasn't going to send the young man away.

"With Father there," said Pate, "I couldn't speak about this with Green."

Clay waited, expecting more. When Pate stayed silent, he realized this must be the young man's way of gauging his willingness to listen.

"Go ahead and tell me," Clay encouraged.

"In his delirium, he seemed to be talking with someone. I think it was those mountain spirits. Father was pleading with them."

"Talked earlier like they was punishin' him, all right. If I was feverish, imagine I'd be tryin' to chase them away from me too."

"Father wasn't pleading for himself. He was pleading for them to leave *me* alone."

"Shows he cares," said Clay.

"That's probably what Green would say too. I'm not so certain Father feels that way."

"Man like him's not the kind to come right out and talk about his feelings. Sick this way, things like that probably come out easier."

"Green told me once that Father's obstinate. He's that way regarding my future as well. He has his mind made up what I'm to do, and he expects me to accommodate his wishes."

Clay couldn't imagine Green using the word *obstinate. Ornery,* maybe. "Mr. Brehmer's just worried what's to come of you, Pate."

"My grandparents died and left him on his own when he was thirteen. He had to make his way working with his hands, and he can't imagine any other way of accomplishing it. I know he just wants to protect me from what he experienced, but he's so controlling that he smothers me."

"Keeps a tight rein on you, all right. Don't know that I agree with it, but at least he's there for you. Lost my father so long ago, not even sure I remember him. Anyway, Mr. Brehmer just wants you to be able to get by when he's . . ."

Clay stopped himself. Brehmer was suffering right now, and Pate didn't need any reminder that things might not turn out well.

"Pate," Clay continued, "you got smarts I'll never have. Yeah, I can usually stay on an ol' bronc when he downs his head, and I'm pretty good at ropin' a steer and draggin' him to the brandin' in' fire. But I couldn't write my way out of a wore-out war bag. You get back, why don't you write up all of this — cave of skeletons, chasin' gold, dodgin' Apaches. Send it back East somewhere and see if some newspaper will print it, pay you for it. A check in your hand might do wonders towards showin' Mr. Brehmer you're ever' bit the expert a top hand is, just in different ways."

"Skeletons . . . gold . . . Indians," Pate repeated, as if committing the list to memory. "Yes, I'll have all that in my notes. And the mountain spirits too. What do you think about what Tats-ah-das-ay-go told Father?"

What could Clay say? That the feeling that the four of them weren't alone was stronger than ever? What good would it do to spook a young man who was already so concerned about his father?

"You think there's really such a thing as spirits here?" Pate pressed.

"Lots that I'm a clabber-head about. Guess that's one of them."

"I had nightmares last night. I think Father was right. They're taking their pound of flesh. I suppose with his dislike of all things literary, he'd be dismayed to know he was quoting Shakespeare."

"Like I say, you know a lot the rest of us don't, Pate."

"I wish I knew more about those spirits. Ever since dark fell, I've felt like the king's son in *The Tempest:* 'Hell is empty and all the devils are here.' That's what Green thinks too — if there are spirits here, they're devils."

For all of Clay's sensation of being watched since entering these mountains, he hadn't felt particularly threatened — until now. Maybe Pate knew a little too much when it came to quoting a passage that set a man scanning the dark with the expectation of something leaping out of it.

Pate soon retired to his bedroll in the piñons, but he had left Clay with something else to deny him rest. If Clay persisted in seeking a day of reckoning for Lucius, would something in these mountains demand one of him?

As his horse carried him in the gloom of

dawn along a rocky game trail over which swaying piñon limbs hovered sinisterly, Dark Man could sense a presence.

It seemed to reach deep inside and touch a corner of his mind where fear lived, and he didn't like it. He wished Fin would do something, for this was a kind of presence that Dark Man had never known before. He wanted it to go away, but instead it grew stronger with every strike of his roan's hoofs in the rubble.

Dark Man was accustomed to getting his way, and he vainly tried to nudge the presence into that part of him where Fin usually stayed. Of course, Fin sometimes wandered into Dark Man's province, but Fin was generally so easy to dominate that Dark Man would often indulge for a while.

But this presence was different. It was a single thing, but at the same time many, and there was a power to it that frightened Dark Man almost as much as his near-drowning at the hands of Clay.

Fin was on edge too, and Dark Man knew it. In many ways, the two of them were alike, even the same person. But while Fin might consider consequences before he acted, Dark Man didn't see the need. He usually did what he wanted and when he wanted, and only rarely could Fin dissuade him.

Things had always been that way, at least as far back as Dark Man could recall. Of course, he couldn't remember coming into being, any better than Fin could remember his own origin. All Dark Man knew was that Fin had been there from the start, the two of them sharing and competing and fighting a fight that Dark Man almost always won.

But he didn't know how to fight against something that was there and not there at the same time.

In a distant way, Fin knew that Dark Man was troubled, just as he knew everything that Dark Man thought and felt. But Fin was shaken in his own right by the distinct impression that he and Pretty Lady weren't alone.

"You feelin' it too, ain't you," Fin said, turning in the saddle to check the brush. "Just like eyes on me, watchin' all time."

Pretty Lady looked around at him from the appaloosa nodding along ahead. "Told you he was coming after you. Told you about the Apaches too. Told you they was going to scalp you."

"Ain't him or no Apaches neither one I'm feelin'." He continued to scan the piñons nervously, finding only glimpses of more brush through wind-whipped limbs. "It's like somethin' seein' inside me, waitin' to pounce."

"Turn around, then. Horses don't have no water. Indians is probably all over. We'll be out of something to drink. Maybe there's ghosts."

Ghosts.

Dark Man didn't like the sound of that, and he whispered to Fin. *Time to leave!*

"No!"

Fin didn't often reply to Dark Man out loud, but this time he did, even though Pretty Lady apparently believed he had been talking to her.

"Then let *me* go back," she pleaded. "Map's done. I told you. Place you're looking for, the gold, how it was drawed, I told you all that. It's just not here. If it is, you can find it good as me."

Inside his mind, Fin fought to restrain Dark Man. Pretty Lady was staring, but she turned away abruptly, maybe recognizing something about Dark Man in Fin's eyes.

Time to leave!

Fin gritted his teeth. *I'll put a ball in my head!* he warned Dark Man.

Time to leave!

Fin drew the Navy six out of his waistband and drove the muzzle into his temple. *I'll do it!*

Time to leave!

Fin thumbed back the hammer. *I'll take you to hell with me!*

Dark Man retreated, and Fin lowered the revolver just as he broke out of the piñons. With stunning suddenness, he saw it all before him, just as Pretty Lady had described: a place that promised so much, if only he could fight away the Apaches and ghosts and the dark thing inside him.

CHAPTER 24

By morning, Brehmer had recovered enough to sit a horse, but even at that, Green and Pate had to help him into the saddle. Now, the three of them were on their animals and ready to start back, despite Brehmer's resistance.

"I have a responsibility to Mrs. Casner," he whispered, still too impaired to lift his head.

"You more than done your part, Mr. Brehmer," said Clay, standing before him. "But your responsibility don't end here. I'm carryin' it on, and I promise you I'll do ever'thing I can, here on out."

Pate and his father rode away through the piñons, but Green brought his horse closer to Clay. There was a lot of emotion in the cowhand's face.

"Wish I could be two places at once," Green said. "You don't know how much I'm a-wishin' it."

"I know it, Green. Sure grateful for all you done. If the Indians don't bother me, I can handle Lucius by myself."

"Just you remember, Good Lord's got His own way of seein' after vengeance, and He'll dish it out better than you or me ever could."

Green stretched a hand down, and Clay shook it. The cowhand's lips trembled as if he had more to say, but then his eyes misted and he wheeled his mount and rode away.

Had Clay let it, the moment could have affected him just as strongly. But he had a job to do, even if he had to do it alone, and he swung up into the saddle and reined his bay deeper into the piñons.

Lucius was ahead somewhere, and he had Lil with him. The map's reference points, sketched totally without regard to scale, were all but exhausted, but whether Lucius was a mile ahead or a hundred, Clay would go on. Maybe his jaded bay would drop dead; maybe he would be set afoot in hostile country where thirst crawled down a man's throat and the blazing sun cooked his skull. The hell with a little hardship! If he had to, he would chase Lucius to the ends of the earth.

Adrift in so many thoughts, Clay didn't know how long he rode through wind-tossed piñons and junipers before he flinched to distant gunfire behind him. He wheeled his horse in the rocky turf and listened — a gunshot, a second volley and a third, six or eight more in quick succession.

"Hyah!"

Clay spurred the gelding and they were away, racing back through the brush, the animal's hoofs drumming against hard rock and scant topsoil. The bay broke through limbs that popped and slapped, once almost peeling Clay from the saddle, but he kept up the frantic pace as he posted with the horse's gait. His course carried him down slopes and up again, alongside low bluffs of sheer rock, across rimrock where the wind howled and the bay's hoofs pounded like an entire cattle herd in stampede.

The gunfire grew ever louder but sporadic: a blast here, two blasts there, quick volleys followed by silence as if a running battle was taking place. Suddenly the reports seemed almost in his ears, and Clay reached for the Colt revolver hanging from the saddle horn and raised it against flashes of horsehide through the limbs ahead.

He was in the vicinity of last night's camp now, and he had the .44 at full cock when he met Pate and his horse bursting out of the final shielding piñons with Brehmer's dapple gray in tow. Brehmer rode slumped in the saddle, but he was still hanging on.

"Pate!" cried Clay, drawing rein.

"Indians!"

The young man never slowed as he barreled past with the gray, but Clay shouted after him. "Where's Green?"

More gunfire erupted at the same moment, and Clay spun back to see another brute form charging out of the brush. Clay leveled his weapon on it, his finger a split second away from squeezing the trigger, and then a bloodied rider was upon him, his shoulders twisted around to the rear and his arm recoiling to the roar of his six-shooter.

"Green!"

The cowhand turned in the saddle as he came abreast. "They's on us! Get out of here!"

Clay caught more movement through the piñons as a rifle ball whirred past. A blue sorrel was there, and so was a rider in gaudy calico and breechclout. The limbs parted, and for an instant Clay looked into the face of a painted fiend behind a shouldered rifle. Clay discharged the .44 at the same instant that fire exploded from the Apache's weapon. Something hot jerked Clay's arm, not enough to affect him, but limbs thrashed

and cracked as the warrior tumbled head-
long from the sorrel.

Clay reined the bay about and spurred it
after Green, whose shoulder was a bloody
mess, starkly red against piñon greenery.

"Green, you're hurt!"

So was Clay, and he just now realized it.
His upper left arm was on fire, and when
he checked he found blood as bright as
Green's. But he could still ride, and he
could still shoot as he glanced back and saw
the Apache sprawled under the broken
limbs.

What Clay couldn't do, though, was fight
off an army, and from what he glimpsed
through the piñons, that's just what they
faced. Flight was their only chance, along
with keeping to the brush where the long-
range rifles of the Apaches were no better
than their own revolvers. He didn't know if
Pate had exhausted his rounds, but Green
seemed to be trying to reload, no easy feat
with a horse at a breakneck run through
grasping limbs.

Clay caught a stirring in the piñons on his
right, an Apache coming abreast on a paint
pony only a few trees away. Clay didn't have
a clear shot but he fired anyway, desperate
to discourage if not hit. It was a wasted
load, leaving him with four, and when the

warrior angled closer, Clay squeezed the trigger again to no effect.

Then the warrior was upon him, a shrieking devil swinging a stone-head war club with a horsetail pendant. Their horses collided as the club fell, altering the weapon's course so that it glanced off Clay's shoulder instead of crushing his skull. Before the Apache could deliver another blow, Clay lunged inside his arms, two men grappling to the death astride jousting horses.

A brown hand reached for a bone handle in a rawhide belt as Clay drove the .44 into the Apache's ribs. For an instant, the close quarters kept Clay from thumbing back the hammer, but just as a knife flashed in the sunlight, he cocked and fired at point-blank range.

Body against body muffled the report as the Apache fell against him. For a few seconds Clay fought even more furiously, expecting the burn of a knife blade. Then the horses separated and he shed the limp form and watched it drop at the paint's hoofs.

Clay had only two rounds left as he gigged the bay into flight again. Things had happened so quickly that he hadn't had time to be afraid, but now the fear came in a wave that set him trembling with weakness. *He had looked two men in the eyes and shot them, and taken a bullet in return.* He didn't know if he could find the strength to raise the revolver again, but when a ricochet sailed through the adjacent piñons, he turned and fired once more at multiple pursuers.

Clay missed, but his shot turned the warriors sharply into the brush. His only hope was that his added firepower and the bodies on the ground had ended this, because the situation was grave. He was down to his last round, and if Green didn't ram in loads of his own in a hurry, a single pistol ball would be only enough for Clay to spare himself torture.

Not only that, but Green's horse was faltering as badly as Clay's, and he knew that either animal could go down with fatal consequences. All the way from the Pecos, the journey had been demanding, but ever since hell's trenches the horses had suffered almost as much as Brehmer. They had been denied water and adequate forage, yet Clay and the others now asked them for more than ever.

But maybe the Apaches' mounts had faded too. When Clay looked, he saw nothing but piñons behind, and the same was true on either side. Still, he pressed the bay for another several hundred yards before he eased the laboring animal into a trot and shouted at Green.

"Don't see them no more!"

Green looked back over his bloody shoulder and relaxed his dun.

"Get Pate slowed down!" Clay added.

Green did so, and the lathered horses trotted on in a single-file formation tight enough for Clay to glimpse Brehmer's dapple gray through the limbs. Clay had a lot of worries as he reached for his powder flask, but Green's condition was the greatest. He rode a little slumped, his arm close to his ribs, and as soon as the cowhand put away his weapon, he clamped a hand across his shoulder.

"How bad you hurt, Green?"

"Hit before I knowed what was happenin'." Green winced to obvious pain. "Got me in a bad way, I tell you they did."

"Got blood all over. Keep your hand on it."

Green glanced back again and must have noticed Clay's wound. "Didn't have to get all shot yourself just so's we'd match."

Clay examined his own arm: the bloody tear in his shirt, the deep gash, the raw flesh that looked as if it had gone through a meat grinder.

"Just cut me is all." The truth was, Clay's arm felt branded, but he wasn't going to complain when the cowhand was in such distress.

"Ain't we in a fix," said Green. "Shoulda saved some cuss words. Been a good time for it."

"How come them to do this, Green? What is it they want from us?"

"Horses, for one. We's in their country, for another. And maybe they's a bigger reason."

As Clay scanned the piñons again, he couldn't imagine what it would be.

"That blessed gold that's s'posed to be here," Green continued. "Maybe them evil mountain spirits ain't the only ones don't want us any closer to it."

CHAPTER 25

Lil had seen only a crude sketch in a shadowy cave, but she knew the place as soon as her appaloosa broke through the whipping piñons.

Rubbly bedrock, punished by the wind, extended sixty yards to a sudden canyon. Near the rim at one o'clock, a jumble of large boulders rose up, guarding a gnarly crucifixion thorn. It was the only thing that had taken root in the bedrock, which otherwise was as bare as a winged thing's perch in hell. With a backdrop of forbidding mountains sheared by the gorge, the scene was enough to take Lil's breath away.

It was more than that. It was awing, considering what she saw to the left of the boulders.

A hundred yards past the cliff's edge, a pinnacle towered out of the canyon to crest a little higher than the rim itself. A hewn spire of rock, cracked vertically by a jagged crevice, it seemed to stand alone. As the appaloosa carried her onto the bedrock, however, she saw a ridge extending out from just below the near rim. The narrow hogback was a natural bridge to the spire, but one that looked fragile. Its thin foundation, rising up from far below, seemed all but hollowed through, and even now the wind carved away at it.

The spire was alive.

The morning sunlight made it that way, setting its spidery veins shining with a warm, yellow hue like the nuggets that Clay had given her. But those had been the size of a fingertip, while these golden veins crawled across the entire upper face of a rock soaring out of a gorge half a mile deep.

The wind seemed alive too. It moaned in an unnatural way that heightened the strange anxiety Lil had felt ever since Fin had dragged her into these mountains. She wanted to turn back into the piñons, but when she reined her horse about, Fin was there, blocking the way. His face was an odd mix of elation and primitive fear.

"You got what you come for," Lil pleaded.

His face without color, his breaths frantic, Fin looked left and right and back at Lil. "Ain't facin' no Indian ghosts by myself. Get down off of your horse."

Fin dismounted with her, and as soon as they tied the animals, he drew his Navy six against a danger neither of them could see, and waved her on.

Lil had just about come to accept what Fin believed about himself — that a devil lived inside him. If that were so, then it must have been at home in this waterless place where Lil could almost feel other unclean spirits walking with them, seeking rest and not finding any.

She went ten steps and tried to turn back again, only to meet Fin's Navy six. "You don't need me no more," she appealed.

"Dark Man and you both wantin' out of here."

Fin's eyes widened as if something occurred to him. He glanced at the appaloosa and surveyed Lil up and down, seemingly appraising her size. When his gaze came up again, there was something even more sinister in it.

"Got plans for that appaloosa," he growled, "and they don't include you."

With the .36, Fin prodded Lil on for the rim, and she proceeded with a terrible weakness because she understood. She stumbled and almost went down, knowing that a searing pain could strike her in the back this very step, or the next, or the one after that. But whether he killed her outright or left her afoot to die, the outcome would be no less sure: Fin would trade her weight for that much more of the yellow metal that drove men mad and maybe roused the sleeping devils.

At the rim, Lil reeled again, this time to a wicked current that howled up out of the depths. Elsewhere the bedrock ended at a precipice, a single pace separating safety from a screaming plummet. Here, though, the rock stairstepped down a series of lechuguilla-infested ledges.

At Fin's order, Lil began to descend, the daggers catching her whipping dress. She negotiated three drop-offs that carried her under the rim at a point a little west of the land bridge. Here, the mountain jutted out, reaching for the hogback, but the only course to it was by way of an inches-wide shelf that angled down the cliff. If she fell, she would miss the hogback entirely — but not the canyon bottom waiting below.

Her cheek against rock, Lil edged out with her heels hanging over open space. She remembered another time she had hugged a wall, and a stranger who had given her a moment of hope in a callous world. Even now, she clung to the memory because it was all she had, and all she would ever have.

As she probed her feelings, she realized something that she supposed she had always known: *She loved Clay, even though he would never find out.* She would die here in a powerful gust, or by gunshot or thirst or Apaches, and he would carry on his search for vengeance and never know what he had meant to her.

Abruptly Lil was there, planting her shoes on the ridge that connected to the spire and the web of veins, shining beside its long, black crack. The hogback, only a few feet wide, stretched dramatically before her, a hundred-yard bridge over a dizzying canyon. If possible, it seemed more dangerous than the ledge, for it caught a strong crosswind that lifted a haze of dust up from below and stirred the white rubble at her feet.

At the jab of Fin's revolver, Lil crept on, her dress slapping her legs and the dust stinging her eyes. She could never have imagined being suspended in the sky this way, the world falling away on either side, but she had taken only a few steps before her alarm grew.

The hogback groaned and shifted to their weight, as if ready to collapse.

She spun to retreat, but Fin was there with his Navy six and a face blanched more than ever.

"Ain't stoppin', Pretty Lady. Not for ghosts or nothin' else. You just pray our way on across."

As Lil went on, feeling the ground quake under her shoes, she prayed, all right. But it wasn't for her or Fin or anyone else except the only friend she had known in all the lonely years.

Every step was nerve-racking, but she made it across to the talus in the shadow of the spire that rose seventy or eighty feet above her. It was maybe half that wide where she stood, a huge rock around which the currents moaned like something in a premature burial.

Now, Fin pushed past her, scrambling in a frenzy a dozen feet up to a shrubby alligator juniper. It grew at the base of the fissure, a crack dark with depth but only as wide as a hand. Alongside, the cliff was sheer and crusted dirty-white with age, and it teased with those spidery veins of warm yellow, just out of reach overhead.

Between glances at Lil to hold her in place, Fin worked his way along the talus, straining and swearing. But always the shining arteries stayed just above his outstretched fingers. He was like an animal, prowling back and forth, leaping at the wall, his cheeks puffed and his sweat pouring.

A mournful soughing seemed to rise up from inside the rock — a wind that wailed through the fissure and stopped Fin in his tracks. When he turned to the juniper, Lil saw a burst of light through the tree's agitated limbs. It seemed to flare out of the fissure's base, a bright display that flickered as the leaves stirred. Fin must have seen it as well, for he shrank from it and stumbled down to her.

As he seized Lil's arm, his face no longer showed elation, only concern. "Ain't just watchin' us no more," he blurted, casting a furtive glance back. "They's wantin' me, same as you."

Maybe Lil felt something, all right. Maybe she felt a strange summons, tugging at her, doing its best to draw her closer to that rock. But it was Fin who dragged her up the talus.

"I can't do nothing," she contended.

"Pistol balls can't either," he rasped. "Pray away them ghosts."

At the talus crest, Fin released her so he could part the juniper's blue-green foliage. Lil watched in strange dread as he clawed through the limbs and set about excavating where the crevice and talus met, his face shining in a dazzling ray. He dug with bare hands like the madman he was, raking away not only flaked rock and dirt, but shiny bits of slag like those in the pouch. The fissure widened the deeper he burrowed, and when the light expanded to his shoulders, he withdrew and dragged Lil down beside him.

"See what's in there, Pretty Lady."

"No."

The barrel of his .36 swept up, gleaming in the mysterious light. Even as she looked down the barrel, she wanted to resist, but maybe there was something at play even more powerful than the threat of a pistol ball.

Spreading the juniper's limbs, Lil crawled toward the blinding light as the wind wailed in her ears.

The Apaches hadn't gone away.

As Clay's horse struggled to maintain a trot behind Green's dun, he glimpsed them over his shoulder. Like a cat toying with a mouse, they teased through the tossing piñons, confident and ruthless warriors who wouldn't give up until the four of them were dead. For Clay, the wait was unbearable, a kind of slow torture worse than anything he could imagine. The devils had the numbers to swoop in and end this, so why the hell didn't they?

He had managed to ram his .44 full, but

he wondered if any of the chambers would fire considering the conditions under which he had loaded. Even now, limbs raked his face, and the saddle punished him with the bay's uneven gait across the rocky turf.

"What they waitin' for?" he shouted to Green, who continued to bleed out despite a hand clamped to his shoulder.

"Don't encourage them none. I expect they'll hem us in soon enough."

"What we got to do, Green? How we gettin' out of this?"

The cowhand turned just long enough for Clay to get a good look at all the blood. "Don't see us doin' it. Lord A'mighty, we's just about done."

"Green, you're the preacher. What's it like to . . . you know, to . . ." Clay couldn't even get the word out.

"Dyin'? Angels go carryin' you off to Abraham's bosom."

"What's that?"

"Good place, is all I know. Lord'll be a-waitin' there, providin' your heart's right."

"What if it's not?"

"Be too late to fix things then. You know, 'tween you and Him. Hell and torments ain't goin' to be pretty."

Clay didn't like the sound of that, considering all the black marks that must have been tallied up against him over the years.

"Green, I . . . I don't know if I'm ready to die."

The cowhand twisted around in the saddle and they looked at one another, two men facing the great unknown and one of them so very scared.

"Times like this, a man better get his house in order. Won't ever go back to my little girl, but it's good knowin' she'll come to me one of these days."

Clay wondered if Molly was already there, looking down and waiting and pleading his cause for all the wrong that might keep him from joining her. But he didn't have time to dwell on it, for a terrible war scream pierced the forest and a staccato of gunfire severed a piñon limb at his shoulder.

"Here they come!"

Clay's cry died in another blast, but Green's horse jumped and ran at the same time as Clay's. Dodging rifle balls and flailing branches, Clay hugged the bay's neck, but he also buried his chin in his bloody upper arm and turned to fire. Apaches were breaking through the piñons furiously, and when Clay thought he had a shot he took it.

The revolver cap popped, failing to ignite the powder, but the Apache's rifle boomed. Pine needles exploded in Clay's face and he thought he was hit, but the whiz of a ricochet told him that the ball had sailed by.

He heard Green shout to Pate, something about the young man's horse, but Clay was too busy cocking the .44 again to listen. This time he took aim on a warrior's mount, and when he squeezed the trigger the muzzle roared, cutting the horse's forelegs out from under it. He watched only long enough to see the Apache fly over the collapsing animal's head, and then Clay spun back to check the course ahead.

Through the brush he saw daylight and a crush of horses, a dapple gray and a dun stumbling over a roan on the ground. Then Clay was there, bursting through the whipping limbs onto bedrock that stretched sixty yards to a canyon with a towering spire. On the other side of the dead roan, he saw Pate down, looking up in helpless panic over the animal's crooked saddle. Another stride told Clay that Pate was pinned, the roan's rib cage shielding him only a little from the lead that exploded out of the piñons.

The dapple gray with a slumping Brehmer trotted on, but Green pulled rein and wheeled his mount to Pate. The cowhand was right in Clay's path, and the two horses collided at an angle that drove Green's animal forward. Green tried to turn back, but when Clay seized the dragging reins of Brehmer's gray, the tide of horseflesh carried Green's dun along.

A jumble of boulders lay ahead, guarding a twisted crucifixion thorn that thrashed near the rim, but before the three of them could reach it, the dun slipped on the bedrock. The horse went down, a sprawling fall that rolled Green across the rock, his shoulder smearing a bloody trail.

Whirling, Clay fired over Pate at a blur in the brush, and then cocked and fired again. It deterred the Apaches just long enough for Green to scramble for the boulders. Chest-high, they formed an exaggerated horseshoe that was all but closed. As soon as Clay squeezed through with the dapple gray in tow, he fell out of the saddle and dragged Brehmer down beside him. Clay came up in a crouch with his cheek against the boulder on the right, while Green collapsed across from him.

Under the piñons across the flat, rifle balls began to pepper the dead roan's saddle, throwing Pate into even greater panic. Flush on the ground, he seemed pinned only by a boot, but no matter how much he squirmed, his foot held fast as puffs of dust rose up from the cantle and pommel.

Pate began to call for Green, a terrified cry that reminded Clay of a goat when a butcher drew a knife across its throat. Before long, an Apache would leap out with a war club, or circle up-canyon and find a killing shot. It tore at Clay's heart, but there was nothing he could do, nothing *anyone* could do except watch and dread and shout for Pate to stay down.

Clay fired twice more before a spent cylinder sent him reaching for Brehmer's Navy six. He had it out and cocked in moments, and when he looked back, Pate had turned his face to Green and was extending a pitiful arm along the bedrock.

Clay knew what Green was thinking even before he saw the cowhand stir. "Stay put!" Clay ordered.

"Green! Green!"

Pate's plaintive cry must have reached a hidden reserve in Green. Clay didn't see how a man who had lost so much blood could even be alive, much less get to his feet. But there he was, pulling himself up against the boulder, painting it red.

"Green! Green!" called Pate.

"I ain't forgot ya!" Green answered, bracing himself against the rock.

"Green, they'll kill you!" warned Clay.

His face wrenched with pain, the cowhand

turned for just a moment — a man ready to die, but also ready to save. "He's all I got. You know he's all I got!"

Then the cowhand lifted his bloody .44 and whirled to Pate. "I'm comin', young'n!"

His revolver spitting fire, Green staggered into the flat, bent for the downed horse and Pate and whatever would come afterward.

CHAPTER 26

It felt unclean, a place fit for Casner and Fin and Dark Man.

Lil stood up inside a fissure that split the entire spire, and from the far crack poured in stunning rays from a sun perched just right in the sky. For a scary minute, she had wormed through a winding squeeze way, but here the fissure widened to six or eight feet, a long, narrow cleft with musty air and rough-hewn walls that narrowed overhead.

Like the veins outside, the chamber seemed a living thing.

It shined in places with the same yellow hue, a warm, buttery tone that basked in the sunlight. The deposits almost seemed to breathe as the rays danced from one to another, but there was something about them that reminded Lil of brimstone ready to burn.

She wanted to leave, but when she turned she found Fin bellying out of the crawlway.

He must have already seen past her, for his jaw hung down and the sunlight glistened in his wide, wild eyes. He snorted like an animal as he clambered up and bumped her aside, and then he stood there trembling and staring, spellbound by Guadalupe gold.

As Lil looked at him, she saw more than a single man or even one with maybe a devil. She also saw all the abuse devised by Casner, another person crazed by the nuggets that had come from here. For six years this place had ruled Lil's life, and even now it wouldn't let her go.

For minutes, Fin didn't move. He didn't seem able, as if something besides Dark Man had taken hold of him. Then the wind wailed louder and he flinched and started forward, his head turning side to side as he took in the fissure's wonders. From above, unstable rubble drifted down around him, evidently stirred by his steps. Twice he stretched quaking fingers toward yellow veins, only to hesitate and withdraw, as if they were things that shouldn't be touched.

Fin stopped before a boulder rising chest-high, a chiseled shelf that all but blocked his way. An arm of rock rested on it, a ridge that ended in a polished fist of yellow that seemed to cast a new spell on him.

Fin took his Navy six by the barrel, and

Lil began to back away. He raised it as he would a hammer, and she turned and flattened herself at the entrance passage. She heard the strike of gun butt against sacred Apache gold, a quick and piercing report that echoed with a rage — and the cave went pitch black.

The rock around Lil began to rumble and move, and in alarm she worked her shoulders inside the squeeze way. She thought she caught Fin's voice, a faint cry lost in the din of falling debris that pounded her legs. Abruptly she couldn't breathe, choked by dust as the passage began to give way around her.

Maybe it had all been happenstance — the sun passing the point where it could blaze through the crack, the impact of the gun butt loosening the debris. All Lil knew was that it was as if they had been lured into a trap from which she might not get away. Even now, something seized her ankles and tried to drag her back, but she kicked and squirmed toward twilight that flickered ahead.

Just as things seemed lost, she found the juniper's gnarled trunk at arm's reach and pulled herself out past her waist. Loose rubble collapsed around her legs, and when she twisted about to dig, she heard a burst of gunfire. Whirling, she looked through the swaying branches at her face and saw dense clouds of white smoke exploding from the rim.

Lil hadn't felt real hope in so long that she had forgotten what it was. In less than a minute, she freed herself and escaped the juniper, a girl bent on crossing the land bridge. She made it only a short distance past the talus before she heard swearing, and she looked back to see Fin rise half crippled from the limbs. He evidently had lost the revolver in the cave-in, but he nevertheless started toward her with purpose.

Maybe he was chasing her. Maybe he was fleeing Guadalupe ghosts. But either way he was just as insane and dangerous as ever.

With the .36, Clay laid down withering cover fire for Green, but he knew it wouldn't be enough.

Rifles thundered from the piñons, the rock flying from the boulders that protected Clay as Green stumbled for Pate through the errant balls. Somehow the cowhand made it to Pate's outstretched arm before his legs suddenly gave way. He collapsed hard and Clay thought he was hit, but Pate helped him squirm up next to him behind the defense of the roan's carcass.

Green lay there in a gathering red pool, his head propped against the saddle so that Clay could see the distress in his face. Pate tendered a ministering hand, but Green seemed all but finished. As for Clay, he was down to his last two or three loads and desperate to measure them out, but the saddle continued to jerk to the impact of rifle balls.

Green, though, had more strength left than all the blood seemed to argue. He twisted around on his hand and fired a quick volley over the cantle, and then set to work trying to free Pate. Clay didn't know what a man in Green's condition could do, but with the two of them struggling, the young man's bare foot slipped free.

Pate scrambled up, pulling Green up with him. Now Clay shot again, and Green too, squeezing off a round into the brush as he guarded Pate with his body. Clay unknowingly expended his last load as they started for the boulders, and when smoke belched from a glint of sunlight in the piñons, all he could do was snap the hammer against an empty chamber. The Apache ball hit home, yanking Green's boot, but the cowhand refused to go down, dragging his leg forward with his hand as he continued to shield Pate.

The two of them were only yards from Clay when another boom threw Green forward. As he went down, the cowhand shoved Pate toward the safety of the boulders — one last act of love from a father who had no one else.

As Pate rolled behind the rocks, Clay heard a distant rumble from down-canyon, as if storm clouds brewed with a growl. But there was something strange in the way it persisted and grew louder, and the Apaches must have thought so too. Maybe they recognized the sound of angry mountain spirits on the prowl, for the brush stirred and the glints disappeared, and moments later came the drum of retreating horses.

Clay couldn't understand, and he continued to surveil the piñons over Green's bloodied body. The cowhand lay with his lifeless eyes open and cast toward Pate, who kept calling his name. Clay stood, knowing he needed to retrieve the powder flask and bullet bag from the bay beside the crucifixion thorn, but the rising clamor drew his attention.

As he turned, he could see the full rim for the first time. He was stunned to find a saddled roan and appaloosa tied a short distance away, and as he scanned on down-canyon, quick movement caught his eye. A narrow ridge connected the rim to the towering spire, and on it were two figures — the nearer one in spotted calico.

"Lil!"

His cry seized their attention, but the next moment both figures were down, clinging to a hogback ravaged by a roaring wind just like Brehmer had described. Seconds later a gust stronger than anything Clay had ever faced picked him up and threw him back into the crucifixion thorn. He was helpless in scourging limbs that bruised and wounded and chastised. The thorns pierced his hands and boots and raked his forehead, puncturing wherever they struck, but he had no choice but to bear it like a lamb at slaughter.

The wind relented a little, and Clay rose quickly to a hip. He felt something streaming down his face, and he didn't have to check it against his hand to know it was blood. Suddenly it was as if he could see a similar scene from the base of an upright hewn timber; he was looking up, and above were ribbons of red, marking the tortured face of a man who was more than a man.

For the first time in Clay's life, the image seemed real. Moments ago, he had worn a dead man's boot, just as surely as the decomposed foot he had pulled from the

Pecos dirt. That find had led him all this way, a dead man drifting and searching in an uncaring dark. But now Clay was alive in a way he had never been before, and he knew that he would always be alive no matter which side of the grave he was on.

The wind rocked him as he clawed out of the crucifixion thorn and sprang to his feet. Pate was inconsolable as he sat up, still calling Green's name as he looked toward the body. As Clay passed, he put a compassionate hand on the young man's shoulder.

"He'll be waitin' on you. Look after your father!"

At Green's body, Clay traded a spent .44 for a loaded one before bolting into the wind, a terrible force that surged and relented and surged again. It battered the hogback, and through raging dust he could see Lil hugging the ridge desperately as Lucius lay spread-eagled a dozen yards behind her.

Clay fought for every step, but he came to a descending staircase of rock and slithered down like a lizard, the only way he could keep from flying off into the canyon. He dropped under the rim where the mountain jutted out, and gained a reprieve from the wind on a sheltered ledge that angled down the cliff. It was his only means of reaching the land bridge, and he put away the .44 and took it. He prayed that the howling gusts didn't swirl around and find him, for his cheek was against rock and he was just a quick step away from joining Green.

Clay began calling Lil, and whether she heard or not, she looked up and started crawling toward him, her hair tossing wildly. Lucius was on the move too, squirming after her across a final stretch of ridge that seemed in danger of collapse. Its wall began to slough, a small rockslide growing larger, and Clay increased his pace, edging down the ledge with reckless abandon. After a harrowing minute, he and Lil were both near the juncture of the hogback and ledge; a few seconds more and he might be able to reach for her. Then dirt and rock flew out below the hogback's crest, a stunning explosion that almost shook him from his perch.

He held on as the mountain kept up its tremble, and when the wind carried away the dust he saw Lil prone and clenching the top of a thirty-foot arch where solid earth had been. He could see the canyon bottom through the opening as the currents gouged away at the arch's underbelly, adding to the debris that rained down.

It wouldn't last. Lord Almighty, the arch wouldn't last!

Lil seemed to know it as well, for she scrambled the last few yards through a mauling wind that wanted to hurl her off. She extended a desperate arm as Clay found a hold in the cliff and stretched out his hand. He gripped her fingers just as the arch groaned and gave way, and suddenly she was swinging at arm's length, her upturned face framed against a landslide roaring into the canyon.

"Mr. Andrews!" she cried. "Mr. Andrews!"

"I'm hangin' on to you! You hear me! I'm hangin' on!"

The dust billowed up, blinding and choking, but with strength he didn't know he had, Clay pulled her up to the ledge. They were still in a dangerous place as the dust cleared, and Clay knew they needed to start for the rim. But he took a moment to appreciate the pinched eyes that turned to him, and the feel of her inside his protecting arm.

"We's a pair, Miss Lil," he said with a smile. "Rivers and cliffs, Indians too, don't make no difference. We get through it all, don't we?"

"Help me!"

The wind had lessened enough for Clay to hear the cry, and as he turned with Lil, he saw Lucius across a chasm where a thirty-foot section of arch had been. Un-armed, he was on hands and knees at the brink and staring down at the impassable gap, while behind him stretched a straight-walled hogback that ended at a spire alive with shining veins of yellow.

"Gold?" Clay asked Lil in surprise.

"Just for a couple of fools, is all."

"Do somethin', Clay! You got to help me!"

Lucius had lifted his gaze, and even from a distance, the panic was obvious in his face. Clay had chased him hundreds of miles from a lonely grave in San Saba, this man who may have taken so much from him, but even though Green's revolver was within reach, Clay grappled with whether he should draw it.

"You need to do somethin'!" Lucius persisted. "We's like brothers!"

"It's not what *I* need to do," shouted Clay. "It's what you never should've done. You and Molly — that's how it was, wasn't it? Straight out, Lucius! You tell me!"

"Wasn't me done it! It was Dark Man! He's the one hurt Molly, not me! I never asked for this!"

"Dog goes mad, you pity him, but you go ahead and shoot him!"

"You shootin' me, Clay? That what you come after me for, so's you can shoot me?"

For a moment, the urge seemed too powerful to resist. Then Clay considered Green's plea and what had happened in the crucifixion thorn, and he saw Lucius as a man already condemned and stranded.

"Guess God's got His own way of dealin' with things," Clay whispered. He tugged on the girl in his arm. "Let's go, Miss Lil."

Lucius's cry followed them all the way to the rim, but Clay never looked back.

They buried Green under stacked rocks with a prayer and a lot of emotion from Pate, and then rode away through angry mountains that must have scattered every Apache.

The events seemed to have triggered a new closeness between Pate and his father, for the young man ministered to Brehmer's every need and the older man responded with a kindness that Clay hadn't seen in him before. By the time the riders spilled out into the desert, Brehmer no longer suffered symptoms other than what might be expected of a man of his age on such a torturous journey.

Clay didn't want to tell Lil what was on his mind until he got her back to safety. But after they struck the old mail road and saw a cavalry patrol approaching, he asked her to stay back with him and dismount. For the longest time, they stood holding the reins of their horses and just looked at each other, but finally Clay mustered his courage.

"I know it's not right — one way, anyway — me sayin' this. But I let you get away back at the Narrows, and I don't want it to happen again without at least tryin'."

"What is it you're saying, Mr. Andrews?"

"I swear, Miss Lil. You ever goin' to stop callin' me that? I think when we get back somewhere, if things go like I hope between us, I'll just take to callin' you *Mrs.* Andrews."

It slipped out unexpectedly, but he was glad it had. Her chin began to quiver, and she seemed to search his eyes. Then she came into his arms, and Clay knew that from some good place up past the clouds where they waited, Molly and Green were smiling down.

AUTHOR'S NOTE

Although fiction, this work is based on actual incidents in the Pecos River country and Guadalupe Mountains region.

For background on early ranching on the Pecos, I drew upon primary sources documented in my nonfiction book *A Cowboy of the Pecos* (Helena: Lone Star Books, 2016, second edition). My description of the Butterfield mail station and corral at the Narrows reflects the recollections of J. M. Browne, "Out on the Plains," *The Overland Monthly Vol. XVI,* November 1890, 495–508. Over a period of more than two years as a young man, Browne spent weeks at a time at the station in his travels between Horsehead Crossing and Pope's Crossing.

My account of a cave of skeletons and supposed gold in the Guadalupe Mountains is drawn from "The Lost Sublett Mine: The Man and His Diggings" in my book *Castle*

Gap and the Pecos Frontier (Fort Worth: TCU Press, 1988), 130–186.

Lastly, my insights into cowboy life would not have been possible without my interviews with seventy-six men who cowboyed before 1932, as well as my study of almost one hundred fifty archival interviews with early cowhands. Documentation can be found in my nonfiction books *The Last of the Old-Time Cowboys* (Plano, Texas: Republic of Texas Press, 1998) and *Saddling Up Anyway: The Dangerous Lives of Old-Time Cowboys* (Lanham, Maryland: Taylor Trade Publishing, 2006).

ABOUT THE AUTHOR

The author of twenty-three books, **Patrick Dearen** is a former award-winning reporter for two West Texas daily newspapers. As a nonfiction writer, Dearen has produced books such as *A Cowboy of the Pecos* and *Bitter Waters: The Struggles of the Pecos River.* His research has led to thirteen novels, including *The Big Drift,* winner of the Spur Award of Western Writers of America, the Peacemaker Award of Western Fictioneers, the Fiction Book of the Year Award from Academy of Western Artists, and the Elmer Kelton Award from West Texas Historical Association. His other novels include *The Illegal Man, Perseverance,* and *To Hell or the Pecos,* a finalist for the Will Rogers Medallion Award.

Dearen lives in Midland, Texas, and has backpacked the Guadalupe Mountains extensively.

The employees of Thorndike Press hope you have enjoyed this Large Print book. All our Thorndike, Wheeler, and Kennebec Large Print titles are designed for easy reading, and all our books are made to last. Other Thorndike Press Large Print books are available at your library, through selected bookstores, or directly from us.

For information about titles, please call:
  (800) 223-1244

or visit our Web site at:
  http://gale.com/thorndike

To share your comments, please write:
  Publisher
  Thorndike Press
  10 Water St., Suite 310
  Waterville, ME 04901